MONSTERS

PRODIGIUM ACADEMY BOOK ONE

KATIE MAY

Cover Design by Logan Keys

To my readers. I know you're all a little bit psycho. Embrace your monster.

CONTENTS

CHAPTER 1

VIOLET

I just barely dodge the onslaught of bullets.

Heart hammering, I duck behind a rusty, old pick-up truck and chance a peek over the hood.

There, in the shadows, my target stands, back silhouetted.

The town is quiet, almost unnaturally so. The peaceful air belies the tension ratcheting up a notch.

Because some *asshole* is trying to kill me. Again.

How did this become my life?

I am a good girl. Promise. I haven't killed anyone in over two years, and I always clean up after I eat.

So why try to kill me?

I duck down once more as another round of bullets fire in rapid succession. Wooden. Of fucking course.

Another glance over the hood confirms what I suspect. Etched into the side of the literal smoking gun is a golden crest.

The Van Helsings.

Fuck me in the asshole.

Hands clenching, I slowly pull myself upwards, hands denting the poor car. I'll have to leave a check for the owner later.

I can feel the telltale sign of my fangs elongating, scraping against my bottom lip.

With a speed that defies logic, I race towards my attacker.

And promptly trip over an orange construction cone in the street.

Here's the thing about my speed: you can't fucking control it. You don't have any extra senses or shit like that as the movies display. You can't know where each and every obstacle is.

Running through a forest? Damn near impossible. You can bet your sweet ass I'll run face first into at least one tree.

So, yeah.

There's that.

Lying face first on the ground, I groan, using my arms to push myself up.

"Freaking tit," I curse, brushing dirt and pebbles off my clothes. My knee stings from where rocks are embedded into the pasty skin my skirt reveals.

Another urban legend. Vampires *do* get hurt. Quite easily in fact, especially if you're like me.

"I'm going to get you!" I call to the Van Helsing who is...nowhere to be seen.

I spin in a wide circle, arms raised to fend off any attack. There could've been tumbleweeds bouncing about with how still the town is. All of the shops have their lights off, shutters drawn.

But haven't you heard? It's night, and the monsters love to come out and play.

I finally drop my hands just as a body tackles me from the side. I squeal, landing once more in the asphalt. Yes, in. As in, my mouth swallows a good handful and a few loose pebbles get in my eye. I really should put a claim to this spot of land. My face is getting well acquainted with it.

"Get off of me, you Van Helsing scum. I. Will. Crush. You." And then I growl, the sound ominously loud and sending unpleasant goosebumps down my spine.

The body above me freezes before pushing off.

I blame it on the growl. What person would respect a monster that sounds like a bat giving anal?

Note to self: don't ever fucking growl. Actually, don't even speak. Speaking and growling are off limits. From now on, I am a nun...of silence.

That's right, bitches.

"What the fuck was that? Were you trying to growl? " a familiar voice says, jumping to his feet and looming over me.

Oh, fuck.

I think I prefer the man trying to kill me.

"Hey, Dad," I say, still awkwardly sprawled on the ground like the badass I know I am. I scramble to a sitting position and brush out my blonde locks, trying to give the impression that *I totally meant to be on the ground*.

Dracula is a scary son of a gun. Movies and shows fail to depict my domineering father. Towering at over seven feet, he is the epitome of classy monster. Bedecked in a business suit with his hair slicked back, you almost fail to notice the blood dripping from his mouth. A few feet behind him is the Van Helsing dipshit who dared try to hurt me.

I glare at his dismembered body.

"Take that, bitch," I say snottily, as if I had any hand in his death. When Dad glares at me, I remember my new life motto.

No. Fucking. Speaking.

Pinching the bridge of his nose, Dad reluctantly offers me

a hand. I take it, pulling myself up, when he promptly releases me, and I land on my ass. Hard.

"You need to practice, Sweet Girl," Dad says, love emanating from his eyes. My asscheeks hurt from where they connected with the ground, but I manage to amble to my feet without his help.

"I'm sorry," I say earnestly. "But did you see me that time? I almost had him."

Even before I finish speaking, he's shaking his head.

"You almost had him an hour ago when he first started shooting at you. Your hands were around his neck, and all you needed to do was snap." His hand pats my blonde mane placatingly, and I duck my head in shame. Dammit. The last thing I need is to fucking cry in front of Dracula. So help me—

"I wanted to play with him first," I lie, kicking my foot out.

Dad is silent for a moment. So silent I almost think he believes me.

Until he speaks.

"You're soft, Violet. Too soft to be a monster in today's world. But we'll work on it. I already talked with the headmaster—"

"Wait what?" I interrupt, glancing up at him.

"Prodigium. Otherwise known as Monster Academy. It will train you. Harden you. Turn you into a monster worthy of my love." As he speaks, he continues to pet my hair like I'm a damn dog instead of his daughter.

"You're sending me away?" I rasp. I'm a fuck up as a monster...and as a daughter. You should just have "fuck up" stenciled into my forehead at this point. I can't stand to see the disappointed look in my father's eyes, as if all his plans never came to fruition.

But dammit! I can conquer the world if he really wants me to.

He just never gives me the chance.

I open my mouth to say all that, to beg him to change his mind, to give me another chance, when his large hands grasp my neck and abruptly snap it.

Parent of the fucking year.

CHAPTER 2

VIOLET

I wake up on a black duvet, my head pounding and stomach churning. One glance confirms I'm in my bedroom in Dad's Romanian house.

Well, maybe house isn't the best choice of words. Gothic mansion is a more adequate description. With a gabled roof, numerous turrets, a silver gate, and a graveyard adorning the front lawn, the house looks as if it's plucked straight out of a horror movie.

My bedroom, at least, has splashes of color—I know, the horror. While my bedspread is black, I have a dozen hot pink pillows. Distressed wood makes up the night stands and dresser.

It's...creepy as fuck. I can admit that. What normal teenage girl has spider webs in every corner of her room? This one, that's for sure.

Heaving out a sigh, I pad on bare feet to the connecting bathroom. After finishing my business (vampires pee, get over it), I exit the security of my bedroom and walk down the labyrinth of halls. Knights in armor line the walls, swords raised to salute me. They're not real, of course. Only King Arthur still remains, and he moved to America centuries ago.

Yes, centuries.

Certain creatures live longer than others—say kings that were enchanted by Merlin himself, or vampires. Yup, you heard me right. Your girl here is slated to live for eternity.

If a Van Helsing doesn't off me first.

The struggle is real.

Entering the retro kitchen, I find my dad sitting at the table drinking from a coffee mug. At his feet, a man lies dead.

I sigh, stepping over his corpse to grab my own mug of blood. It's still warm and smells vaguely of chocolate. I'm not normally a blood snob—blood is blood, after all—but I can admit when it tastes better than normal. I don't know what it is, exactly. Just some people have tastier blood than others, just like some animals have tastier meat than others...

And that makes me sound really creepy.

"What did he do?" I ask, nodding towards the dead man.

Now, before you start judging me, let me point out that most of these men and women aren't upstanding citizens. Dad has a deal with the local prison. They get a generous donation, and we get the worst of the worst.

"Raped and murdered ten little girls," Dad replies, voice tight with disgust and righteous anger. We may be monsters, but even we have morals, though they may be somewhat skewed. Hurting little girls? Hurting anyone defenseless? That's a big no-no in our metaphorical book.

I hum my disapproval, drowning the rest of the blood with grim satisfaction. Serves the asshole right. Burping—and receiving a disapproving scowl from Dad because of it—I focus on the matter at hand.

"You're not really going to make me go to the Academy, are you?" I ask, not above pleading to get my way. Hell, I'll even throw in a few tears here and there. No man, not even my father, can resist the tears.

He scowls at me once before turning back towards his newspaper. The front page describes Frankenstein's newest creation. Contrary to popular belief, Frankenstein isn't the green monster with earplugs. He's actually the scientist who *created* the green monster with earplugs. He discovered immortality some two hundred years ago. Interesting man. Genius, for sure. And a little crazy.

And…

I got distracted.

Again.

And somewhere along the way, I spilled blood down the front of my shirt.

Awkwardly, I grab a napkin out of the dispenser and begin to dab at the growing stain. Dab. Not scrub. That's no way to get blood out of clothing.

Father rolls his eyes towards the heavens as if he's waiting for someone to grant him patience.

"*This* is why you need to go," he declares, returning to his newspaper and mug.

"Okay, look. I know I'm not the best monster in the world. But who the hell would be? I'm young. And I'm learning." I scramble to my feet, fully prepared to get onto my hands and knees and beg. Instead, I trip over the edge of the Arabian rug and land face first on the floor.

Because, yeah. I can't even fucking walk without screwing it up.

So how the hell does he expect me to "monster?"

AT THE END OF THE DAY, IT'S A LOSING BATTLE.

I take one last helpless glance at my cute canopy bed, the

severed head on my dresser (because everyone has one), and the spiderwebs on the wall. I named the little guy Peanut. The spider, not the head.

The head's name is Bob.

"I'll be back," I say sadly, wheeling my luggage out of my room and into the hall. I wanted to bring my furniture, but Dad insisted it wasn't needed.

"They'll have bedding and shit there," he said, ever the eloquent one. "Just grab some clothes, and let's go."

Dad's waiting by the car when I arrive, meticulously groomed in a suit, tie, and cufflinks. I'm wearing my trade-mark pink skirt and black jacket ensemble, my blonde curls brushed away from my face. Tiny bats are embedded throughout the material.

As the car pulls away and towards the direction of the airstrip, I find myself bouncing with tension. My knee bobs, and it takes considerable effort to keep it still. My stomach continues tightening to unbearable levels threatening to expel the meager contents of my breakfast.

While I've been out of the country before, I haven't exactly been around other people.

Well, other monsters.

Dad decided to homeschool me, and my few friends have all been human. Humans I can deal with. They pee and eat and bleed. But monsters?

Fuck no.

I continue to bounce in the backseat, trying to dispel my nervous energy. The only thing it serves to do is annoy my father, if the glances in the rear view mirror are any indication.

As the airstrip comes into view, I allow my body to relax marginally. I know deep in my gut, the way I know the sun is going to fall before rising once more, that my life is going to change irreparably. I'm not certain what I'm going to face at Prodigium, only that it'll alter my life forever.

And for a girl that'll live for eternity? That's scary shit.

With bated breath, I prepare myself. You never know what fate awaits a monster like me.

CHAPTER 3

FRANKIE

The pungent stench of sulfur permeates the air.

I shift awkwardly on the stool looking everywhere *but* at my patient. The man's—whose name I have already forgotten—top half is separated from me by a white sheet hanging from the ceiling. It makes my job easier if I can't associate a face with...well...with other body parts.

"Did it work?" the man exclaims excitedly. "It feels different."

I remain silent, lips pursed into a thin line.

Because how do I explain to someone that I sliced their dick in half?

People come to me if they need something. A way to stay up at night to study. A love potion. A way to see into the future. A monster to clean their dorm room.

A larger penis.

I have a pretty good success rate, I'll say. Nine out of ten.

But sometimes...

Well...

Sometimes I get a dick cut in half, slithering like the snakes on Medusa's head.

At least I didn't set it on fire this time.

"The ladies are definitely going to notice your cock," I decide on at last, and he lets out an enthusiastic whoop. Pulling my gaze away from the forked dick—seriously, it resembles a snake tongue—I slide my stool towards the top half of my patient.

We're in my lab in the basement of the school. Bleak white walls cage us in on all sides, and an assortment of machinery sits on a long white counter against the far wall. In the center of the room is an operating table, and it's where my patient is currently sprawled out on.

"I just need you to sign the contract here, here, and here," I say, procuring an enchanted document I had Mikey— Merlin's son—create.

"What does it say?" Snake Dick asks, and I nonchalantly shrug a shoulder.

"Nothing much. Just that you won't ever harm me or threaten me or hurt my loved ones. The usual." Another shrug. Without preamble, Snake Dick signs, and I tuck the paper and clipboard beneath my armpit. "And payment?"

He nods towards his pants discarded on the ground, and I hurry to grab his wallet out of his pocket. Two-hundred dollars sit in crisp bills at the very top, and I don't hesitate before shoving them into my own pocket.

"Pleasure doing business with you," I say, quickly ducking around him and out the door. I can hear the sound of him shuffling, pulling back the blanket that obscured his lower half from view…

"What the fuck?!?!"

I continue listening to him curse up a storm as I emerge from the maze-like basement and into the bustling halls of Prodigium.

Now, Prodigium in Latin means port or portal. It's rumored that Prodigium itself was once built on the biggest portal ever created, one that led directly to the Underworld. That, of course, is superstition.

And yes, the son of Frankenstein is talking about superstition.

It's a strange, new world.

Strolling languidly through the halls, my hands in my pockets, I partake in two more trades before I reach the exit.

A cheerleader—and a distant cousin of Wolfman—needed a potion for hair removal. Instead of money, she offered me front row tickets to the Roaring. Mason needed another beanie magically fitted to remain on his head. As a friend of mine, I was generous.

Instead of two-hundred, I charged him one-hundred.

Pushing my glasses up with the pad of my thumb, I step out into the courtyard.

I'm always in awe of the academy grounds. They're surprisingly cheerful for such a melancholic place. Manicured grass spreads out in all directions and is adorned with rose bushes and the occasional tree. A marble fountain sits in the center of the paved walkway, the statue currently spouting water depicting Dracula himself. Horrid creature. Honestly, I hate vampires.

Blood-sucking pests.

In the back of the school, the cemetery rests, headstones crumbling with age. It's designed to keep the ghosts at the school until they're permitted to roam freely.

It's then that I see *her*.

She steps out of a taxi, an older man—her father more than likely—walking beside her. My tongue turns to cotton in my mouth, and my hands shake.

What the fuck is happening to me?

Her blonde curls fall to mid back, and I have the

strangest, irresistible urge to brush them behind her ear. She wears a hot pink skirt darkened with bats and a black leather jacket.

The blood drains from my face and rushes straight to my cock.

And fuck, I don't know what to do. I've never had this reaction before. To anyone.

In my line of work, I see a lot of naked bodies, both male and female. Sure, I can admire a good cock or a set of tits, but I never became hard before. I was afraid there was something broken in me, something Frankenstein failed to create.

But seeing her…

Sensations I never knew existed course through me. White hot pleasure. It encases me completely.

Her brilliant blue eyes, the color of the sky during dusk, flicker to where I'm standing…

…awkwardly groping my cock through my jeans.

Fuck.

Cheeks blazing, I race back inside, practically plowing over students in my haste. I hurry inside the unisex bathroom and lock the door. Breathing belabored, I press my back to the door and attempt to get myself under control.

I've never had this reaction before. To anyone. Sure, she's beautiful, but I've met a lot of beautiful people in my life.

My hand snakes to the zipper of my pants, grabbing my rock hard cock in my fist. Stroking, I envision the blonde-haired beauty once more. She was ethereal—plucked straight from a stained-glass window. She could be an angel sent from Heaven itself.

My hand strokes faster and faster as I suddenly imagine *her* lips around my cock, plush and full. I can feel myself reaching the precipice, the need to crest over that edge overwhelming.

Fuck.

I explode, my cum landing my stomach. For a moment, I remain there, panting.

What is happening to me?

My mind reels, trying its damnedest to catch up. My heart seems to be growing in a rapidly shrinking vise.

Cursing, I move to the bathroom sink and grab a handful of paper towels, dabbing at my cum.

I wonder what her name is.

Unbidden, my eyes flicker to my reflection in the mirror, and horror swamps me. There is no way in fuck I'll ever capture her attention. I'm not...I mean...I'm not...I'm just me.

I don't have a six-pack or even a one-pack. I'm not fat by any means, but I'm a good handful. My hair is curly and disheveled. No matter what I do, it can't be tamed. And I wear glasses. What monster wears glasses?

Self-pity and something akin to loathing cascades through me until I'm nearly drowning in it. My breathing is embarrassingly heavy.

Those thoughts are immediately cast away, washed away, in a tidal wave of anger.

When have I ever felt this way before about a female? About anyone?

No, my visceral reaction to her is unnatural.

She must be a witch.

Hmmm.

I tap my chin with the tip of my finger.

Maybe it's time for our school to go on a witch hunt.

CHAPTER 4

VIOLET

I grumble as the taxi pulls up in front of Prodigium.

To the humans, including our taxi driver, they believe Prodigium is a boarding school for rich kids. They're not entirely wrong.

Half the students who arrive at Prodigium *are* rich as fuck, my family included.

"Do you need any help with your bags, Miss?" our driver asks, swiveling in the driver's seat.

After a bumpy, turbulent flight to the United States and a two hour car ride to the academy, I'm exhausted. I'm about to take him up on that offer when Dad gives me a pointed look.

Don't let humans know of our existence, blah blah blah.

Forcing a smile, I shake my head. "No, it's fine. Thank you."

At that, Dad looks positively aghast. As a general rule, monsters don't say "thank you" to humans. Hell, it's more than a general rule. It's simply unheard of.

Emerging from the car, I grab my one suitcase from the trunk before finally taking Prodigium in.

The brochure failed to encapsulate how beautiful the campus actually is, how large. The main academic building is three stories of brick and ivy, the entrance a set of white, narrow stairs and two rails twined with flowers. A pebbled pathway weaves off to the side, into a small forest. A large dormitory crests the top of tree boughs.

"What do you think?" Dad asks as the taxi drives out of the silver gates.

There goes my only escape.

"Cute," I say dismissively. "Wait...what are you still doing here?"

Please don't tell me my dad is staying. I might die a slow and painful death.

"I have someone I need to meet," he answers evasively.

"Someone you need to meet," I parrot, my eyes still traveling around the campus. My wandering gaze pauses at the sight of a man standing on the front steps of the academic building. He has light brown hair, unruly and cascading to his shoulders, and his hand...well...his hand is groping his cock.

That sight shouldn't turn me on as much as it does, but my face burns hotly.

Even from this distance, I can see his eyes widening in horror seconds before he scurries away.

"Violet!" my dad snaps, tugging on a strand of my hair. I immediately wrench my gaze away from Cocker (his new nickname) and follow my father up the curving trail bogged down with weeds.

We arrive at the dormitory just as someone is coming out.

A headless someone.

"How's your father doing?" Dad asks the young man. Obviously, my father recognizes the headless...

The Headless Horseman. Well, his son anyway.

How the man can hear remains a mystery, but he does a weird half bow thing. When Dad nods and continues walking into the dorm, I realize that must mean his dad is doing good. Noted.

I officially can speak Headlessness.

We enter what appears to be a lobby, complete with an assortment of couches around a flatscreen, a pool table, and a small kitchen. A desk is adjacent to the kitchen, and a translucent female sits behind it.

It's there Dad strides to, ignoring the stares and hushed murmurs he's receiving.

You see...Dracula? He's sort of a big deal in the monster world. You can't have hundreds of movies dedicated to you and *not* be.

As if he relishes in the attention, Dad straightens his shoulders imperceptibly. He seems even taller, even larger, like a plant that has grown after being exposed to sunlight. I trail behind him warily, kind of wishing the Shadow Monster would eat me alive.

The ghost's eyes widen fearfully when she catches sight of my domineering father. Unlike me, she's capable of disappearing into the floorboards and never returning. Lucky bitch.

"We're here to pick up the housing information for my daughter, Violet Dracula. The greatest monster that ever lived." He sounds so fucking proud of me, his smile abnormally large, and I feel heat rush to my cheeks.

"Dad..."

Parents always embarrass their kids. It's a given.

But for the most fearsome monster in the history of monsters to brag about me—a fuck up—in a room full of actually fearsome monsters?

I kind of want to die.

"Yes, of course." Ghost Girl moves her fingers over the keyboard, but she never actually types anything. Probably because she's dead and incorporeal and all. After a minute of watching her ineffectually pass her fingers over the keyboard, she turns to us with a soft smile. "Second floor. Room 276."

Without bothering to say thanks, Dad stalks towards the staircase. I wave awkwardly goodbye to the girl before following behind, my suitcase banging against each step.

I have to give myself credit: I tripped only once going up the stairs.

By the time I reach the second floor—not even the fifth floor or anything but the goddamn second floor—I'm panting and out of breath. Dad, of course, is standing against the wall pinching the bridge of his nose to fight off the impending headache.

"The carpeting was loose," I defend, scrubbing at my blonde tangles with my free hand. He mutters something indistinguishable beneath his breath before hurrying down the hall.

So maybe not *hurrying*, per se. Hurrying implies that he's doing anything except walking.

But man, can my dad fast walk with the best of them.

Room 276 is adorned with two golden nameplates above the number. The first reads Cynthia Clit. The second one is blank.

Cynthia Clit.

I snort.

What type of name is that?

I wasn't given a key, so I instead try the handle. It opens easily, and I step into a stereotypical dorm room complete with two twin beds, two desks, and two wardrobes.

Ms. Clit is sitting on the far bed against the wall, gaze on a textbook in her lap. When we enter, her head snaps up, long, dark hair cascading in front of her face like a shield. I lift my hand to wave when she releases an ear-splitting scream.

An   ear-splitting,   blood-fills-your-ears-and-mouth scream.

As I slam into the wall, my head snapping painfully, two things become clear.

One, my roommate is a banshee. And not just any banshee, but the Woman in White.

And second, she just fucking killed me.

How's that for a first day?

So yeah. Here's the thing about dying: it sort of sucks.

Not that I actually *die* die—at least, I don't believe I do. It's like falling asleep. You close your eyes, and unconsciousness washes over you like a wave. When they reopen, sunlight is filtering through the blinds in your room and birds are chirping.

But, like, in my case, my snapped neck slowly rolls back into place. It's a lot of grotesque, creaking noises and pained grunts. A few curse words here and there.

When I orient myself, I realize I'm sitting on the bare mattress in my dorm room. Dad is leaning against the wall talking to an unfamiliar man with a cascade of dark brown hair. Both of them either are oblivious to my...*awakening* or choosing to ignore it.

Ms. Clit sits on the bed opposite me, eyes intent on my sleeping—previously dead—form.

On closer inspection, I see that she wears a long white gown embedded with jewels. It dips low to reveal a generous amount of cleavage. Her thick black hair hangs in clumps in front of her abnormally pale face. When she notices me staring, she winces.

"Sorry about that. I'm not usually...well...I haven't really committed murder. I mean, not in a couple weeks. Honestly, I thought I was past that phase." She rolls her dark eyes. "So yeah. What I'm trying to say is, I'm sorry for accidentally murdering you. I hope this doesn't make things awkward between us." She twists her fingers anxiously, uneasily, in her lap. Yellow teeth chew on her bottom lip.

"Err...yeah. Don't worry about it. Accidental murder happens all the time," I reply.

Because, really, what can I say?

"You're much nicer than my last roommate," she muses, tapping a finger to her chin in consideration. I can't help but notice the yellow pallor to her skin, almost as if she's sick. It must be a trait of all banshees.

"Who was your last roommate?" I ask, flicking my gaze to my father and his companion. Both haven't turned to me yet, but I know they're aware I'm awake. It's not like I'm being exactly subtle about it.

"Big Foot's daughter," Ms. Clit answers. "Amelia."

I don't know a lot about Big Foot, but from what little I garnered, he's an immense beast who lurks in Canada. Why anyone would want to harm Canadians remains a mystery to me.

"Was she...?" I don't even know what I'm asking. Is it socially acceptable to ask if some strange girl was hairy and monstrous?

"She looked normal," Ms. Clit—Cynthia—says with a thoughtful expression. "I mean, sort of normal. Her body was normal, but her feet...well...she wasn't Big Foot's daughter for nothing." Leaning closer, she adds conspiratorially, "One foot was the size of the twin bed you're sitting on. After only a day as my roommate, they realized they needed to move her to a bigger location."

"No way!" I screech, bouncing to my feet and eyeing the bed distastefully. I try to picture myself with feet that big, and the image constantly eludes me.

As Cynthia and I engage in "girl-talk," any and all thoughts of my death by her hand—scream—diminishes.

If all monsters became angry every time we killed one another, what type of world would we live in?

"You should see her dad. Big Foot himself," she continues, voice low. When I quirk a brow, urging her without words to continue, she adds, "You know the saying. Foot span correlates with other body parts."

I know my eyes are impossibly wide.

Good Lord.

Now, I'm picturing a man with twin-size mattresses for feet and a similarly sized dick. How can someone even walk with a dick that large? I imagine it just sort of drags behind him, collecting grit and other unsavory substances from the floor. He can probably use it as a beanbag chair if the need arose...though, that might hurt. I can't imagine sitting on your dick would be fun.

And does he just *not* wear pants?

"Violet!" my dad calls, dragging me out of my thoughts. My cheeks are on fire, but I revert my gaze quickly.

"Yes, Dad?"

"This is Headmaster Lupine, and a close friend of mine." My dad levels me with a no-nonsense stare, and I bob my head once to show him I understand. No talk of Big Foot's dick is allowed in this conversation. Duly noted. Extending a hand towards the new man, I flash him my best smile.

"How do you do?"

Because I'm super respectful and shit.

He eyes my hand warily as if he thinks I'm capable of

transmitting a disease through touch alone. After a moment of awkwardly holding my hand in front of me, I drop it to my side and perch back on the edge of my bed.

He hasn't told me to sit yet, but the expression on his face? Yeah. I made that bed my bitch with how fast I sat.

"We have some rules at the academy," he begins, interlocking his fingers behind his back. Like my dad, he's dressed in an impeccably pressed suit, devoid of wrinkles, and a bright red tie. Unlike my dad, this guy has facial hair *everywhere*. A full-on unibrow, for one, and a beard/mustache combination that extends from his cheeks to his thin lips.

He must be a werewolf of some sort, maybe even descended from the original Wolfman. Unlike vampires, werewolves don't live forever. Their bodies grow and age just like a human's does.

"The first and only rule at the academy—no killing someone permanently." His eyes flash yellow, his wolf materializing behind his impassive mask.

"No killing," I say, gulping. "Should be easy enough."

It's hard to kill a lot of monsters. For the most part, we bounce right back as if it was any other Saturday night. But sometimes? Sometimes, the death is permanent. A stake to the heart. Decapitation.

And that's just two ways to kill a vampire, the most formidable of monsters.

"The punishment for killing another student is immediate death. I made the Van Helsings on campus aware of that too," he continues on, and my heart stutters once before flatlining. My breath leaves me in a shallow gasp.

"Wait," I say, cutting off whatever he's going to add. "*Van Helsings* are here too?"

Well.

Fuck.

CHAPTER 5

VIN

I spin the blade between my fingers, enjoying the licks of pain that erupt from each press of the knife to my skin.

"I'm tired. Do we have to keep doing this?" Vanessa whines, dropping her own blade and putting her hands on her hips. She's covered in sweat, and her normally sleek ponytail is beginning to loosen.

Frankly, she looks like shit.

Keeping my expression blank, I nod towards the target against the far wall. Dozens of knives are already embedded into the human-sized dummy.

"Again," I instruct.

My twin huffs, rolling her eyes, before grabbing another throwing dagger. Maintaining eye contact, she tosses the dagger, and it hits the bullseye.

"Again," I say stiffly, folding my muscular arms over my chest. I'm attempting to intimidate her, but she meets my glare haughtily, never one to be cowed.

"I said. I'm. Tired." Each word is a bark, a slash of a whip.

We partake in a stare-off, her golden green eyes—the same shade as my own—locked with mine. After a moment, her lips twist into a malicious smirk, and she breaks eye contact with me. My victory is short lived when she whispers, "Viper alert."

I stiffen, muscles locking together, as the clink of heels echoes behind me. Vanessa wiggles her fingers in a wave before striding out of the gym.

"Vinny Poo!" an annoyingly chirpy voice sings. Immediately, thin arms wrap around my waist from behind and cold lips press to my neck. I shake in revulsion, quickly trying to detangle myself from the she-demon.

Schooling my expression into something neutral, something that doesn't hint at my intense loathing, I turn towards the newcomer with a forced smile.

Cheryl fucking Ness.

Descendant of the original Loch Ness monster.

She looks normal enough, pretty even, with shimmering orange hair, bright red lips, and thick lashes. The only indication that she's anything *other* is the gills sprouting from her neck and curling down her chest. I would know.

I've seen that naked chest more times than I care to admit.

Cheryl Ness.

The bane of my existence.

I stiffen briefly when her fingers brush my arm, and she pushes out her plump bottom lip. I imagine she thinks she's being seductive, but the poor girl looks like she needs to take a massive dump.

"I miss you, Vinny Poo," she whispers, that skeletal finger of hers trailing up and down my bicep. It takes considerable restraint not to rip it off and shove it up her ass. It'll fit quite nicely with the stick currently there.

And that damn nickname…

If I have to hear Vinny Poo one more fucking time…

Ignoring her, I bend down to pick up one of my fallen daggers. I can feel her eyes on my ass, but I don't bother to give her the satisfaction of responding. Bitch doesn't deserve anything from me. Not after what she did.

"Did you hear?" the viper inquires, taking a step closer. This time, her finger travels up and down my back. Fucking cunt.

I know she wants a reaction, a response, but I refuse to give her one. Not this time. She can take my silence and shove it up her ass alongside the finger and stick.

Displeased with my lack of response, she releases a growl. The sound only serves to make my smile broaden.

"I just thought you, of all people, would know. Being the heir to the Van Helsing's fortune and all." She's trying to bait me, putting the worm on the hook and watching it bob in a turbulent ocean.

But I'm not stupid enough to snap down on it and impale myself. Not again.

Still silent, I move to the target and pull the daggers methodically from where they're deeply embedded in the plaster.

One dagger.

Two daggers.

Three daggers.

At dagger number ten, Cheryl finally explodes.

"Dracula's daughter is here!" Her voice is a screech, grating on my nerves, but her words have the desired effect. My brain shuts off, going numb, and ice encases me in an impenetrable chokehold. I spin on my heel, searching her face for any signs of deception. Her red lips are curled into a cunning smirk at having finally gotten a reaction out of me.

"Are you sure?" I ask darkly.

She rolls her eyes.

"Of course I'm sure. Hayley saw her and—"

Before she has even finished speaking, I'm racing out of the room. My stomach is churning, tightening, and my thoughts are running rampant. I pray this is some sort of practical joke. Cheryl's way of getting back at me.

Dracula's fucking daughter.

My hand immediately goes to my favorite wooden stake, one I always keep in my belt. It was crafted from my grandfather himself, the only person besides Vanessa who has ever loved me, and given to me on my tenth birthday.

The same birthday Grandpa was murdered on.

Red coats my vision.

If Dracula's daughter is here, that means the vampire is as well. The monster. And if he is, I will not hesitate to do what I wanted to do for years.

Stake the murderous bastard. Right in the heart.

I FIND MASON IN THE CEMETERY BEHIND THE SCHOOL, SITTING in his usual spot beneath the willow boughs. He's languidly smoking some potent fairy shit, eyes glazed over. He doesn't even bother to look up when I approach.

"Are you high right now?" I demand without preamble, towering over him. Mason's not a small man by any means, but he has nothing on me. He's wearing his signature beanie, a flannel shirt opened over a gray tank top, and fitted jeans unbuttoned, his cock sticking at attention.

"High as a fucking Valkyrie," he murmurs, taking another drag. He breathes out, and a cloud of smoke engulfs us both.

I wheeze at the scent permeating the air.

Yup. Definitely the top-notch fairy shit. Probably sold to Mason by Frankie himself.

"Come on. Get your lazy ass up."

"After she's done," he drawls. A moment later, a figure flickers to life, her mouth over his dick. She slurps once, before releasing his cock with a loud "pop" noise. As the Invisible Man's daughter, Natasha has a reputation for being the "other woman." Being invisible makes her the perfect cover. She can suck your cock right under your girlfriend's nose.

Not that Mason has a girlfriend. He has fuck buddies—we all do. Him, more than most.

Can't really have a girlfriend when you have a fated mate somewhere out there.

Not all monsters have mates. I don't, for one, but that's mainly because I'm more human than beast. I'm the creature that the *monsters* fear.

So yeah. No mate for me, thank fuck.

"Hurry the fuck up. And put your dick away!" I snap, trying to look anywhere else. Seeing my best friend's dick billowing in the breeze is *not* how I want to start this investigation/assassination attempt.

"Hey, Love. That's enough." He pushes at Natasha's shoulders, and she falls to the ground with a "humph", turning invisible once more. A moment later, she rematerializes, her perky breasts on display for the world to see.

"Aren't you going to get me off?" she pouts, lower lip trembling. Ignoring her, Mason ambles to his feet and sticks his now flaccid dick back in his pants.

"I'm afraid that's not how I work," he proclaims unashamedly with a shrug. "I'm a pretty damn selfish lover."

She sputters, face growing red with indignation, before hurling a list of insults at our retreating backs.

Only when we exit the cemetery, does Mason's shoulders slacken with relief.

"I thought she would never stop nagging," he laments,

offering me a hit. I decline, already focused on the job at hand. And getting high is not on my list of things to do.

"How much of a liability are you going to be?" I ask my high-as-fuck friend. He considers, the silence stretching to the point I'm afraid he's fallen asleep.

Finally, he admits, "On a scale of one to ten, I'm a solid eighty. And not just in the good looks department. Honestly? I feel pretty good right now. Mellow. Chill. I kind of want to take my dick and wave it around like a flag."

I close my eyes briefly. "Don't take your dick—"

Too late.

With another sigh, I leave Mason to his Pledge of Allegiance and hurry to the dorm building. As an upperclassman, I'm fortunate enough to live in a house off campus. I remember how shitty these dorms were with their waterstains, cold showers, and uncomfortably hard mattresses. I'm pretty sure I got an STD from them once.

I press myself flush against the ivy climbing up the brick building, content to wait in the shadows until night fell.

Contrary to popular belief, vampires *are* able to travel in sunlight. It only irritates the skin in the same way it'll irritate a freckled, red-headed person's skin. Of course, that makes *my* job ten times harder. If only they'll spontaneously combust in the sunlight and save me the hassle of killing them.

But alas, I'm not that lucky.

After only about an hour of creepily lurking, the front door of the dormitory opens and closes. I prepare myself for another bout of disappointment—after all, it could be one of the fifty-some other students currently living in the dorms.

Instead, two familiar figures step out. The first I'll recognize anywhere as the headmaster, his curly hair untamed and disheveled. Just like his wolf.

The second figure is tall and intimidating, his chin raised

imperiously. He's the type of man who looks like he gives zero fucks about anyone and anything.

Anger, red hot, cascades through my veins. Vibrates within me. It's like I'm seeing in tunnel-vision, my entire focus on him and him alone.

Dracula.

The monster I've been trying to kill my entire life.

The man who murdered my grandpa, my best friend.

My hand tightens around the stake.

I understand perfectly the punishment for killing. Not just in the academy, but in the monster community at large. And killing a man as powerful and connected as Dracula? I'll be brought down faster than I can blink. In the monster world, I'll be labeled as a traitor and an enemy. But in my world, as a Van Helsing, as a hunter, I'll be declared a hero.

I'm sorry, Vanessa.

My muscles shift, preparing to spring at the unsuspecting man, when the wind changes direction, bringing with it a delectable scent. Goosebumps erupt on my arms, and my cock instantly hardens.

What. The. Ever. Loving. Fuck?

I'm about to murder my nemesis, and I'm sporting a raging boner. Am I really that kinky?

The smell assaults me again, and my eyes practically roll up into my head.

It reminds me vaguely of the cookies Mom used to make. Melted chocolate. Smoke from the hearth in our living room. The floral scent from our collection of flowers on the dining room table.

It smells like...home.

I can't stop my body's visceral reaction. It's something carnal, primal, within me. I can't quite understand it, but I know I want to jump the distance between us and kiss the everloving fuck out of—

I sure as fuck hope it's not Dracula.

A moment later, the door opens once more, and the object of my desires manifests itself. She's everything I never knew I wanted, a vision of elegance and grace.

Right as I think that, she trips over a rock and faceplants on the ground. Wincing, she rubs at her forehead and scrambles back to her feet.

"I'm okay!" she calls to Dracula's retreating back.

He doesn't even slow down.

The need to run to her, to claim her, to kiss her, is nearly overwhelming. My hands grapple with a loose brick, using it as a handhold to hold me back. To stop me from doing anything rash and reckless.

I know what this is. I've read about it hundreds of times in my textbooks.

But it's utterly impossible.

Mate bonds don't exist between creatures of different species, and never in the history of monsters did a Van Helsing get a call.

Deep in my bones, however, I know exactly what it is. I can feel it settling in my gut like a ball of lead, mixing with the tangle of nerves already there.

This girl—this blonde-haired, dewy face girl—is my mate.

And if her close proximity to Dracula is any indication, she's his daughter.

As a wise man once told me, "Fuck me sideways, backwards, and everywhere in between."

CHAPTER 6

VIOLET

After an hour of awkwardly sitting and pretending I don't exist, I'm finally dismissed back to the dorm.

I leave the main academic building—which also serves as the offices for administrative staff—and wander down the numerous pathways branching off from the main one.

I take the one that leads to the graveyard, a surprisingly popular hub with the students. I see a crowd dancing merrily around one of the crypts (picture Children of the Corn) and what appears to be a sports team doing push-ups where the graves end and the forest begins.

"They're practicing for the Roaring," a quiet voice mumbles from behind me. I turn, heart hammering, to see a young man sitting beneath a tree. Thick, black glasses accentuate the cerulean eyes gazing back at me framed by long lashes. He scratches absently at his nose, pushing a strand of unruly dark hair away in the process.

He's beautiful. I know it's a strange thing to say about a guy, but he has beautiful, delicate features. Almost feminine.

When he meets my gaze, his cheeks burn hotly, and he ducks his head. After a moment, he glances back up at me through his fringe of lashes, a tentative smile playing on his full lips.

"What's the Roaring?" I inquire, moving a step closer. He scrubs again at his nose, hitting the edge of his glasses, before dropping his hand into his lap.

"It's a game us monsters play." He pauses, picking at the skin on his wrist. He doesn't even seem to realize he's doing it, the gesture reflexive. "Are you new?"

"You could say that." Before I can stop myself—because, really, when have I ever cared about personal space?—I sit cross legged in front of him. He gulps, instinctively shifting away as if my female cooties are contagious.

Hell, for all I know, they might be.

There's a reason us girls bleed out of our vaginas: to warn away monsters. Show them how badass and deadly we can be.

Oh, your cock shoots out cum. How quaint. My pussy? Yeah. We have blood, motherfuckers.

And...I'm getting off track.

"So the Roaring," I repeat, smiling disarmingly at the man to show him I'm not going to kill him. It takes real skill to perfect such a smile. I had to practice for days in the mirror before the humans stopped running from me. Apparently, grimacing malevolently while holding the severed head of your enemy is *not* the way to make friends. Who knew?

I still have that head, if you want to know.

My first accidental kill.

In my defense? He totally deserved it. The man cornered me in an alleyway when I was fourteen and slapped me.

When I began to scream, he slapped a hand over my mouth and pulled down my pants.

So I killed him.

Accidentally, of course.

Once again, I attempt to focus on the here and now. Namely, Glasses nodding towards the athletes. They're all dressed in color-coordinated red shorts and shirts. It seems to be a mixture of girls and guys, all various ages and monsters.

There doesn't seem to be anyone with abnormally big feet which is a shame...for...reasons.

"They hold it every year at the Academy," the man says dryly. He sounds less than enthused by this. "It's a chance for the top dogs to show off. Lick butt cracks. Whatever floats their boat."

"I take it you don't compete," I say, glancing once more at the athletes.

"No, I totally do compete. I just hate every second of it." He sighs heavily, a hand ruffling his already disheveled black curls. "I'm Jack by the way."

"Violet."

He doesn't ask me who I'm related to, and for some reason, I'm extremely grateful. I surprisingly enjoy the anonymity of being just Violet. Not Dracula's daughter. Not a pawn in this ever-changing game board.

Just Violet.

I must've said that out loud, for Jack's lips twitch.

"Well, Just Violet, I need to get back to my studying." His face slackens with horror suddenly, as if he has only just realized how his words could be construed. "Not that I don't enjoy your company...because I do. It's just...um...frick!"

He scrambles to his feet, dropping papers everywhere in his haste. To escape me? To escape himself?

Still sitting on the ground, I lean forward to help him pick up the fallen papers just as he does.

Now, in the human movies, this would be the part where our fingers touch and long, extended eye contact is made. The world would freeze around us, trapping us in an eternity of our own making.

In reality, my forehead smacks against his nose, and we both fall to our backs, groaning in pain.

"I think you broke my nose," Jack declares, voice muffled. One glance confirms that, yes, there is an ungodly amount of blood dripping down his face.

"Oh shit," I curse, crab-walking backwards until I'm a safe distance away.

Jack seems nice and all, but I know how monsters work. An eye for an eye. Blood for blood.

And dammit, I like my blood in my body where it belongs (yes, I see the irony).

Jack chuckles good-naturedly.

"It's fine. It was an accident. Don't look so...oh crap." His eyes widen in horror, and I whip my head from side to side, desperate to see what has ensnared his attention. Noticing nothing that wasn't there five minutes ago, I turn back towards Jack.

His glasses are gone, discarded onto the textbook beside him. His wild hair, once curling into his eyes, is now pushed behind both ears to showcase a sharp jawline, stubble, and a wicked scar on his left cheek.

He smiles down at me coldly, the radiant warmth previously emitting from his eyes all but gone. Vanquished.

"Well...well...well. What do we have here?"

CHAPTER 7

HUX

I roam the labyrinth of my host's mind. There's a small section I'm regulated to, a tiny portion bathed in darkness.

No lights.

No warmth.

I wouldn't say that it's cold, just empty. The monotony of darkness is only broken apart when he sets me free. A pocket that opens up whenever he experiences a strong emotion. Hate. Anger.

That pocket—that hole of pure, undiluted light—calls to my battered soul. It's nearly impossible to resist. Not that I want to.

When it comes, cracking open the black floor, I jump.

It always takes me a moment to orient myself. The sudden light is almost blinding, and I squint my eyes to adjust them. Next, I have to get used to my limbs. An arm and a leg. A head that can turn from side to side. Eyelids that blink.

A cock that is currently rock hard, straining against the jeans I am—he is wearing.

Dark hair is obscuring my vision, and I hastily push it behind my ears. I don't know why Jack is so against the scar marring his face. He sees it as a flaw, a constant reminder of who and what he is.

I see it as a trophy.

My hands snag on the hideous glasses, and I drop them onto one of Jack's ridiculous books. I'm not a big enough dick to break them—though the prospect is tempting. He doesn't actually *need* glasses. I think he believes it makes him look smarter.

Cracking my stiff neck, I raise my arms above my head to stretch the taut muscles.

And then I notice *her*.

She sits across from me, blonde curls flowing around her like a halo of golden silk. Porcelain skin. Red, pouty lips. A cute nose currently scrunched.

Ah. Now I understand the reason for Jack's strong emotion.

Lust.

I can't deny the appeal of the feminine creature sitting delicately across from me.

"Well...well...well. What do we have here?" I ask. My voice sounds weird. Deeper, almost. Has it really been that long since Jack set me free?

"Jack?" she asks tentatively, tilting her head to the side. Her hair reflects in the sunlight, highlighting the streaks of lighter blonde and tawny red.

"Not Jack," I say. It's surprisingly difficult to speak, to form the words that want to leave my mouth. My tongue feels like cotton.

Her eyes widen slightly, almost imperceptibly, but she doesn't immediately run away.

Strange, stupid monster.

"Then what's your name?" she inquires curiously.

My name. No one has ever asked me that. They refer to me as the beast, the monster.

"Hux," I reply at last. "They call me Hux."

"They call *me* Violet." She extends a small hand—a hand easily capable of being crushed. She should be more careful.

And what exactly does she want me to do with the hand?

Scouring my memories, some of them long buried, I lean forward and inhale her fingers deeply. Her breath catches, her heart beating unevenly.

Hmmm.

She smells like...like sunshine. Like the grass I'm sitting on, the tree behind me, the flowers surrounding the nearest stone...grave.

But also…

"You smell like death," I muse, dropping her hand. "You should shower."

The dreamy, glazed expression in her eyes vanishes. Her brows raise, and her mouth opens in indignation.

"It's a good death smell," I assure her, confused by her reaction. Why is she getting so defensive? Females have always been strange creatures. Even my limited knowledge of the world tells me that. "Is it the smell of your…" I search for the appropriate word. "Period?"

I mentally pat my back, pleased I had gotten the terminology correct.

Her face turns darker, angrier, a banked fire resting just beneath the surface.

"Excuse me?" she says slowly.

"I know there's a certain time of month where the female population experiences the Great Period." I sift through my memories. "They partake in sacrificial blood rituals designed to enhance their...their anger." I shiver. "Are you experiencing your Great Period?"

"What the fuck, man!" she snaps, jumping to her feet and placing her hands on her thin hips. They're abnormally small —the girl must be malnourished.

I have to feed her.

As she continues to rage on—further proving my Period theory—I dig around in Jack's backpack. Surely, my host has some sort of sustenance.

Sadly, there's no severed hands available for the lady.

At the bottom of the bag, I find something that seems promising. Holding my treasure in my hand, I turn towards the blonde-haired beauty—Violet—who is still babbling about the feminist movement.

Feed her.

Quickly, I shove the food source into her plush mouth, and I watch her eyes widen as she bites down. I breathe out a sigh of relief at having been able to—

She spits the food source out, gagging.

"Why the fuck did you feed me an eraser?" she asks in disbelief. She scrubs at her tongue, eyes crossing.

"An. Eraser?" I say each word separately, succinctly, tasting them on my tongue the same way she had just tasted the apparent *eraser*. "Is that not a food source?"

"No!" she groans, her tongue sneaking out to lick her lips. "Erasers are *not* food."

When I continue to stare at her blankly, she sighs, reaching into her pocket to grab a small...thingy.

"It's a candy bar," she explains as if that's supposed to mean something. "Chocolate."

"Chocolate." I have heard about this chocolate. Apparently, it's a common cure for the Great Period.

"Have a bite." She extends the "chocolate" to me, and I feel my heart begin to beat erratically. I've never been offered a gift before.

"Thank you," I say, emotion clogging my airway. "I'll treasure it always." I hold the diminutive piece of "chocolate" to my chest, over my heart. I know I will die for this gift. No one will take what's mine, not even Jack.

Her brows furrow in confusion.

"No, you're supposed to eat—"

I feel the change coming over me, pushing me back into my darkened corner. For the first time ever, I fight it. I kick and claw and scream, attempting to stay with the captivating girl with the golden hair and eyes that seem to hold me captive.

"No!" I roar. I know that if I'm to go back into my hole, my abyss, I'll forget.

And I can't forget.

Not her.

I'm plunged into an inky darkness that slithers across my skin like thousands of snakes.

"No! No! No!" I scream, pounding at walls I don't see. Don't sense. Panic coils in my gut, but I push it down.

I won't forget. Not her. Not the pretty monster who gave me my first gift.

My gift…

Which is currently still in my hand.

I fall to the ground, a sob breaking free, and cradle my treasure to my chest. It came with me.

Violet.

Her name reverberates through my head.

Violet.

CHAPTER 8

VIOLET

I toss and turn in the lumpy bed, the scratchy blankets the school provided rubbing at my sensitive skin.

The weird exchange with Jack and Hux plays on a loop in my mind.

After Hux had retreated to...well...to wherever the hell he goes, Jack had returned, flustered and red-faced.

He also hadn't seemed to realize that time had passed. He'd seemed shocked to find his glasses gone and his hair behind his ears.

Does he not know about Hux?

Dozens of questions are rattling together in my brain, and it's increasingly difficult to separate and ask them.

Welcome to Prodigium, my friends, where you learn to expect the crazy.

Finally, my phone alarm rings, and I jerk upright in bed.

"Motherfucker with hairy penis balls," Cynthia curses from the bed beside me. She's beneath a mound of blankets, a solid lump of female banshee. As if feeling my gaze on her, she rips off her blanket and...

Oh God.

"What are you looking at?" she asks suspiciously, and I quickly try to school my features.

"Nothing," I say quickly. Too quickly.

"No, you're definitely looking at something. What is it? Do I have something on my face?" Her hand scrubs at her cheeks and then her hair, as if searching for whatever had captured my attention.

"So breakfast...will I be able to eat my—errr—special food?" I ask, changing the subject. Cynthia scoffs at me but graciously allows the topic change.

"They have a little bit of everything in the cafeteria," she says, reaching onto her bedside table to grab her nose and eyeballs.

Yup.

Cynthia apparently doesn't sleep with her facial features.

Her face twists as she pops one eyeball into its socket and then the other. I can't help but watch, enraptured.

She twists and turns the eyeball, wiggling it deeper into the socket. It sort of reminds me of that children's toy I used to play with—where you have to place the shaped block into the correct hole.

"I'm craving pancakes with a side of human liver," she says solemnly, popping her nose back into place. It's initially twisted to the side, a bone protruding outwards, but she works to get it straightened.

Satisfied, she rubs a hand down her dark hair, though it does nothing to tame the stringy locks.

"Seriously. What are you staring at?" she asks, and her eyes—now back in her face—darken dangerously. Her mouth parts slightly, a whimsical noise escaping.

Shit.

The last thing I need is to piss off a banshee, the historic Woman in White at that, and die. Again.

"Nothing."

Throwing off my covers, I hurry to my dresser and pull out my favorite outfit. The neckline is low, revealing an indecent amount of cleavage, and the hem stops just above my belly button. The knee-length skirt is hot pink decorated with black bats—I have *way* more bat clothing than I care to admit.

I turn just in time to see Cynthia slip on her trademark white dress, shrugging a backpack over one shoulder. White, of course. I'm fortunate the academy doesn't require uniforms. The last thing I want to wear is a short skirt, knee-high socks, and a jacket that suffocates my boobs.

No, thank you. We may be monsters, but we believe in individuality. If the human world taught me anything, it's that it's fun to stay at the YMCA. Oh, and that people should be free to express themselves however they see fit.

"Where's the cafeteria?" I ask, following Cynthia out of the dorm building. The sun hasn't fully crested the tree boughs yet, so the entire school is engulfed in a grayish sheen. A slight wind stirs my unruly blonde curls.

"Down this path." Cynthia nods towards a fork in the surrounding forest. The trail is overgrown with weeds, long branches obscuring the exit from view. It looks like the type of trail she would lead me down seconds before she murdered me.

"Okay!" I say happily, skipping along beside her.

If I'm murdered, at least I'll die knowing ahead of time that I'm a dumbass.

The pathway seems to go on forever, the lack of sunlight causing the trees to appear malevolent and oppressive. Their skeletal branches dig into my arms and cheeks as I walk.

Finally, we reach the end where a surprisingly modern

building rests. Monsters of all kinds—I even spot a few vampires—wander in and out.

"Huh. So you didn't plan to murder me and hide my body," I murmur, eyeing Cynthia in a new light. Is this the start of a beautiful friendship?

Ignoring me, she hurries towards the entrance, and I reluctantly trail behind.

The inside is exactly how I'd imagine a human cafeteria to look like. That is, if human cafeterias had various rooms labeled "live donors" and served severed body parts on trays for students.

"You'll probably need to find a blood source," she says. "They have a few on site for the vampires." I follow the direction of her gaze towards where a few humans sit in chairs facing the cafeteria. The majority of them have their necks obediently canted as vampires drink from them.

Fuck, I'm starving. I can't even remember the last time I drank directly from the source.

Licking my lips, I bypass Cynthia who is standing in line to grab her liver and head towards the donors.

The only available donor is a man a few years older than me. He's handsome, I suppose, with honey-toned hair and mossy green eyes. His teeth are blindingly white when he smiles.

Fuck, what do I say?

Hey...so, not trying to be weird or anything, and I don't want to make things awkward...but...can I sit on your lap and drink from your neck?

"Vampire?" the donor queries, a wicked glint in his eyes.

Eyes that are currently devouring me from head to toe.

"Yeah...um…" I fiddle with a strand of my hair, unable to make and maintain eye contact.

"Come here." He pats his lap, tilting his head to the side. My eyes fixate on his pounding pulse. Instinctively, I lick my lips before scrambling towards him and straddling his waist.

There's numerous ways you can feed, but the easiest—and least messiest—is facing the donor. You can stand and bend down, but that leads to a kink in your neck. No, the most practical way to feed is by sitting on the donor's lap and tilting his head to the side.

A donor who is very, *very* happy to meet me if the mini donor poking my cunt is any indication.

I lean forward, breath caressing his neck, and he tenses beneath me. His hands come to rest on my waist…

Abruptly, I'm pushed off of him, just barely managing to stay upright.

"What the fuck?" I yell, glaring at the asshole who interrupted my meal.

He stands between me and the donor, body trembling with fury.

Ignoring me, he directs his full attention on my scared shitless donor. Well, not *my* donor. Especially not now.

"Leave," Newcomer says darkly. I don't even bother to see if the donor obeyed. When some creepy ass, scary man says "leave" you fucking run.

Finally, the newcomer turns towards me, and I get my first look at him.

He has dark brown hair cut short and tan skin. He's big—intimidatingly so—and his muscles are clearly defined beneath his gray shirt. His body seems to be hewn out of stone. When he crosses his arms, I spot intricate tattoos clamoring up his biceps. The pattern undulates, ripples, as he flexes.

"Um…hi," I say awkwardly. Because, really, what else can I say? He totally just scared my breakfast away with his big, sexy muscles and his big, sexy smirk and his big, sexy cock —y smile.

Head. Out. Of. Gutter.

When he remains silent, staring at me as intently as I'm staring at him, I cross my arms over my chest. That only causes his gaze to dip to my breasts.

"You scared away my donor," I say stiffly, silence settling and stretching between us like a taut rubber band.

His nostrils flare, eyes flashing to mine. "He's not *yours*."

Okayyyy...someone drank too much cult kool aid.

"Well, um, I'll just head over to him instead." I point towards a second donor who had just finished up. His eyes are closed in bliss, the wounds on his neck already closing over. Perks of vampire venom.

"No," the newcomer says sharply. Indecision flashes across his face for a brief moment, and his eyes anxiously travel around the cafeteria. Fortunately, no one is paying attention to us.

There's an incubus and werewolf fucking a few tables over. That's a sure way to hold the cafeteria's attention.

"*I'll* be your donor," he says quickly. Panic momentarily flitters across his striking face, but he smothers it down, buries it beneath lock and key. He's scared of me...and yet he's offering to feed me?

My bat senses are tingling.

Without waiting for my response, he sits stiffly on the seat the previous donor had abandoned. His body is rigid, almost as if he has a stick the size of Kansas up his ass crack.

"Are you sure?" I ask, shifting from foot to foot.

Through gritted teeth, he hisses, "Do it quickly before someone sees."

Okay, so I don't really understand a lot of what's going on in my life. I'm sort of like a video game character being controlled by a child. I trip over air, accidentally kill the good guy, and genuinely look like a complete fucking idiot.

But, dammit, I'm starving. And here's a handsome man

offering me his neck on a silver platter.

How can I refuse?

His heart is beating so loudly I can hear it from where I stand. His breaths saw in and out.

"Hurry." He clenches his jaw.

"What's your name?" Before I can second guess myself, I awkwardly straddle his lap. His hands move to my hips, kneading the flesh through the thin fabric of my skirt.

He hesitates briefly before conceding with, "Vin."

"That's a cool name," I say, grabbing a fistful of his hair and tilting his head to the side. The smooth, dark skin of his neck is just begging to be licked and sucked. After a moment, I do just that. My saliva marks the sensitive skin there, and his breath hitches sharply.

I can still sense his underlying fear in the way a predator can sense fear in their prey. A sixth sense.

But beneath that, I can sense something else, something potent and heady and settling between the two of us like a live electrical wire.

Lust.

"The first bite might hurt," I warn breathily, my lips inches from his neck.

"Just do it already," he growls.

Before common sense can win, I bite down.

His blood enters my mouth, eliciting feelings and sensations I have never felt before. He tastes like chocolate and whisky, the two contrasting flavors causing a moan to reverberate through my body.

"Fuck," he breathes huskily, his hips jerking upwards. His own moan rumbles through his chest.

I gyrate my hips against his. Each thrust causes his cock to hit my sweet spot even with the two layers of clothing separating us.

More. I need more.

Faster and faster I rock, and he meets me thrust to thrust. Sexy-as-sin noises escape his parted lips.

I can feel myself on the precipice. So. Fucking. Close.

He explodes first, biting down on my shoulder to contain his roar. I continue to ride him through our clothing, my hands caressing his broad shoulders. The orgasm shatters me, and I come with my mouth still connected to his throat.

At some point, I must've stopped drinking. My lips simply rest against his sweat-soaked skin.

"Fuck," Vin whispers. He's gripping the edge of the chair so tightly his knuckles turn white. "Fuck."

"Fuck," I parrot stupidly.

Abruptly, Vin grabs my chin and pulls my head away from his neck. Blood still drizzles down my face, my mouth, and his eyes heat as they assess me.

"Does that happen every time you feed?" he asks, tone unreadable.

An intense orgasm? Lust permeating the air like a smoke bomb? I fucking wish.

"No," I say with a quick head shake. "Nothing like that has ever happened to me before."

His eyes trace my features, and his hand comes up to cradle my cheek.

"Don't let anyone else feed you but me, understand?" he orders.

That shakes me out of my lust-induced haze.

I narrow my eyes at the little shit—*very large shit*—and use the back of my hand to wipe away the remaining blood.

"Who the fuck do you think you are?" I hiss.

He opens his mouth to respond when he suddenly snaps it shut. As quickly as the lust appeared, it abates. Before I can react, before I can comment on his strange behavior, I find myself deposited on the floor, my ass bouncing on the cold linoleum tiles.

"Don't ever touch me again, vampire scum," he says darkly, and his abrupt change in demeanor makes my head spin. All I can do is gape at him like a bloody—pun intended —imbecile. Turning away from me, he addresses the group that has just arrived. "The vampire bitch compelled me."

What?

The?

Fuck?

The group is led by a striking girl with obsidian hair and a voluptuous body. The similarities between Vin and her are unmistakable. She must be his sister or cousin. Unlike Vin, she looks mildly concerned as she stares at me, lips tightening into a thin line. A combination of men and women stand behind her, all various ages and ethnicities.

But all hunters.

Vampire hunters.

I finally turn back towards Vin who is standing over me with a hideous sneer distorting his handsome face. Any warmth and lust I thought I saw in his eyes has all but vanished. The guy who has fed me is nowhere in sight. What remains is a stranger.

"What the fuck is going on?" I question stupidly.

"Vampire bitch," one of the hunters snarls. He leans around the pretty black-haired girl and spits on me. Spits. On. Me.

Vin looks murderous for a second before his impassive mask once more returns.

"She doesn't deserve our attention. Ignore her." He steps over me, unintentionally—or perhaps very intentionally— blocking me from their view.

"She's Dracula's daughter," another hunter, this one female, protests. Vin makes a scoffing sound.

"She's nothing," he says dismissively...as if he hadn't just shot a load in his pants and made me orgasm as well. I hope he's super uncomfortable right now walking around with cum pants. "Leave her."

It's only when he raises a hand do I see the signet on his finger. The golden band glistens in the artificial lighting, as damning as his words. I'd recognize that ring anywhere. Two crossing swords etched into the gold.

Van Helsing.

Vin is a Van Helsing.

And I…

I swallow the sudden lump in my throat, refusing to cry.

And I'd just been played like the strings on an out-of-tune guitar.

Our exchange has now garnered the attention of the entire cafeteria—of fucking course. Apparently, the very happy couple had taken their sexual escapade into a private room. With nothing else to watch, we have become the prime-time drama.

Cynthia smiles at me sympathetically, but even my scary roommate doesn't jump to defend me.

"Don't ever fucking touch me again," Vin hisses darkly. He can't quite meet my eyes.

As he rejoins his friends, his fellow hunters, he doesn't bother to glance back. Not once. For some inexplicable reason, that hurts. Fucking *kills* me. This feels like a one night stand where the guy says he wants a serious relationship seconds before stealing your money and never calling again.

Vin's sister *does* glance back, and her expression is curious. Concerned.

But I stop looking at them. The second a beautiful woman with gills wraps her hands around Vin's bicep, I have to look away. It stabs me like a knife to the gut.

Note to self: don't ever, not ever, trust a man.

Instead, cut up their bodies and bathe in their blood.

CHAPTER 9

MASON

The Fairy Blossom rushes through me, dipping everything into a silvery sheen. Before, the world was in shades of black and white, the monotony of colors making my head whirl. Now, it's a kaleidoscope of color—pink, red, yellow, blue, and sparkle.

Yes, sparkle.

They're *everywhere*.

I reach a hand out to pluck one from the nearest tree, but my hand goes through it ineffectually.

"Fuck," I murmur, determined as shit to get my damn sparkle. A surge of confusion courses through me, and I stumble.

This has been happening more and more recently.

This morning, as I was getting dressed, I experienced a horror that liquefied my veins. There was no rhyme or reason for it. The emotion came out of nowhere, assaulting me in its intensity.

Is it the Fairy Blossom? A bad batch? I'll have to talk to Frankie about it.

The confusion I initially felt turns into lust. My cock is suddenly rock-hard, straining against my pants. I groan, staggering, and can't stop myself from cupping my bulge through the material.

What the fuck is happening to me?

In the distance, I catch the familiar sight of Ruby's iridescent pink hair. She's an old fling I had...until she decided she wanted us to be more. I ditched her faster than you can say fairy sparkle. But before that, she was a good fuck. Great with her mouth and hands.

I begin to make a beeline over towards her, but stop.

Wrong. All wrong.

My cock is still uncomfortably hard, but the thought of her mouth around it fills me with revulsion. Disgust. Horror, even. I try to imagine myself buried in her wet cunt, but the image escapes me.

I immediately turn before she can catch sight of me and lean against the nearest tree. The scratchy bark digs into my skin, but I welcome the pain. It's a nice and welcoming change to the confusion plaguing my thoughts.

Maybe I can find Serena and have her...

Fuck! My cock throbs painfully at the prospect. And not a good kind of throb either. A full-on, blistering pain type of throb that feels as if I had dipped my cock in acid.

So, Serena's out...

"Say hello to my little friend," I whisper, holding my hand in front of my face. Chancing a glance in both directions—and assuring myself that the forest is empty—I release my dick from the confines of my pants and begin to stroke.

My hand has barely touched the head when I suddenly explode. Fucking detonate, my cum whitening the forest floor.

What the hell?

I came quicker than a twelve year old boy. And by my fucking hand!

All I can do is stare at my cock in betrayal. It stares back at me all cocky—snort—and shit.

It must be the Fairy Blossom. I'll fucking murder Frankie when I get my hands on him. Cut off his head and sell it for profit. Drain him of blood and dance—oh shiny!

I feebly grasp at the sparkling dot dancing just at the edge of my vision. No matter how hard I try, no matter what I do, I can't catch it.

Motherfucking shiny asshole...pain. So much pain. Loneliness. Alone.

Alone.

Alone.

I grab at my head, fingers fisting in my beanie, as the thoughts come to me in rapid succession. I know innately that they're not my thoughts. Well...motherfucking shiny asshole *was* mine, but everything else? Nada.

I stumble over a tree root, suddenly determined to get to the cafeteria. I can't say why, only that I need to.

I fucking need to.

The sunlit building comes into view, surprisingly cheerful for a monster academy. With a flat roof and floor-to-ceiling windows, the cafeteria rests a respectable distance away from the dorm rooms, campus houses, and the main academic building. Some monsters get rather anal when they're forced to smell decaying flesh on the daily.

It's there I walk, picking up speed the second I'm inside.

The feeling of embarrassment and pain is stronger now. Louder. It echoes in my eardrums until it's all I can focus on.

It's mostly silent when I step inside scanning the dozens of rectangular tables scattered throughout. A few girls wave to me, flashing identical sultry smirks.

But it's not them my eyes are drawn to like a magnet being propelled towards a refrigerator.

It's *her*.

She sits on the floor, her skirt pulled up to her thighs and flashing a sliver of lacy, pink underwear. Her blonde hair is disheveled, and blood coats her mouth.

A vampire.

And my mate.

I know that as surely as I know my name is Mason and I'm the son of Medusa. Everything about her calls to me in a way I didn't think was possible. I can feel her, sense her, deep in the abyss of my tattered soul. Just seeing her mends something within me, something I can't articulate into words.

My mate.

Who has just been humiliated.

Anger like no other thrums through me as I search for the culprit. The last traces of Fairy Blossom diminish from my system leaving me alert and coiled, ready to spring like the snakes hissing on my head.

But before I do all that, before I murder the asshole who hurt my mate, I need to make sure she's okay.

Now, how to do that without scaring her off…

My stomach clenches when I spot a male crouching beside her.

Not just any male.

Frankie.

Strangely enough, it's not jealousy I feel. Not exactly. Sure, I'm jealous he got to her first, but a part of me knows that he'll take care of her. He'll protect her and comfort her when I can't.

But how do I fucking know this?

It's not like Frankie has a good track record when it comes to girls. Come to think of it, I don't think he has ever actually been in a relationship with anyone, male or female. I don't think he has ever even *kissed* another person.

So why is he whispering comforting words to my mate while patting her back? As I get closer, I see her hair isn't just blonde, but a variety of colors. Strands of white woven with honey brown and russet red. The curls bounce when she swivels her head to stare at me.

"Who are you, and what do you want?" she asks scathingly, her gaze nervously flickering around the cafeteria. It suddenly occurs to me then that this girl, my mate, has enraptured the entire student body. Everyone is staring at her intently.

At her panty-clad pussy.

That bothers me immensely. It more than bothers me—I feel a murderous rage at the thought of others seeing what doesn't belong to them. Before I can stop myself, I crouch in front of her—shielding her from view—and flash a smile.

"Hello, little miss. Correct me if I'm wrong, but are you having a shitty day?" When she stares at me blankly, mouth agape, I continue, "Then you need the new and improved Mason Medusa. Satisfaction guaranteed. If he breaks, or if he doesn't perform to your standards, feel free to return him to get a full refund. And if you act fast, I'll throw in a Frankie as well."

There it is. That singularly beautiful smile I didn't even know I needed to see crosses her face, revealing dimples on both cheeks.

Frankie, still kneeling beside her, purses his lips.

"Don't throw me into this," he says stiffly. "I was merely asking the lady if she would like a new ass. I have a two-for-one special on those without the crack in it."

My little mate and I exchange an eloquent glance. Then, as one, we break into laughter. I laugh so hard tears fester in my eyes, one breaking free and cascading down my cheek.

Her hands are wrapped around her stomach as she chortles, the laughter adorably turning into snorts. That only makes me laugh even harder.

Frankie glances between the two of us with barely concealed disgust. And...and is that fascination? His eyes are uncharacteristically tender as he turns towards my mate. He still has Resting Asshole Face, yes, but the first sign of life I've ever seen sparks in his gaze.

"She was just telling me what transpired," Frankie says, pushing his thick glasses up his nose. She smiles softly at him, and I see his face scrunch up in confusion. When she takes his hand, squeezing it once, he doesn't pull away.

"Thank you for coming to me," she tells him sincerely.

Has the world gone to hell, or did Frankie just blush?

"So...recap. Not that I trust any of you, keep in mind. I already made a mental promise to myself that I'll bathe in the blood of all men. But anyway, so I'm hungry and all that, and I find a nice little donor who's happy to feed me the goods."

"Is this donor male or female?" Frankie asks the question I've been thinking. Her brows furrow adorably.

"Male."

My stomach muscles tighten, and my hands clench into fists.

"No males will be 'feeding you the goods,'" I say curtly, and when she turns towards me, brow raised, I add, "You deserve more respect than that?"

Yup. When in doubt, talk about respecting a lady. Fucking nailed the whole "mate thing."

She glances at me as if I'm an exotic specimen, and I meet her gaze with an impish grin. After a moment, she sighs and rolls her eyes.

"Back to the story. So, here I am, preparing to feast on him—" My cock hardens while I simultaneously plan ways to murder the donor. "—when some asshole shoves me to the ground."

Frankie's expression turns dark. Turning towards me, he says, "I have ways to dispose of a dead body."

"And I have ways to kill a body," I add. The easiest way will be turning him to stone, but that might make it obvious who the murderer is. I can't very well be loving my mate when I'm dead, now can I?

"What?" my mate asks, alarmed. "No! No killing! What the fuck is wrong with everyone?" The last statement is said as a hushed murmur, unintended for our ears. "*Anyway*, so this asshole starts dictating who I can and can't drink from. Namely, everyone. Especially people with dicks. And then he offers me his neck, we orgasm like synchronized swimmers, and then he calls me horrible names and tells his friends I compelled him! And get this, he's a fucking Van Helsing. Vin fucking Van Helsing." Her breathing is heavy, chest heaving. I know I shouldn't, I really fucking shouldn't, but my eyes are drawn to her impressive breasts straining against the small top she wears.

"So you *don't* want us to kill him?" Frankie asks carefully.

"Ugh! You two are impossible! And I don't even know your fucking names."

The strap of her pink bra slides tantalizingly low on her shoulder, and I have the sudden urge to slip it back up. Or all the way off.

Fuck, she has a nice rack.

The girl stares at me, eyebrow raised, and I realize she must've asked me a question. Whoops.

"Are you staring at my boobs?" She doesn't sound aghast, thank fuck. More curious than anything.

Deciding for honesty—important in any new relationship —I say, "Fuck yes. You have the best rack I've ever seen."

Her neck and cheeks turn red, but a sly smirk tilts up her lips.

"Oh...well...thank you. I'm Violet, by the way."

"Mason," I introduce.

"Frankie," the little asshole adds.

"It was nice meeting you both." Violet scrambles her feet, smoothing down her skirt and straightening that precariously hanging bra strap. I don't know whether to feel relieved or disappointed. I settle on relieved. I don't want just any asshole staring at her boobs. "I need to get to class."

She awkwardly waves at us, fingers snagging on her blonde locks. I watch, amused, as she moves through the cafeteria attempting to untangle her fingers. She doesn't seem to notice the attention she is garnering from just about everyone. Females are staring at her with envy and unveiled contempt. Males are staring at her like she's a tasty morsel and they're starving.

Or, if she notices, she pretends not to.

"Fuck," Frankie mumbles, his eyes trained intently on her ass. It does look rather nice in that short skirt.

I don't know why I'm okay with him looking at her like that. I want to murder all of the other guys who do it.

"Fuck is right," I reply.

"I have a thousand questions, and I don't even know what to begin asking." He uses his middle finger to push up his glasses.

"I do." My gaze slides towards Vin who is sitting at the Van Helsing table next to Vanessa. His attention, however, isn't on his sister nor the girl practically draped on his arm. It's on us.

More specifically, on where Violet had once been.

"What the hell type of game is Van Helsing playing with Dracula's daughter?" Because now that I've seen her up close, now that I sensed the magic thrumming through her veins, I have no doubt that's who she is.

It's no secret that the Van Helsings live their lives slaying monsters, particularly vampires. They deem themselves protectors of humanity, and Dracula is public enemy number one. Numero uno.

But one thing is certain.

Van Helsing or not, best friend or not, I will not hesitate to kill him if he tries to harm my mate.

My loyalty has changed in the last five minutes. She doesn't know it yet—she doesn't know *me* yet—but I have just become hers unconditionally.

At the same time, Violet is mine, and I'll always protect my own.

After all, how can we be monsters if we're not selfish assholes?

CHAPTER 10

VIOLET

B oys are weird.

Monster boys? Even weirder.

I'm determined more than ever to follow my internal promise to sacrifice all men and wash in their delicious blood. Not that I'm a psychopath, mind you. Just moderately psycho.

The events from the cafeteria play like a movie reel in my mind. Vin's heated gaze followed quickly by his hostile one. Frankie coming to perch beside me, awkwardly patting my back and whispering, "There, there." Mason arriving with his impish smirk and glittering eyes.

As if compelled by my thoughts, I hear the crackle of twigs getting trampled on a second before Mason appears. He wears a purple flannel streaked with gray over a matching shirt. A dark brown beanie rests on his head, concealing his hair from view.

"Mind if I walk you to class?" he asks, reaching into his pocket to grab out a pipe. He places it in his mouth, inhaling once, before removing it. When he blows, the smoke is almost iridescent in color, swatches of red and pink and orange mixed throughout.

"What's that?" I ask, nodding towards the pipe. He smiles deviously, eyes glowing, before offering it to me. I eye it for a long moment with disdain before shaking my head. "No, I don't do drugs. Especially not the monster kind." When he quirks a brow, waiting for me to continue, I add reluctantly, "My mom died doing some fairy shit."

"Oh fuck!" Mason looks horrified and quickly shoves the pipe back into his pocket. "Sorry, Pinkie. I didn't know."

And I don't know why I told him. Maybe this Academy is fucking with my senses. That's the only logical explanation.

"You didn't know," I say point-blank. And then…"Pinky?"

His cheeks turn red, but a lazy smile tips up his lips. He really is handsome. That mischievous smirk he loves to wear makes it seem like he's telling a constant joke. Only the shadows in his eyes belie his easy-going nature.

"You just seem to…um…like pink." He scrubs at the back of his neck awkwardly, refusing to meet my gaze burning a hole in his face. I tear my eyes away reluctantly and glance down at my outfit. Only my skirt is pink, though that color is nearly overtaken by the black bats. And, of course, my panties and bra are pink, but Mason hasn't seen them.

Changing the subject, Mason inquires, "What class do you have first today?"

We step out of the gloomy forest and up the stone steps of the main academic building. My stomach is a tumultuous mixture of nerves as my hand tightens on the rusted railing. My first day of class.

My first day as a monster.

Fuck, I'm nervous. Terrified. It feels like an icy finger is traveling from the nape of my neck to my back.

"Proper ways to dispose of a body," I recite. "You?"

"Mythological studies," he replies. "Need to study my origins and all that shit."

"Wow. Studying shit. I'm sure that's riveting," I tease, elbowing him in the stomach. His face twists for a moment before understanding dawns on how his words could be construed. He chuckles, opening the front door for me.

"Did you know that almost all monsters crap like a human?" Mason says conversationally, leading me down a hall. The interior consists of roughly hewn cement blocks splashed with cream paint. The carpeting is a hideous shade of gray sprinkled with green and red flecks. Christmas carpeting.

"You said almost," I point out as the carpeting ends and white ceramic tiling begins. I work to step over each crack, dancing on the tips of my toes. Don't want to break my dead mother's back. Mason watches my antics with a small smirk of amusement.

"Apparently, werewolves don't shit. Ever."

That makes me pause, and I spin towards him incredulously.

"What? No way. Werewolves totally shit."

He presses his lips in a tight line to fight off his impending smile.

"Nope. Apparently, the food they digest goes out a secret hole in their wolf tails."

I skip back to him—still being careful not to touch any cracks—and whack his arm lightly.

"You're so full of shit. Ha. Shit." I giggle at my own joke.

"And fairies? Instead of shit, they just release glimmering pieces of candy." He casts a conspiratorial look in both directions. "Fairy candy? You heard of it? That's just fairy shit."

This time, I pinch his arm. His very muscular arm.

"You're such an ass. There is *no* way fairy candy is actually fairy shit. No way."

"Yes way," he says, mocking me. "My ex used to—" He breaks off suddenly, picking at the skin on his hands. Why is he acting so weird? Is it because he mentioned his ex? I barely know the guy, and I sure as shit don't care who he dated in the past.

He glances at me through his fringe of lashes, clears his throat once, before murmuring, "Sorry about that. That was inappropriate."

If this was a cartoon, I would have a thought bubble above my head with dozens of questions marks inside of it.

This just confirms what I already know: guys are weird.

We stop at a door halfway down the hall.

"This is your classroom," Mason says, fiddling with the collar of his flannel. "You'll like Ms. Stevens. She's a vampire, like you, but from a lesser family. I'll meet you here after class, okay?"

All I can do is nod. Is he wanting to be my friend? Is that what this is about? Does he expect me to give him a blowjob or something? Fuck. I hate peopleing.

Mason smiles tightly before leaning forward and pressing his lips to my forehead. My skin tingles, heat traveling straight to my core. I can't help but wonder how those lips would feel on my own...or connected to my pussy.

With a whack on my ass—is that how friends behave? should I be ass whacking Cynthia?—Mason pushes me inside the half-filled classroom before sauntering away, hands in his pockets.

"Oh, look. It's the slut that can't get a boy without using compulsion," a sly voice tuts as soon as Mason's out of hearing range. One glance at her confirms it's the same girl who threw herself at Vin. Gorgeous red hair, a body to die for, and gills on her neck. "We should just kill her and end all our suffering."

"Oh, enough," someone else retorts. It's the black-haired

beauty from the cafeteria. Vin's sister. I could've sworn I left before her…

"Shut your face, harpy," the red-haired girl snaps.

"I don't even know what to say to your stereotypical, high school mean girl insult," she replies snarkily before turning towards me. I prepare myself to be on the sharp end of her verbal knife, but instead, her face softens and confusion once more settles on her features. "I'm Vanessa. And you must be Violet."

Oh shit, she's talking to me. Say something normal, Violet. For the love of Dracula, say something fucking normal.

"I gave your brother an orgasm," I blurt.

There you have it, folks. The reason why I have no friends.

Fucking shit, brain. You had one job to do, and it was not *that.*

Her lips curl in disgust, and I'm pretty sure her eyes twitch. Gills, a few seats over, scoffs, expression thunderous. One look from Vansssa has her clamping her mouth shut.

"Um…not what I expected, but okay. You can sit next to me, if you want."

I eye Vanessa warily, instinctively lowering my gaze to the golden ring on her finger. Why would she want me sitting beside her? I'm Dracula's daughter, and she's a Van Helsing. Unless…

Unless she plans to murder me.

"I'll warn you, I'm really hard to kill," I babble, moving down the aisle to sit in the empty seat beside her. "Like, my nickname is Indestructible."

"And my nickname is Kill Shot," Vanessa says with a wry grin. I gulp. "But don't worry. I'm not going to kill you. Sister or not, he'll kill me."

"Who'll kill you?" I question just as the door opens and a familiar face enters. Technically, two familiar faces.

Based on the hair obscuring half his features and thick

glasses, I know I'm looking at Jack. He doesn't notice me at first, shuffling towards a seat in the far back. When I call his name, hand raised and waving, he stiffens, shoulders rising to his chin.

His piercing eyes lock on me as heat comes to his cheeks. I smile placatingly and pat the empty seat beside me.

"I guess she's friends with all the losers," Gills—I really need to figure out her name—drawls. "First Frankie and now Jack."

Jack tenses at her words, but I continue smiling, gesturing for him to join me. Vanessa watches the exchange with an unreadable expression. But if I had to guess, I'll say she looks intrigued.

"Jack, come sit by me," I say, keeping my voice light. The last thing I want to do is scare him away by being overly aggressive. Jack hesitates a moment longer before grabbing his bag and books and moving towards the desk beside mine.

One of the monsters sitting on the opposite side of the aisle extends his foot just as Jack passes. My weird, sort-of friend stumbles, bracing his hand on the two desks surrounding him. His eyes momentarily flash with anger, something dark and unmistakable, but Jack quickly shoves Hux down. He takes a deep, calming breath before righting himself, straightening his sweater and tie combination, and sliding into the seat beside me.

I glare at the asshole smirking indolently. His teal hair and scaly face hints that he might be descended from a sea creature. When he smiles, I notice his teeth are abnormally sharp and sit in a strange circle formation in his mouth.

"What the hell, asshole?" I snap, hands balling into fists. The urge to wipe that smug grin from his face is nearly overwhelming. Maybe I'll even sit on him until he bleeds and dies.

"You talking to me, princess?" he asks, lips twisting malevolently at the nickname.

"Yes, I'm talking to you." I jump to my feet, fully prepared to kick some ass. I guess this will help me see what type of friend Vanessa will be, if any. Will she hold my earrings while I kick major reptilian ass or will she join in?

"Violet, it's okay," Jack cajoles.

"No, it's not okay! He was acting like a major asshole!" I throw my glare at Jack who winces, shrinking further into his seat, before leveling it once more on the dick head. "Why are you so mean? Are you compensating for something, fish boy? Maybe a lack of working dick?"

"Hey!" A hairy girl scrambles to her feet. Based on the fur sprouting from her arms and legs and glowing yellow eyes, I label her as some type of werewolf. "That's my boyfriend you're talking about, bitch!"

"Oh...now I understand why he's such an ass. Having to put up with you," I quip because, yeah, I'm just that good. I have just patted myself on the back when Vanessa lets out a strangled noise and Jack screams my name. I only have a second to brace myself before the wolf girl pounces, claws extended.

Jack leaps to his feet, preparing to throw himself between us, eyes wide with fear. Still, his jaw is set with determination.

But he never has the opportunity, and the werewolf girl never reaches me. The second her claws would've connected with my face, she's shoved to the ground and lands with a thump on her ass.

"Ali! No fighting in my classroom!" a strident voice yells. A tall woman stands where the werewolf once was, hands on her hips. She has a sheet of orange hair curling around her shoulders and violet-tinted eyes. When she snarls, flashing her incandescent glare onto Fish Man, I see a hint of fangs.

Vampire.

She must be the teacher Mason told me about.

"And what is this about, Nep? Are you involved?" she continues.

Fish Man—Nep, apparently—glares at me before smiling sweetly at our teacher.

"No. I'm just a...a bystander." His lips twist, and our teacher frowns at his reply. Still, what can she say? Call him out on a crime she didn't see? After a moment, she straightens and turns towards Ali.

"Ali, Headmaster's office. Now." She points a manicured finger towards the door, and Ali sputters, face red.

"But...but…" She gestures helplessly towards me, and if I was a lesser being, I would've stuck my tongue out at her and flipped her off.

Wait. I'm a monster. I *am* a lesser being.

My tongue is still out, my finger waving in the air, when she exits the room. I'm a classy bitch, what can I say.

The teacher shuts the door behind Ali and turns to face the class. Her smile is kind, eyes radiating warmth.

"Hello, class. Now, I know for most of you this isn't your first day. However, we *do* have a new student, and I'd be remiss if I didn't introduce myself." She smiles at me. "My name is Ms. Stevens, and I specialize in the legal side of being a monster. Hiding a body, evading the law, developing legal avenues to retain what you need in the community. Violet, dear, please grab the previous class notes from one of your classmates."

She turns towards the whiteboard just as Jack places a notebook on my desk. It's filled with delicate script—swooping curves and straight lines. Jack blushes and ducks his head.

"Thank you," I mouth, grabbing my own notebook to copy his notes. I'm only halfway through the first page when a crumpled up wad of paper appears in front of me. I stare at it before glancing towards Vanessa—who's sleeping—and then to Jack. His ears are red, head ducked down to obscure his face...his scar.

After a moment, I open and smooth out the paper.

Jack's familiar handwriting stares back at me.

Thank you for standing up for me. I never had someone do that for me before.

My heart hurts as I read his words. Nobody ever stood up for him before? Well, if I have my choice, that'll change. I'll be the protector, the champion, he never had.

We're friends, right? I write, my handwriting considerably sloppier than his. *At the very least, we're acquaintances. What's that dude's problem anyway?*

I wait until Ms. Stevens is turned away before tossing him the paper.

I only have to wait a minute before the paper is in front of me once more.

Some people are just assholes, you know? He's always hated me. The entire school hates me. I'm kind of a weirdo. I don't really have a lot of friends.

I chance a glance at his face, hoping to gauge his reaction. His hair still curtains his face, but I can see that his lips are curled down.

Well you have one now. Violet Dracula, at your service.

He unfolds the paper and glances towards me in surprise. I offer him a cheeky smile. A long beat passes as he continues to stare at me, expression inscrutable. Finally, he bends his head down and writes a quick reply.

Are you sure? It's social suicide.

I smile softly at him.

"I'm sure," I whisper, reaching across my desk to squeeze his hand.

I'm already a social pariah. If being friends with a sweet

boy causes me to become even more of one, then so be it. I can befriend him, understand him, and maybe even talk to Hux again. The more I think about it, the more my resolve straightens, cements itself.

At this school, you need all the friends you can get. The good and the bad. The monsters and the saints.

I chance a glance at Jack out of the corner of my eye only to find his head bent over his notebook as he studiously scribbles the teacher's lecture.

The question is: which one is he?

CHAPTER 11

VIOLET

After a riveting lecture on the networks and connections needed to dispose of a body and evade the cops, Ms. Stevens releases the class.

"Violet, could you stay back here a moment?" she calls from where she now sits behind her desk. I chance a glance at Vanessa and then at Jack. Vanessa is staring at her phone, very pointedly ignoring me. Huh. What an end to a beautiful five minutes of friendship.

Jack meets my gaze and loiters in the doorway. His hand scrubs at his glasses, pushing them further up his nose.

"She'll be out in a moment," Ms. Stevens tells Jack, smile still firmly in place. He blushes, ducking his head, but glances at me with a quirked brow. I nod subtly, both pleased and confused by his protective behavior.

When he's in the hall and the last student shuts the door behind her, Ms. Stevens turns towards me with a bright smile. It's *unnaturally* bright, unnaturally happy. She seems like the type of person who would laugh and smile at a funeral. Granted, my father does that too, but the point's still there. Probably claps when an airplane lands as well.

"I just wanted to see how you were fitting in," she tells me. "I remember when I was a student...oh gosh. How long ago was that? A few centuries?" She snorts with amusement. "How times have changed..." Shaking her head, she offers me another pearly white smile. She has really good dental care. I wonder who her dentist is and if he is included with the health insurance the Academy provides. I'll need the best of the best to assure my blood diet doesn't discolor my teeth.

I rather like my teeth.

And...

I'm distracted again. During my internal ramblings, Ms. Stevens had stopped talking and is now staring at me in concern. Even anxious, she has a damn smile on her face. I didn't know whether I wanted to be her best friend or punch her.

Or both.

Best friends can punch other best friends, right?

"I'm sorry. I zoned out," I admit sheepishly.

Her smile turns sympathetic—as if I'd just admitted to dying instead of merely not paying attention. She goes as far as to pat my hand resting on her desk.

"Being a vampire is tough at this school," she admits. "You deal with a lot of prejudice and bigotry. A lot of people *will* look down on you, but you just have to remember that you're stronger."

I nod my head eagerly, but mentally, I'm thinking about how hungry I already am. Vin's blood has rejuvenated me. Given me life. Maybe I can find him and beat the shit out of him before sucking him again (snort). Make him beg for another orgasm.

Listen up ladies and gentlemen. Don't ever, not ever, allow a guy or girl to treat you like Vin did me. You're not trash, and the minute someone starts treating you like it, carve out his heart and eat it.

This concludes my public service announcement.

Suck dicks. Don't be one.

"If you ever need anything, come see me. There are only a dozen or so vampires at this school. We want you to feel comfortable, especially being Dracula's daughter," she says, eyes burning with excitement. Ah. Now it makes sense.

She doesn't actually like me, but my dad. Figures. Everyone wants to get on Daddy's good side. And what better way than taking his clumsy, fuck up of a daughter under your wing?

Spoiler alert: it would be a pretty damn good idea if my father wasn't big on independent monstery. And no, I'm not making that up. Dad truly believes that to be a good monster, you have to climb to the top using your own fangs—or some other profound saying—and that anyone who helps you deserves an immediate death. His words, not mine. Being a monster isn't about the connections, but the way you can kill the people in your way.

Or something.

I zone out a lot when he talks.

"I need to get to my next class," I say, hiking the backpack further up my shoulder.

"What do you have?"

"Um...fight class," I recall. And that's literally all it says on my schedule. It doesn't tell me who we're fighting or why. Hopefully, I get to punch Vin in his stupid face. Maybe Gills and Fish Boy too.

I wonder if they're related. Not Gills and Vin—ew, that's gross even for monsters, for I saw them practically hanging off each other at breakfast—but Gills and Fish Boy.

Ms. Stevens smiles, the slightest curl of her thin upper lip. Her eyes are dreamy, wistful, as if my words had pulled her into a pleasant memory. She shakes her head rapidly and clears her throat.

"Have fun. Be safe."

Smiling awkwardly, I hurry out of the classroom to find both Jack and Mason waiting for me. They both glance up from their phones when I exit, and in eerie synchronization, shove them into their pockets.

"Ready for your next class, Pinkie?" Mason says with a devious smile.

"Ugh I hate fighting," I groan, throwing my head back. "I always end up accidentally stabbing or punching myself."

With a sly grin, Mason jabs his elbow gently into my side.

"Well, I'll be there, and I can assure you that I won't let any harm come to you. Even harm you do to yourself."

"I always keep a first aid kit on me," Jack whispers, and I turn towards him with bright eyes. I can guess how tough this is for him—talking around strangers. He seems unbelievably shy and soft-spoken, almost to the point where even his hands don't want to be seen. He's making an effort, though, and as his self-appointed best friend, it's my job to encourage him.

"We're going to need it," I tell him with a small smile. His smile is more tentative, more hesitant, but it's still there.

Mason watches our exchange with a curious look, but when I turn back towards him, he replaces it with a shit-eating grin.

"Race you to the gym?" he challenges wickedly, the question directed at both Jack and me.

Jack's face turns sheepish. "I'm not really the best runner," he admits. "I'm more like Violet on that front. I trip more often than I stand. But you two can go! I'll be right behind you with my first aid kit. I think you'll need it." And then, the shy, quiet boy *winks* at me. Winks!

I'm so distracted that I miss Mason's quick, "Go!" He's

already halfway down the hall, shouldering through students, when I regain my bearings. Cursing at the expanding distance between us, I pick up my speed...

And promptly run into a chest of solid muscle.

Vin places his hands on my shoulders to steady me.

"You okay? I saw—"

Before he can finish whatever he's going to say, I lift my leg and knee him in the balls.

Motherfucker shouldn't have messed with a monster.

CHAPTER 12

JACK

I stumble to a stop just in time to see Violet knee Vin in the groin and grab a fistful of his hair. She speaks to him, too softly for me to hear, and I watch in rapt fascination as she then shouts to the gathering onlookers, "Does anyone have a removable arm I can use to beat the shit out of him?"

One of Frankenstein's creations—a large green monster with thread woven into his face—removes his arm and hands it to her like an offering. She takes it with an easy, slightly sardonic and sociopathic grin, before turning back towards Vin.

And proceeds to hit him with the arm.

I watch quietly for a moment, admiring the petite female the way I had only ever admired my paintings. I have the sudden, irresistible urge to draw her. Those plump lips I yearn to kiss, memorize. Her luscious breasts straining and bouncing beneath her thin shirt. Her shapely legs.

The students begin to chant, "Fight! Fight! Fight!" A few men race forward, eager to see the bloodshed, and I'm shoved against the wall brutally. My anger festers briefly, materializing in a cascade of white hot fury. I push it down just as quickly. The last thing I need is for Hux to appear now.

Hux.

My heart hurts when I think of my older brother, but I bury those emotions under lock and key—so deep that not even a necromancer can raise them.

Straightening my glasses that have been knocked sideways in the hustle, I focus on Violet who is currently sitting on Vin and...tickling him?

Yup. My little monster is using the borrowed arm to tickle Vin's side, and Vin—the epitome of cool and collected usually—is laughing hysterically, attempting to bat her away.

Oh, how the mighty have fallen.

"Alright, back it up. Nothing to see here, folks. Just your average day at the Academy." Mason rejoins the group, shooing people away with a wave of his hand. A couple gripe and groan, but the majority seems to realize that no murders will be occurring at this point in time.

Unless someone can be tickled to death. There's a very real possibility that is happening before my very eyes.

Only one person stays behind. Vin's sister. Vanessa, if I remember correctly. She stares down at her brother, arms folded over her chest and one eyebrow raised.

"Really?" she asks. Vin's laughter begins to die off...only for Violet to find a new spot to tickle, and it returns with a vengeance. He half-heartedly swats her away, but I know he'll never truly hurt her. How I know that is a mystery, but I know in my heart that Vin will do everything in his power to protect the scary beauty.

Violet.

Her name sounds like music to my ears, and that in itself is strange. I've never been the romantic type, so to suddenly compare her name to music is weird as frick.

Violet, a reverent voice repeats in my mind. I jump, glancing over my shoulder with wide eyes. I have only ever heard this voice on camera. Darker than mine. Raspier. The hints of an accent from his days in England.

"Hux?" I whisper, trying to nonchalantly glance down both hallways. The halls have emptied, everyone else having already entered their classrooms.

There's a beat before, *Jack?*

The voice is coming from inside my mind.

But...

But that's impossible. I've been dealing with Hux for hundreds of years, and never, not even once, has he manifested himself in my mind when I'm still occupying my body.

Where's my precious treasure? Hux demands, tone curt. My confusion only grows.

Precious treasure?

In the last few centuries, I have released Hux more times than I care to admit. He has taken a few lovers during that time, but he has never once referred to them as his "precious treasure."

Unless...

I recall my lack of time in the cemetery. The curious look in Violet's eyes. Something inside my mind snaps into place as understanding dawns.

Frick, I think, and Hux's answering chuckle reverberates through my head.

Still not using swear words, I see? he notes with veiled amusement. My cheeks flame, and I turn towards the wall to hide my reaction from the others.

I've missed you, brother, I admit. The truth of that statement surprises even me. It's hard to miss someone you never truly met. For as long as I can remember, he has been an extension of me. Another side of me I never had the pleasure of meeting. When we were younger, we would exchange notes. But that all changed after…

I clear my throat, reinforcing the walls around those horrid memories.

Let me see her, Hux demands, and with great reluctance, I turn back towards the fight at hand. Violet is now being restrained by Mason, and Vanessa is helping her brother up. Vin himself looks wildly disheveled, his hair tousled and his normally immaculate clothes wrinkled, but his eyes are bright. Heated.

Aroused.

The Van Helsing stares at Dracula's daughter as if he has never seen a girl before. As if he never *wants* to see another girl. I imagine his expression is similar to my own.

She's glorious, Hux praises, tone awed. I can't help but agree with him.

Perfect, I agree. Because, really, what sane monster would take on a Van Helsing…and win? Only someone like Violet Dracula.

Perfect for us, Hux states. An image jumps to the forefront of my mind, and heat travels through my veins. The visual isn't mine, however, but Hux's.

Her body under mine as I thrust into her, those perfect tits bouncing in my face. In the vision, my demeanor changes, and Hux takes over, pounding into her brutally and savagely. She goes from crying my name to Hux's, easily able to differentiate between the two.

I shift uncomfortably, aware that it would *not* be appropriate to sport a raging boner at the moment.

She's ours, Hux says darkly, and I can hear the conviction in those two words. The need.

For the first time ever, I agree with my brother.

Yes. Ours.

"I'm fine," Violet is reassuring Mason, patting his arms to indicate he should release her. "I'm not going to murder Vin...yet." She flashes the Van Helsing a sharp-toothed smile, and I notice the bulge in his pants jump.

Is she experiencing the Great Period? Hux asks me seriously.

The what?

Before he can respond, Vanessa speaks up. "I like you, Violet. I like you a lot." She throws her silky dark hair over her shoulder. "It'll be a shame when I eventually have to kill you."

Hux roars in my mind at her threat, demanding to be released and set fire to the girl. Mason stiffens ever so slightly, subtly pushing Violet behind him. Even Vin whips his head around to glare at his sister.

"I'm kidding," Vanessa says with a roll of her eyes. "I'm not murdering the little vampire." She grabs her backpack from where she'd deposited it on the floor during the tickle fight and winks at Violet. "Yet."

With that ominous statement, she sashays away, humming beneath her breath. Violet watches her go with more amusement than fear on her face. She turns back to us eagerly.

"Does that mean we're best friends again?" she asks indicating the hall where Vanessa has disappeared down. Mason sighs heavily, and Vin pinches the bridge of his nose.

Let me know if the slayer ends up being a threat, Hux warns darkly. *I'll take care of her.*

Um...I'm not sure Violet will be happy if you killed her apparent best friend.

Hux doesn't reply, and for a moment, I think he's retreated to wherever it is he goes when he's not in my body.

But no, I can sense his presence hovering at the edge of

my awareness. A pesky fly buzzing around my head but never landing.

I protect my precious treasure, he replies at last, and the words send a chill through me. Fuck, Hux is a scary mother-fucker when he wants to be. His letters didn't tell me *that.*

CHAPTER 13

VIOLET

How did this become my life?

Beating a boy with a severed, grizzly monster hand. Planning murder of the painful variety. My new best friend threatening to kill me.

I don't *think* I'm a horrible person. On a scale of one to ten on the murder scale, I'm a solid four. A perfect number, if I do say so myself. Definitely not deserving of all this shit.

Vin continues to stare at me, expression unreadable. After a moment, he tangles his fingers through his hair and releases a pent-up sigh.

"Are you going to apologize?" I ask, irritated. Honestly, I don't really care if he apologizes. I just want to hear him talk again in that sexy-as-fuck Romanian accent. I can listen to him talk all day. I'm pretty sure he could call me a toilet-plunging cockroach and I would still swoon.

It doesn't change the fact that I'm fucking furious at him and want him to suffer.

When he remains stubbornly silent, muscles flexing and

lips in a thin line, I dismiss him. I won't give him the time of day anymore.

"Wait. That's it? You're just leaving?" Vin calls to my retreating back.

Ignoring him, I turn towards Mason who has fallen in step with me, a smug smile on his handsome face. "Where's the gymnasium?"

"Violet, don't fucking ignore me," Vin warns darkly, still a few steps behind. Jack moves to stand on the other side of me, brows drawn in confusion. He looks to be deep in thought, his mind a million miles away.

I nudge him inconspicuously and offer him a timid smile. "You okay?"

"Yeah." He matches my smile with one of his own. Again, it isn't a full one, but it's better than nothing. I'll make it my personal mission to make him smile and to have that smile meet his eyes. He just needs to be more confident, to know that he doesn't have to hide with me. He winces suddenly, rubbing at his temples with his fingers. "Just a headache."

"Do you have anything in your medical bag? Fairy drugs or something?" I know fairy medicines—a combination of herbal supplements and magic—are ten times more reliable and potent than human medications.

Jack surprises me by taking my hand in his and giving it a reassuring squeeze.

"I'll be fine. Seriously."

"Violet, can we just talk about this?" Vin demands, still behind us. Still in my shadow because I'm a vindictive bitch.

"What do we learn in fight class?" I ask, volleying my gaze between Mason and Jack. Mason has his lips pressed together to fight off his encroaching smile, but he still answers.

"Usually, they teach us proper ways to defend ourselves."

"Sometimes they have us work on offensive maneuvers,"

Jack adds quietly, scrubbing at his nose. "There are more monster hunters than just the Van Helsings. We never know when we'll have to fight for our lives."

"My favorite is when we play games," Vin adds, eager to implement himself into the conversation. He trails behind us like a besotted puppy. "Sometimes we play an epic game of Capture the Flag or Tag."

When I don't respond, staring purposefully ahead, Mason clears his throat and repeats, "My favorite is when we play games. Sometimes we play an epic game of Capture the Flag or Tag."

I smile at him brightly. "That actually sounds like a lot of fun. I love games...but I can't say I'm excited to get my ass whooped."

Vin groans. "Are you fucking kidding me? Real fucking mature, Violet."

We stop in front of large red doors, and I hesitate. Sitting behind a desk, filling out notes, no one can see how much of a fuck up I am at monstering. It's completely different from fighting with other monsters, *proving myself* to other monsters. Using my brain, I can do (somewhat). Using my fists? Yeah, just prepare me a bodybag.

"You okay?" Jack whispers. He gives my hand another reassuring squeeze—I haven't even realized they were still interlocked.

"I'm fine," I tell him, and I try to infuse as much sincerity into my words as I can muster. Straightening my shoulder and raising my head, I try to recall one of the many life lessons my father has given me: act confident, and you'll begin to *feel* confident.

That, and don't just bury a body. Burn it.

I can do that. I can act like I'm not wanting to run in the opposite direction, find a colony of ants, and become the queen of the fucking anthill.

With great trepidation, I push open the gymnasium doors.

No one looks up at me when I enter. Not one single person.

Well, that was anticlimactic.

Various monsters are grouped together around the abnormally large gym. They tend to stick with similar species—water monsters in one cluster, giant monsters in another, and so on. The divide between the monsters is meticulously clear.

I spot Vanessa and a few other hunters in one corner. All of them—minus Vanessa—glance up when we enter, and their lips twist into hideous, matching sneers. I barely resist the urge to flip them off, instead choosing to be the bigger person, and walk briskly towards the bleachers. I'm momentarily surprised when Mason and Jack follow me. And I'm even *more* surprised when Vin trails behind all of us, still grumbling beneath his breath.

We sit as a group on the bleachers, me in the center like their motherfucking queen. Okay, maybe I've been reading too many romance novels, but can you blame me? With this many hot guys, I'm on sensory overload. I need to live vicariously through the protagonists of my novels. The last one I read was about a queen and her harem of guardians.

Sigh.

I want a harem.

"Frankie?" Mason calls. "What are you doing here?"

Frankie steps up to our little huddle, as always stylishly groomed. He's wearing khaki pants, a button up plaid shirt, and a cute little bow tie. His hair is slicked away from his face with gel.

He's not as muscular as the other men, but he's still handsome. There's something captivating about him, something that ensnares my attention and holds it hostage.

"I have fight class during this hour," Frankie says stiffly. He, like Jack, wears a pair of glasses, but while Jack's are a means to hide his face and eyes, Frankie's are designed specifically to call attention to his handsome features. The black frames are thicker and more stylish than Jack's.

"You never showed up to class before." Mason's voice is heavy with amusement. "What changed?"

"Yeah, I thought you got some sort of pass because you were supplying the teacher with drugs," the wind adds.

That shall be Vin's new name. He doesn't deserve any other title.

"I decided I wanted the exercise a class like this would offer me," replies Frankie.

Both Mason and the wind chuckle.

"Okay, buddy. Okay." Mason slaps him on the back, and Frankie winces, brushing his hand away. "And it has nothing to do with a cute girl's attendance?"

"Cute girl?" I snap, white hot jealousy surging through me. Who the fuck is Mason talking about? Who does Frankie think of as cute? And why am I acting like this? "Who's the cute girl? Let me at her, and I'll show her just how cute she is. I wonder how 'cute' she'll be with my fingers in her eye sockets and her eyeballs in her ass."

Mason attempts to put his arm around me, but I shove it off.

"Violet," Jack whispers, and I turn to the only guy not on my shit list. "You're the cute girl."

Oh.

Ohhh.

I flick a glance at Frankie who is smiling sheepishly and then at Mason who still looks amused.

"Welp…" I begin, rubbing the back of my neck in embarrassment. "That was an overreaction."

"You don't say," Vin—shit, the wind—drawls bitterly.

"Sometimes you just need to tell my hormones to tone it down a notch," I tell Mason seriously who sputters and widens his eyes. "They're everywhere. Just look them in the eye, and tell them to calm the fuck down."

"Your hormones," Mason confirms slowly.

I nod.

"You make my hormones your bitch."

Before he can respond, the gym doors open and a scary looking man enters. He's covered entirely in white wrappings, only his eyes visible through the bandages. A mummy. An honest-to-God mummy.

I only say it's a man because of the bulge down below. Unless the mummy's using his pelvis as sausage storage, I'm looking at a male.

"Line up, class!" he calls in a rasping voice, slightly muted from the bandages. Everyone *runs* towards the white line painted across the center of the gym. Even my guys run like their lives depend on it. I try to run—I honestly do—but there's a reason my father hates me.

Running I cannot.

Seconds before I would've reached a spot in line between Frankie and Mason, I trip over nothing. My arms sort of windmill in the air, desperate to find purchase and keep me upright, and for a moment, I think my agility actually worked. But then Gills (still don't know her name) smiles at me maliciously and whispers to her similarly gorgeous friend. Her friend smirks and blows, propelling me the remaining distance to the ground.

Now, keep in mind, I'm still wearing my skirt, so my dick-taker clad only in pink panties is on display for the entire world to see. Well, entire school to see. I'm not too dramatic.

When someone whistles, there's suddenly a flurry of activity. Namely, said whistler getting knocked on his ass by the wind and three other guys surrounding me in a protective circle.

You'd think no one has ever seen a girl's vagina before. Geez. Is it really such a novelty?

I straighten my skirt and then check the boobage, confirming they haven't fallen out.

Note to self: don't ever wear skirts and crop tops to the gym again. Seriously. Don't.

They're practically spilling out of my shirt and bra, resembling two plump muffins fresh from the oven.

After I'm sure everything's back where they're supposed to go, I wobble to my feet and say cheerfully, "I'm okay."

I can count on my ass cheeks how many people actually *care* that I'm still alive. I'll give you a hint: I only have two.

Well, maybe more than two. I'm pretty sure Mason has an interest in me, and Jack, of course, is my new best friend. Frankie seems to tolerate me (which apparently is a pretty big deal), and the wind defended my honor by punching the whistler. And I can't forget Hux who treasured my chocolate.

"You okay?" Jack asks worriedly.

"Peachy," I say with a smug smile—trying to give the vibe that I looked death in the face and conquered it.

Because falling in gym class is totally the equivalent of death. Duh.

I skip into line, aware that I have *now* received the grand entrance I'd expected to have when I first arrived. Everyone is staring at me and whispering. Snippets of conversations float to my ears.

"That's Dracula's daughter."

"She's hot."

"Did she just fucking fall?"

"What a whore." That last one is of course said by Gills. That's rich coming from the girl who dated the wind. He probably just blows in her vagina to get all that dust out.

Jack's hands curl into fists beside me as he listens to the onslaught of accusations and remarks thrown our way. *My* way.

I see the exact moment the change takes over. The exact moment he becomes someone else, someone other.

I think my classmates recognize it as well. Or, at the very least, they realize something is wrong. The hushed whispers intensify, and the monsters begin to flash anxious glances in our direction. Even Mr. Mummy looks concerned, stumbling back a step.

Maybe it's a change in the air, an electrical charge coursing through each and every one of us. Maybe it's the twisting and contorting of Jack's face as he first removes his glasses and then brushes his hair behind his ears, revealing the jagged scar. Maybe it's the way prey always know when a predator is approaching, that sixth sense demanding survival.

Hux peers down at me, a salacious, seductive smile on his thick lips.

"Hello, my precious treasure."

CHAPTER 14

VIOLET

Hux's different from Jack in the fact that he's more confident, more sure of himself. He doesn't slouch, and he seems to wear this metaphorical cloak of imperiousness. Sort of like: fear me, peasants, or I will smite you.

Sexy as fuck, I'll admit.

There's something endearing about both the timid, soft nature of Jack and the holier-than-holy side of Hux. In some people, like the wind, their confidence comes across as being cocky. With Hux, I see merely a damaged, albeit powerful, young man. Not only does his shit not stink, but he takes said shit and lathers it on the walls.

And yes, even to me, that's a gross analogy. Sue me. It's not like I'm working with the top brass here.

"Hello," I say, licking my lips. His eyes fixate on that minuscule movement with fascination.

"Hello, precious treasure," he purrs, and I detect a hint of a British accent.

My vagina fans herself, and I have to physically press my thighs together to quell my intense reaction. There's something about a man and an accent that causes me to want to give birth.

"Are you done disrupting my class?" Mummy hisses, the words guttural from his face wrappings.

Hux turns his attention towards our fight class teacher, all the warmth he had given me diminishing. In its place is an ice so sharp it can cut glass.

"You *dare* threaten my precious treasure?" Hux asks, taking a threatening step forward.

As much as I find his despotic, kick-ass attitude attractive, I don't want him fighting my battles. And I *especially* don't want him getting in trouble because of me.

"Tone it down there, Tarzan," I say, placing my hand on his chest to push him back. "He's my teacher. He's not actually going to harm me."

"Wow. The freak, too?" Gills says to her blowy friend—any relation to the literal wind? "I suppose she'll open her legs to just about any cock."

Hux lunges towards her, only to be stopped by Mason and Frankie—of all people—pulling his back.

"Nah, only the big ones," I say to the pretty redhead, and she sputters.

"Knock it off, Cheryl," the wind snaps.

Cheryl.

Now I know the name of the female with the incandescent gills.

"Yeah, Cheryl," I remark with a curl of my lips. Because I'm just *that* classy.

"Come at me, bitch." Her hands ball into fists, and I know we're seconds away from coming to blows.

"ENOUGH!" The mummy is practically roaring. His eyes, slitted through the intricate wrappings, glow brightly. It has the desired effect—Cheryl winces and steps back in line with her fucking blowjob best friend, and I turn to face our professor. "This is my class, not a schoolground. Is that understood?" When no one immediately responds, he screams, "Is that understood?!"

"Yes, sir," we repeat dumbly, like five years olds being reprimanded by a parent. Cheryl flashes me a scathing glare before facing the front. I place my hand on Hux's bicep, holding him back. The last thing I need is for him to get all murderous on a bunch of dumb bitches because they insulted me. Honestly? They're not worth it. They live their lives putting other people down because they themselves don't believe they'll amount to anything. It's pathetic, really, and only serves to make me feel sorry for them. How miserable must your life be if you go around intimidating others?

Hux crosses his arms over his chest, and I glance at his bulging biceps. He almost appears to be *larger* than Jack...which is impossible, right? They have the same body.

I realize that there's still so much of this world I don't know about it. This horrifying, mysterious world. There's so much about *them* I don't know about. All of them.

"Now that these petty, schoolgirl fights are over—" Wow, sexist much? "—we can begin discussing the Roaring," Mummy says with a glare fixed firmly on me.

There are enthusiastic murmurs from the crowd. Even the viper—my bad, Cheryl—is smiling eagerly.

"What's the Roaring?" I ask the person closest to me...which just so happens to be the wind. Fucking dammit.

He smirks cockily, as if he knew I wouldn't be able to resist his sexual prowess as long as I have. He opens his mouth to speak, but I turn towards the male on the other side of me.

"What's the Roaring?" I ask Hux, and I hear the wind

make a sound of indignation followed by a huff of annoyance.

Hux looks just as confused as I do, his brows furrowed and eyes narrowed.

"I don't know, my precious treasure, but I can find out for you." He goes as far as to bow his head in submission.

And my God, does that do wonders for a poor girl's self-esteem.

"It's a competition. A game, so to speak," Frankie says, moving to stand between me and Hux. I worry for a brief moment that Hux will retaliate for the unintentional diss, but instead, the scary man looks thoughtful. He regards Frankie like one would study a science experiment at a fair: with wonder and bewilderment. Almost as if you can't quite figure out how it works but want to play with it anyway.

"It's what we train for here. The reason for the games and fight training," adds Mason from farther down the line.

Frankie clears his throat, once more reclaiming my attention. "All monsters are allowed to participate. Students from other schools, students from here, parents, relatives. Everyone can play."

"It tests you as a monster," the wind says.

Silence. I kind of wish crickets would start chirping to add to the badassness of this moment.

Note to self: buy crickets.

"Um...it tests you as a monster," Frankie repeats, forking his fingers through his hair uncomfortably. The wind lets out a string of curses behind me, all of which I ignore.

"What does that mean?"

"Everything you learn at the academy is put to the test," Mason adds helpfully. "Fights against other monsters. Scenarios you may find yourself in. Tests that...well...test your intelligence." He shrugs.

"Are you guys competing?"

"Hell yeah!" Mason says with a fist pump and whoop. The sound is loud enough to capture Mummy's attention who turns a piercing glare on us. Mason *really* needs to work on his whispering.

Only when Mummy Man turns away to discuss today's games do I ask, "Anyone else?"

"Of course not," Frankie snorts. "I'll never resort to playing such childish games."

"That's because you know you'll never win," the wind retorts, and if I wasn't ignoring him, I would've flipped him off, especially when Frankie's face turns crimson. Then again, Frankie sounded *pretty* condescending. "But I'm playing. And winning."

Now, *that* sounded pretty condescending.

What a cocky asshole.

"We're playing too," Hux says, the skin between his brows scrunched together.

"You are?" I ask, confused. Just a second ago he hadn't even known what it was. His face goes slack once more, eyes glazing over, and then he nods his head decisively.

"Yes, we are."

Is he...?

Is he talking to Jack?

I guess I never really considered the logistics of two people sharing one body. I suppose it'll make sense for them to be able to communicate mentally.

"It's why we came to the school," Hux explains. "To train. Our father...he's very strict with us. Wants us to win."

I don't know how to respond to that declaration, mainly because I have a thousand and one thoughts fighting for attention in the deepest recesses of my mind. I feel...upset. Heartbroken.

I can't imagine what it's like to be a prisoner in your own body.

The wind nudges me, directing my attention back to the mummy. I never did catch his name.

Damn, I'm horrible at this whole "monster/people" thing.

"To prepare us for the Roaring, I have designed today's class to be a scavenger hunt. I have hidden red flags around campus. Your job is to find them and bring them here within the hour. The team with the most flags will get an A for the day."

"And?" Cheryl asks snarkily, obviously not impressed with the prize. Mummy stares at her coldly, a silent battle of wills. Finally, he relents with a heavy sigh.

"And...the winning team will be able to skip this class for the rest of the week."

That captures the class' attention. Everybody begins chatting excitedly. If there's one thing that can compel students to try their hardest, it's a promise that they'll be able to skip class with no repercussions.

"I call being on a team with Vin," Cheryl says smugly, waving her hand in the air. The person in question—He Who Shall Not Be Named—mutters something unintelligible.

"*I'll* be picking your teams," Mummy tells her, and she pouts. Actually pouts. What is she...five? "Now, as I was saying, you'll be separated into teams of four—"

Hux makes a rumbling sound deep in his throat, and Mummy whips his head to face the dark-haired monster.

"Umm...three?" Mummy tries, and Hux's growl intensifies. He's scaring *me*. And also turning me on.

But then again, I'm a kinky bitch.

"Five?" Mummy questions, and Hux nods his head. Clearing his throat, Mummy attempts to gain control of the situation he already lost. "Okay, I'll pick the teams—"

Another growl echoes from my scary friend.

"*You'll* pick the teams," Mummy concedes with a sigh. Clearly, he realized he has no say in the workings of his class.

Poor guy. He probably didn't expect to go to class today and get verbally manhandled by a guy with a split personality.

The divisions I saw when I first entered the gymnasium are the teams for this assignment. Monsters almost seem to gravitate towards others with similar traits as them.

Cheryl—the bitch—tries to get the wind on her team, but he rebuffs her with a firm glare. With a huff, she stalks towards her friends and Blowy.

The guys stay around me. Apparently, we're a team.

Who would've thought?

They better not fucking slow me down. Those flags? They're mine. I'm going to win this competition, and not only for the prize and good grade. I'm going to prove myself to these monsters, to Blowy and Gills, to Mummy, to these men surrounding me, to myself—I'm going to prove that I have what it takes to be a monster.

CHAPTER 15

VIOLET

"So we have an hour?" I clarify as we emerge outside. The sun is high in the sky, illuminating the tree boughs in sprinkles of gold. While the sun doesn't burn me alive like the stories will have you believe, it *does* irritate my skin. I scrub at my arms with my fingernails, trying—and failing—to be inconspicuous.

As the guys move farther ahead, discussing their game plan or whatever the hell men discuss—dick sizes? ways to make a female orgasm? how to milk a cow?—I hang back. Fuck. I wish I had a jacket or something.

Frankie surprises me by staying beside me. His hands are shoved into his pockets as he attempts an air of nonchalance, but his eyes betray his concern.

"It's just the sun," I answer his unasked question, keeping my voice low to hold off any and all wayward boys. I have the distinct impression Hux would physically tackle me to the ground and shield me from the sun. Maybe he'll even try to destroy it, plunging us into endless darkness.

The man's pretty fucked up.

"Hold on," Frankie says, dropping to his knees and pulling off his backpack. He pulls out a couple of strange looking vials and what appears to be...eyeballs? And a...and a goat horn? Just what the fuck is Frankie doing with that stuff in his backpack?

Procuring an empty tupperware container, he begins to put all of his—errr—ingredients into the bowl just as the other guys realize we haven't been following.

"What's going on?" the wind demands.

"Is something wrong with my precious treasure?" Hux roars—damn, someone needs to tone it down a notch.

Just kidding. I—and my vagina—love it.

"It's just the sun," I assure them. "Burns me worse than a redhead in summer."

"That's an easy fix. I've been making this cream for years now," Frankie says distractedly.

He uses a spoon (who the fuck keeps spoons lying around in their backpack?) to stir the creamy liquid. It's thickening, turning a deep red color. Hopefully, that red isn't from the blood of the eyeball.

"Here." He lathers a generous amount on his hands before turning towards me. The second he would've touched my skin, he hesitates. "May I?"

"As long as this doesn't make me grow hair or something."

He snorts, seemingly offended by my accusation. "Of course not!" He begins to rub it into my arms, paying extra attention to each individual finger. "That requires pine needles, which I clearly didn't add to this."

"Clearly," I respond dryly as his hand travels to my shoulders. I'm not going to lie—his hands feel really, *really* good.

"I only did it once," Frankie continues bluntly, and I stiffen. Not what a girl wants to hear when he's currently balls deep in rubbing it on her. Either oblivious or ignoring my body's reaction, he says, "Had a bunch of pissed off clients. A few death threats. The usual."

His hands lower, brushing against my bare stomach. Goosebumps pebble on my skin, and my breath hitches. I know he's merely applying an ointment, probably doesn't feel anything himself, but I can't stop my visceral reaction.

I need to get laid.

When he scrubs it into my face, licks of fire following the path of his fingers, I can barely hold in the instinctive moan.

Yup. *Definitely* need to get laid. With a big, fat cock.

Frankie finally pulls his hands away from my skin, and I'm surprised to hear his breathing as ragged as my own.

"There. You should be all set. Just make sure to reapply it every twenty four hours. Or I can. You can come to my lab in the basement at anytime. No charge."

For some reason, his proclamation causes the other three men to inhale sharply. Well, two men. Hux is still staring at me intently, eyes roaming my skin and checking for an injury that doesn't exist.

I wrap my arm around Frankie's waist and smile gently.

"Thank you, Frankie. Truly."

His eyes meet mine, and I'm struck by the color. They appear to almost be *golden* flecked with spots of brown. They're beautiful, ethereal, and I know I can stare into them for hours and never tire. He's staring at me just as intently as I am him. Finally, he clears his throat and scrambles to his feet.

"It's whatever," he mumbles sheepishly, cheeks burning.

"Ohhh...Frankie has a crush," Mason says in a singsong voice, earning himself a punch from both the wind and Hux.

Straightening to his full height, Frankie pushes past Mason and stomps forward, towards the edge of the woods. Only when he's out of earshot, lingering at the tree line with his head lowered, do I glare at Mason.

"Don't be an ass," I warn him. "He was being nice."

The wind snorts in derision, pulling my attention off of Mason. "Frankie is *never* nice. You may think I'm a dick, but that man? He always has an agenda. A plan. I rule this school with my strength, but he rules it with his brains. A liar and a crook."

Finally, I can't take it anymore. I jump to my feet and stand toe to toe with the asshole.

"He's my friend. Don't talk about him like that."

"Oh, so *now* you're talking to me," he snaps, his face inches from mine. His breath caresses my face; his nose is nearly touching my own.

"And I already regret it."

"Don't fucking be like this." His tone turns pleading, desperate. "I let you beat me with a fucking arm. What more do you want from me?"

"An apology would be sufficient," I say.

"Speaking of arms..." Mason's head appears over the asshole's shoulder, and he smiles encouragingly. "What happened to the arm you borrowed?"

"Left it for him in the lost and found." I wave my hand dismissively, still focused wholly on the asshole and his asshole hair and his asshole perfect body. And his actual asshole.

I have no restraint.

"Do you know what you do to me?" the wind asks me, stepping even closer. I can see fireworks of brown in his eyes.

"Irritate you?" I guess.

His lips quirk.

"Among other things, yes." The smile fades, and he takes my hands in his. "Violet, I'm sorry for the way I treated you in the cafeteria. I was just trying to protect you, I promise. My friends and family can be..."

"Evil?" Mason pipes in helpfully, once more ruining the moment. Both Vin and I whip our heads in his direction.

"Shut up, Mason," we quip in unison.

"Okay, but why?" I question, focusing once more on Vin. And yes, he's Vin now. He's not completely out of my shit bowl (i.e. a toilet), but he's no longer public enemy number one. "Why me? Why did you come up to me, of all people? Did you come to kill me?"

His face slackens with horror at my final statement, and Hux, behind me, inhales sharply.

"No!" Vin says vehemently. He shakes his head. "No, it's not like that. I want to protect you. I *need* to."

"Why is that, brother?" Mason asks suspiciously. If even *Mason* is suspicious, you know shit's about to go down.

Because in a span of days—hours?—four guys have clung to me like a bunch of spider monkeys, and I've been helpless to resist them. Now, I just need to understand why.

"Look, can we talk about this later?" Frankie asks, storming back towards us. Apparently, he got bored waiting by himself. "I hate fight class. It would be nice if we got a pass for the rest of the week."

"You already have a pass," Mason mutters, but he drops the accusatory glare he was aiming at Vin.

"I worked hard for that pass," Frankie retorts with an imperious upwards tilt to his chin.

"You sold drugs," counters Vin, stepping away from me. One step. Two steps. Three steps. It's only then do I feel like I can breathe again.

"Hard. Work," Frankie stresses. "Now come on. We're down to forty minutes. And we haven't found *any* flags."

"Frankie's right," I reply. This confrontation can wait for a later date. I need to get straight answers from each and every one of them...but not now. Now, we need to kick some flag ass. "I want an A in this class, so let's get to work. Where should we look first?"

Vin seems relieved for the conversation to be over.

"We were thinking maybe inside the student houses. Or around that area. Everyone would've found the ones in the forests, in the academic buildings, and in the dorms," a soft voice says, and I turn towards Jack in surprise. His hair once more hangs in front of his eyes, and his glasses are back in place.

"Jack?" I ask. "Where did Hux go?"

His face falls in disappointment.

"Oh. I can grab him if you want."

He sounds so depressed, so forlorn, that all I want to do is take him in my arms and hug the shit out of him. Maybe buy him a puppy. Puppies can make even the loneliest person happy—just look at the Grinch.

"No!" I say quickly, lifting my hands up. When he blanches at my sharp tone, I work to soften it and my features. "I'm sorry. I just meant I like both of you. In different ways, of course. I just wish you could both be here at the same time." I sigh wistfully, and Jack echoes it.

I wonder if Hux is there right now, looking out through Jack's eyes. Seeing what he's seeing. Feeling what he feels. I wonder if Jack was there when I talked to Hux.

Would it be rude to ask?

The rest of his words come to me then, and I turn towards the boys in surprise.

"Wait. What fucking houses?"

APPARENTLY, THE UPPERCLASSMEN HAVE BIG, FANCY HOUSES A mile away from the school. It's a bit of a trek, cutting through the cemetery and forest, but it is so fucking worth it.

All shapes and sizes, the off-campus houses have everything from balconies to wrap around porches to stained glass windows. One house stands a little taller than the rest with a gabled roof and numerous turrets. Mason elbows me slyly as we step in front of it.

"That's our house," he says, indicating the three other guys.

"Your house? You guys live together?" If my voice sounds incredulous can you blame me? I didn't even know they knew each other let alone liked each other enough to be roomies.

In answer, Mason winks.

Numerous images assault me. Namely, being the fifth roommate to this gorgeous bunch. Emphasis on the *room* part of the equation. This freeloading bitch won't need her own room. Nope, not me. I'll be perfectly content to hop from one room to another like a mythical tooth fairy collecting orgasms instead of teeth.

Wait...

Is the tooth fairy real as well?

"I found one!" Frankie calls, and I'm pulled from my inner ramblings. He stands in front of a flagstand with a billowing flag raised. Just underneath it, tied to the pole itself, is the red flag we've been instructed to grab.

"Fuck," Mason curses. "How are we supposed to get it?"

If I were to estimate, I'd say it was about twenty feet off the ground—give or take twenty feet (I'm not a good estimator). Either way, it's too tall for us to reach up and grab.

"We might have a ladder in the basement," Vin says, nodding towards their house. He jogs through the wrought iron fence and disappears inside.

"I can see about a potion," Frankie mumbles, already pulling off his backpack and digging through it. This time, he pulls out a...is that a liver? A Barbie doll head. Something that resembles a vintage record. A bunch of pine cones.

I'm beginning to think Frankie's backpack is spelled to be a clown car or something. Hmmm. Maybe I should speak to him about doing the same to my purse.

I could hide a body in there.

And with that…

"Let me get it." I crack my neck from one side to the other. I don't really need to crack it, but I think it makes me look cooler. More badass.

"Um…what exactly are you planning on doing?" Jack asks with concern.

"Running and jumping, of course." I thought the neck cracking made it obvious.

"Are you sure that's a good idea?" asks Frankie, still crouched over his clown backpack. "I mean, you did trip while walking in gym class."

"*Running* in gym class," I correct snottily. "Have a little faith in me."

"Pinkie, I want a lot of my things in you, but is this the best idea?" Mason chimes in.

"Just watch me be a total badass," I assure them with a wicked grin. Keeping my eye on the pole—and our prize—I begin to back up until I'm at the edge of the lawn about twenty feet from the pole, give or take twenty feet (again, I'm terrible at estimating). "You ready?"

"I can't watch this," Frankie groans, turning away. Mason gives me a thumbs up. Jack just looks pained.

Before I can chicken out, I break into a run. For a moment, I feel suspended—weightless. The rest of the world disappears in a blur around me until all that exists is the flagpole and me. My *prize* and me. When I'm in close enough range, I kick off from the ground, using my strength to give me a much needed boost, and jump.

I can see it, a hair's breadth away. So close. So. Close.

My head bangs against the flagpole, and I fall unceremoniously onto the concrete.

"Ow…" I moan, holding my forehead. Everything hurts. My back, my legs, my fucking head from the damn, traitorous flagpole. Even my vagina hurts from that fall.

Three sets of feet surround me, and I peer through the blinding sun at Jack, Mason, and Frankie. Mason winces when he meets my gaze, and Frankie crouches down, handing me a pink concoction.

"For the pain," he explains.

"She hit the flagpole?" Vin calls from wherever the hell he is.

"Yes," all three men say together. "Bring the ladder."

"I fucking hate you all," I gripe, still holding my forehead. I hear the clink of the ladder, the pounding of footsteps, and then—

"Got it!" Vin says only a second later, and I turn to see him waving the red flag in the air.

When a monster loses to a fucking ladder…

Violet: zero.

Ladder: one.

CHAPTER 16

FRANKIE

I've dealt with my fair share of monsters. My entire job is dependent on forging these connections and evoking trust in my clients.

But never, in all of my history, have I met someone like Violet.

While she's a monster, she isn't cold. If anything, she's *warm*. Real and vibrant, slowly melting away the icy fortresses erected around my heart with painstaking finesse. And while I have seen numerous bodies before—male and female, naked and fully clothed—I've never experienced such a carnal reaction as I do with her. I've never before wanted to strip someone completely and learn their body through touch alone.

These feelings are immensely dangerous—ones that should be discouraged.

She's going to burn me, of that I have no doubt, but I'm going to welcome the pain.

To my utter amazement, her body heals itself right before

my very eyes. If this had happened to anyone else, I would've wanted to study her in detail, plan a way to profit off of the unimaginable.

But with Violet, all I can do is marvel and be relieved she has this protection.

What the hell is wrong with me?

Now, she's a few feet ahead of me, skipping through the forest like some real life Red Riding Hood. Mason, of course, is skipping right alongside her with a raucous laugh patented only for her.

Vin and Jack hang back with me.

These men have been my roommates since my first year, but I've never felt as close to them as I do now. I would've considered ourselves mere acquaintances only a day or so ago. Not friends, but not necessarily enemies.

"She's...enthusiastic," Vin says, watching Violet jump off the ground in a feeble attempt to catch a butterfly. She falls to the ground, laughing hysterically, and Mason picks her up by the waist and spins her around.

"She's in a lot of danger," Jack murmurs softly, and both Vin and I whip our heads in his direction, trying to discern if what he just said is a threat or a warning. He isn't looking at us, however, but at the golden-haired beauty currently clinging to Mason's back. "Hunters. Other monsters. She's Dracula's one weakness, and the other monsters know that. It's a wonder why Dracula sent her here in the first place."

"I can handle the hunters," Vin says resolutely, and I give him the side-eye.

"But—"

"I said I can handle the hunters," Vin repeats with a dangerous glint to his eyes. This motherfucker is scary on most days, but add in that glint? He's downright terrifying.

"We need to protect her," I reason. Violet has now taken

to...to somersaulting? Why the fuck is that girl somersaulting on the forest floor?

"Agreed," Jack and Vin reply in unison. When Vin pulls his attention away from us, becoming fully enamoured with Violet's antics, I turn towards Jack.

"I might be able to help with your little issue," I say with a shrug of my shoulders. His brows scrunch in confusion, but he doesn't cease his walking.

"What do you mean?"

"You and Hux," I explain. "I might be able to help with that."

His eyes widen slightly, marginally, as hope and fear dance within their depths. He looks as if he desperately wants to believe me...but doesn't want to hope for a whimsical fantasy.

But I make a career out of whimsical fantasies.

Before he can reply, a scream ruptures the serenity of the forest. Not just any scream.

Violet's.

Ice cold terror steals all the warmth from my body. It reminds me of the Abominable Snowman trailing a finger from the nape of my neck to the middle of my back.

I break into a run—yeah, I'm just as shocked as you are—a few steps behind Vin and Jack. Curse my chubby legs.

The tension thrumming through my muscles somewhat alleviates when I see Violet safe and sound, snuggled into Mason's chest. He's holding her tightly, one hand stroking her mane of hair and the other wrapped around her waist. His attention, however, is on the forest floor.

Correction: the dead body on the forest floor.

From an analytical standpoint, I see that the death was recent, the color having yet to drain completely from her face. I also note that it's a female with an abnormally generous amount of hair.

The last thing I catalogue away is the way she died. The bite marks evident on her tan neck.

"Fucking hell," Vin murmurs, anxiously running a hand through his hair. He backs up a step, pauses, and then stumbles forward. With hopeless abandon, he presses his fingers to the woman's neck, checking for a pulse. I know, even before he solemnly shakes his head, that he wouldn't find one.

"I know her," Violet cries softly, voice muffled from where they're being spoken into Mason's shirt. Mason shushes her gently, still stroking her hair, but she continues on dogmatically, "Her name is Ali, and she was in my first class with me. Do you remember, Jack?"

She lifts her gaze to meet Jack's. His nod is more hesitant, more calculating, but it only makes the wheels in my head spin faster and faster.

"She tried to attack me," Violet continues, voice edging on manic disbelief. Has she never seen a dead body before? I realize immediately that sounded heartless, even mentally, and focus instead on the matter at hand.

This girl tried to attack Violet...and now she's dead.

With vampiric-like wounds on her neck.

I exchange a long, loaded glance with Vin before glancing once more at the body.

With clinical detachment, I lean down and—being careful not to touch anything—survey her body and wounds with renewed vigor.

The wounds haven't scabbed over yet which means the perpetrator hadn't actively tried to heal the bitemarks. Only a lick from a vampire is capable of that. Not even their salvia —though heavy in venom—can heal a wound completely. These two are still bloody and raw, but no longer bleeding as profusely as I had no doubt they once were.

And...

And the cuts are too meticulously clean, the type of work you would get from a knife.

A vampire did not kill this woman.

"They're trying to frame me," Violet says in horror, obviously coming to the same conclusion I had.

"Can't we test the venom or something? See who actually killed her?" Mason asks anxiously, clutching Violet even closer as if he wishes to meld with her and become one.

"It's not a vampire," Vin responds tiredly. I can see his mind rapidly sifting through possibilities, through suspects. People who want Violet dead. People with an agenda against Dracula.

The list is too long.

"It's not?" Mason buries his face in Violet's hair, his body shaking. Or hers is shaking. It's becoming increasingly hard to differentiate.

"Someone obviously wanted to frame the vampires," I say. "And if I had to wager a guess, I'll say that they placed Violet's venom on the 'bite marks' just in case it was tested."

"Who the fuck would do that? How would they have even gotten my venom? The only person I drank from was Vin. So who did this? Who's framing me?" Violet rapid-fires, parroting all of our thoughts. She finally removes her head from Mason's chest and glances at each of us before lowering her gaze to the body. "And what do we do now?"

We. I've never been a 'we' before, and despite the terror of what we found, the fear of what is to come, I feel an excited tremor reverberate through my body. I really wouldn't mind being a 'we' with Violet.

"If they find this body, you could get accused of murder," Vin tells her with a detachment I know he doesn't feel. He meets my eyes, and I nod subtly, already removing my backpack. "So we need to get rid of it. Now."

CHAPTER 17

VIOLET

You've heard of stain-be-gone?

Let me introduce you to the new and improved version: body-be-gone.

That's right, folks. Pour it on any body—young or old, male or female, the body-be-gone doesn't discriminate—and watch it disappear before your very eyes.

Frankie could make a *killing* (get it?) selling it on the black market.

To my utter horror and morbid fascination, Ali's body begins to deteriorate before my very eyes. It starts at her legs, burning through the flesh and bone with the same ease you'd burn paper. Actually, it sort of reminds me of that. The body curls in on itself like charring, burning paper seconds before it dematerializes, becoming nothing more than soot and ash. Not even the bones remain.

Hell, not even the *ash* remains as a strong gust of wind carries it through the tree branches.

All I can do is stare in horror at the forested ground that

once housed the dead body of my fellow classmate. Stare and think.

Somebody killed Ali, but who? And why? What could be the reason behind murdering an angry werewolf? And why would they frame me?

And, the most pressing issue, what do we do now?

"People are going to realize she's missing," Mason murmurs, echoing my own thoughts. His hands tighten around my waist, kneading the tender flesh, seconds before he buries his head in my hair and inhales.

I don't move away from him. Apparently, I *like* physical comfort. Who knew?

"We act like everyone else," Vin reasons stoutly. "We haven't seen her since…since…"

"Since last class with Ms. Stevens," pipes in Jack. He shifts uneasily from foot to foot, his glasses sliding down his nose. He uses his middle finger to push them back into place.

"We tell everyone we went to the houses, grabbed the flag, and went immediately back to the gym," Frankie adds. He straightens to his full height, running a hand through his unruly brown hair. He seems tired, I realize. The sort of tired that comes from being out in the sun all day. Is it possible for someone to gain bags under their eyes in seconds?

The silence stretches as awkward eye contact is made and retained. All of the men give a sort of macho head bob that I try—and fail—to replicate. Seriously, who knew that head nodding could lead to a kink in your neck?

With that consensus, we head back down the trail and towards the gymnasium.

Fortunately, we are not the last team to arrive.

Unfortunately, we only found one flag.

When Mummy arrives, wrapped arms crossed over his chest, he gives us a disapproving look as if he genuinely thought we would do better than that. My mood sours further when he announces Cheryl and her merry band of monsters the winner at three flags.

Nothing like seeing and disposing of a dead body then losing the competition to your nemesis to put a damper on your day.

Cheryl sashays over to our group, hair shimmering like rubies in the artificial gymnasium lights. Blowy the Best Blowjob walks behind her alongside two people I don't know. Taking up the rear of the group is Ali's boyfriend, Fish Face. He doesn't look upset or anxious or any other emotion you would normally feel if you suspected your girlfriend had been murdered. So, bonus?

"Should've been on our team, Vinny Poo," Cheryl says with an exaggerated hair flip. If there was an Olympic sport for hair flipping, I have no doubt that Cheryl would come home with the gold. Me? I'd probably whip my hair so hard that I lose an eye. And then, with my noticeable lack of eyes (yes, somehow it turned into losing two eyes instead of one) I'd fall into an abnormally large garbage disposal. Of course, I'd survive.

But talk about embarrassing.

"Don't touch me," Vin hisses as the beautiful girl places her delicate, albeit scaly, fingers on his arm. Her lips contort into a sneer, but she composes herself quickly.

"What happened to you? You're a *Van Helsing*," she emphasizes the name with a sardonic twist to her mouth. Her declaration garners the attention of a small group walking by. Their faces are unmistakable—the assholes from breakfast, minus Vanessa.

Hunters.

Now, hunters don't usually go after just vampires. They consider themselves the police of the monster world, putting down any monster that goes too far. At the Academy, their curriculum consists of appropriate monster responses, ways to kill every breed, and the unspoken laws regulating the monster world. Kill one human? Sure, that's fine. We're monsters, after all. Wipe out an entire town? The hunters come, guns blazing.

But the Van Helsings?

They focus on vampires, believing us to be a lesser breed. They look at Dracula, the leader of the vampires, as the devil himself. The epitome of evil.

Some hunters, like the group slowly converging on us, follow the strict regiment implemented by the Van Helsing family: kill all vampires. Hell, they might even be Van Helsings themselves. Heaven only knows how large they are—cousins, aunts, aunts of aunts, cousins of cousins, a brother's friend's uncle's grandma's cousin.

The Van Helsings are a fucking *tribe*.

And this tribe?

They want my blood.

Vin tenses significantly as the hunters approach, more upset now than he was when we had found the body.

These were the assholes with Vanessa and Vin in the cafeteria, when Vin had embarrassed and accused me of compelling him. That memory momentarily exacerbates my rage, but I push it down.

"What the fuck are you doing?" the male leader snaps, eyeing Vin like he's a disgusting pimple on someone's nose. A healthy dose of fear and disgust combined with the "should I say something or should I leave it" mentality. But combined with all *that* is anger. Lots and lots of anger.

Cheryl grins like the cat who finally got the cream. Mason and Jack both stand in front of me, attempting futilely to obscure me from view. Frankie takes a step closer to me, our shoulders brushing.

Fuck, this could go really, really bad. These men will tear Vin alive for being my sort-of friend.

"I'm giving him sexual favors in exchange for protection," I blurt to the man and his friends.

Everyone blinks at me.

Everyone.

Even Mummy has stopped talking to a student on the opposite side of the gym to stare at me. Vin's mouth is agape, eyes comically wide, and Cheryl just looks pissed.

Welp, you got this far, Violet. Why not finish the mile?

"I knew I needed protection because I'm a poor, defenseless vampire," I say, sniffling. Jack is trying inconspicuously to shake his head, to warn me against talking, and Mason is covering his mouth to hide his smile. I can't see Frankie's face, but his grip is suddenly tight on my hand.

Wait, when did we start holding hands?

I kind of want to swoon, but I figure that would ruin the badass, sexual vampire image I'm trying to portray.

"I'm really, really good at, um—" My eyes land on Blowy. "—blowjobs. Super good. I think it's the teeth." I allow my fangs to poke my bottom lip and then bite the air seductively.

Okay, not *seductively*, per se.

But I don't think I look too shabby either. A solid six on the whole sex-o-meter scale.

Again, another round of synchronized blinks.

"Vin's offering you protection...in exchange for blowjobs," the man says slowly, carefully, as if testing the truth of my words on his tongue.

"Yes." I nod my head vehemently—before realizing I look over-enthusiastic and need to tone it down a notch. "I decided to create a...errr...um...I decided to hire bodyguards," I decide on quickly. "Yup. Four bodyguards. You never know when you're going to need protection."

Sounds perfectly plausible, if I do say so myself. And these guys *have* been kind of following me around. Huh.

Maybe I should start offering blowjobs and shit as payment. Make this whole thing legit.

Cheryl's face is bright blue in rage. Yes, blue. Her gills are ten times more pronounced as she bristles.

"What the hell, Vin?" she screeches, turning towards a shell-shocked Van Helsing. He's still gaping, stunned into silence.

The new guy's predatory gaze slides over my body before resting purposefully on my breasts. He nods his head with something that resembles approval.

"Not a bad idea, Vin. Not a bad idea at all."

CHAPTER 18

VIOLET

The men are *not* happy with me.

"What the hell, Vi," Vin snaps as soon as we're in the hallway and away from other students. Frankie and Jack stand behind him, expressions carefully blank. Mason leans against the wall, but unlike the others, he has a huge ass smile on his face.

"I didn't do anything wrong," I defend, annoyed. "But even you guys can admit it looks pretty damn suspicious." I turn my pointed glare onto Vin. "You *kill* my kind for sport—"

"And you do the same to mine," he interrupts.

Ignoring him, I continue. "And I still don't even know why you guys are hanging around me. Is it because I have big tits? Because I promise you, they're not that great. I'm pretty sure my right is bigger than my left. Don't say I didn't warn you."

Mason groans, scrubbing a hand down his face. "Pinkie,

please stop talking about your tits. Please, for the love of all that's good and holy, stop."

I totally have the urge to fondle my breasts, but I dismiss it.

Later, I tell my boobs very seriously.

"Look, can we talk about this later? I have to get to class."

Vin looks as if he wants to argue—fuck, he even opens his mouth *to* argue—before conceding with a sharp nod.

"What class do you have?" Jack asks gently, and I throw him a grateful smile.

"Urban legends," I reply, having already memorized my schedule.

"I have that too. I'll walk with you," Frankie volunteers.

"With Dimitri?" questions Vin.

"Errr...I believe it's Mr. Gray, but I'll have to check."

Frankie squeezes my hand before I can check my class schedule.

And...

We're holding hands again.

I totally want to have a girly moment where I swoon and make a wedding scrapbook.

"It's Dimitri," Frankie assures Vin. "But we probably should start heading over there. It's on the opposite side of the academic building."

"We'll meet you outside the classroom." Vin's voice leaves no room for argument. Turning towards me, his eyes soften considerably. "Be safe, okay?"

"Um...yeah, okay."

Vin is a strange, strange man. A *confusing* man. One second he's throwing me on the ground and accusing me of a despicable act, and the next he's following me around apologizing, concerned for my safety. I almost think he cares about me which is strange by itself. For one, Van Helsings don't care about vampires, least of all Dracula's daughter. And second, we barely know each other.

Yet there was no hesitation, no fear, when he decided to dispose of the body and then cover for me.

They should seriously consider making a manual for men. The do's and don'ts. The on and off switch. You know, normal stuff.

Mason wraps me in his strong arms, nuzzling against my neck like a needy cat. Come to think of it…

Maybe Mason is just an overgrown cat.

Nailed it.

Jack waves at me once, blushes, before hurrying down the hall in the opposite direction of Mason and Vin.

"Today has been a strange day," I muse to Frankie once we're alone. He takes off his glasses to rub at his eyes.

"Tell me about it."

"Oh I will," I say teasingly. "But you were witness to like ninety-nine point nine percent of it."

"What's the point one percent that I missed?" Frankie asks, falling in step beside me.

Leaning towards him, I conspiratorially whisper, "I woke up at two in the morning and…" I cast a quick look in both directions.

"And?" he asks, leaning closer to me as well.

He smells good, I realize somewhat distantly. Almost like peppermints. If I was weird, I might start inhaling him like one would inhale cocaine.

But I'm not weird, so I just lick him instead.

He jerks backwards, head slamming against the wall. When his wide eyes fall on me, a single eyebrow raised, I shrug sheepishly.

"You smelled good."

Because *that* explains everything.

I really need to work on my excuses. Or I just need to stop licking random people.

Actually…

I rather *like* licking random people. And sucking.

Okay, so maybe not random, *random* people. I don't consider Frankie a stranger anymore. It's not like my tongue is a magnet and the men are the fridges.

Frankie is staring at me blankly, and I realize I missed half of what he said. Correction: *everything* he just said.

"You're a strange monster, you know that, right?" Frankie asks, but his tone makes me think he's not upset by that. If anything, he sounds amused. Maybe a little tender.

"My dad said I was dropped on my head as a child," I reply very seriously.

Frankie's lips twitch as he reaches for my hand, propelling me along. "Come on. Let's get to class before we're late."

The halls are beginning to empty out, but there are still a few students loitering about. More than one do a comedic double-take as we walk by.

"What's up with them?" I whisper to Frankie after a pretty female staggers to a stop, eyes fixing first on our interlocked hands before rising to glare daggers at me.

Am I mistaken, or does Frankie blush?

"I don't usually…" He runs a hand through his hair. "I don't usually associate with females."

"But you associate with males?" I ask. I want to understand everything there is to know about Frankie. His secrets and fears. His desires. I want to bare the man beneath the mask.

"No," he sighs. "I don't usually associate with anyone. Male or female." When I give him a quizzical look, he reluctantly explains. "I'm committed to my work. I never felt the need to...partake in activities with members of either sex." He shrugs his shoulders.

I have so many things I want to ask him—namely, his kindling relationship with me and what it means.

I don't, though. His face is drawn, cheeks still rosy. I know when a conversation needs to end, and this one? This one has hit a fucking cement wall.

"So I heard you have a lab here?" I say sweetly, and he notably deflates in relief at the subject change.

"Yes, in the basement." He grabs my shoulder to stop me and points down the hall, towards a door labeled as *Employees Only*.

"Down there?"

"Down there," he agrees, resuming our steady pace.

"What do you do down there?" I ask just as we turn at a fork in the hall. Frankie shrugs, but another blush darkens his cheeks.

"A lot of things," is his evasive reply.

I once more nod understandingly.

He doesn't need to spell it out for me. "A lot of things" does not necessarily mean good things.

It's no secret that Frankie is the school's most esteemed drug dealer. Even Cynthia knows about him—he deals everything from fairy drugs to human organs.

"Can you take me there sometime?" I ask tentatively, unsure if I'm encroaching on taboo territory. When Frankie whips his head around to stare at me, eyebrows raised, I hurry to elaborate. "Your lab. Can you take me?" He doesn't answer right away, a dumb-struck expression on his face, and I feel myself grow self-conscious. "I won't touch anything, promise! And I won't talk if you don't want me to. I'll just sit there and watch."

He looks away quickly, clearing his throat. "It's not that.

It's just...no one has ever wanted to watch me work before. No one has ever cared."

"I care," I say immediately, and then blush.

Play. It. Cool.

"I care about you, Frankie."

Dammit.

He clears his throat harshly once more before opening the door to one of the classrooms. My cheeks are still on fire, and I duck under his arm to enter.

I have only taken one step into the classroom, towards a set of empty desks near the back, when Frankie whispers, "I'd like for you to join me."

My smile is wide as I practically dance to my seat. I add a few extra butt shakes along the way—there's not really a reason. My butt just likes to move and show off. And not trying to toot my own horn or anything, but I personally believe I have a damn good one.

Frankie slides into the seat beside me...and then moves his desk even *closer* until his thigh is touching mine.

I glance around at my fellow classmates, wanting to see if any of them are staring at us. Fortunately, I don't recognize the majority of them.

I think if I had *another* class with Cheryl, I'd be liable to murder her. Wait. Is it too soon for a murder joke?

I notice, somewhat absently, that the majority of students are females, all scantily-dressed. The ones wearing blouses have the top few buttons undone, showcasing their bras. Others are wearing skimpy shirts and short skirts.

I only have a moment to ponder about their strange clothing attire when the door to the classroom opens...and the most perfect guy I've ever seen enters.

He has light blonde hair, so blonde it's almost white. His body seems to be hewn from stone, muscles rippling as he places a stack of papers and his briefcase onto his desk.

Dimitri Gray.

Dorian Gray's only son.

I don't know much about that particular legend, but I do know the curse extended to his son. Beautiful and perfect...with a dark soul only visible in a painted portrait. Apparently, the men of the family are unable to look into mirrors for fear of seeing their monsters personified.

He stiffens, back hunching, as if he can feel my eyes caressing his skin.

Slowly, ever so slowly, he turns around.

I'm not going to lie: I totally expected a Hallmark movie moment. Our eyes meeting, and the attraction between us becoming undeniable. Maybe a slow motion skip towards one another.

Alas, reality hurts like a bitch.

Dimitri Gray—sex and sin personified—glares at me. His eyes are thin slits, and his face is hard.

The man's tall, almost abnormally so. Tall and lean and so heartbreakingly gorgeous I feel my heart speed up.

His eyes sweep over me as if I'm an insignificant bug. Not even a bug he'll want to smush—just an annoyingly pesky bug that happens to be in his classroom, one he doesn't care enough about to kill.

Without a word, he grabs the stack of papers and begins distributing them to the class. A few of the girls flutter their lashes at him, reaching for his arm. He ignores them all with a frosty glare.

When he drops the paper onto my desk, I could've sworn his fist hit the table harder than necessary.

I exchange a look with Frankie, one that eloquently states, "What the hell is his problem?"

Frankie shrugs one shoulder, eyes fixated firmly on the smoldering professor. His gaze can almost be described as challenging. Dimitri meets it with an impassive one of his own.

"You have one hour," Dimitri says curtly, moving back to his desk in the front. "Begin."

Begin?

I glance down at the stapled paper, shocked to see it's a motherfucking exam. An exam on things I've *never* learned before. Even Frankie is diligently bent over his test, though his eyes flicker to me occasionally.

How the hell does Dimitri freaking Gray expect me to complete this when I've never studied the material?

I hesitate for a brief moment, shifting uncomfortably in my chair, before grabbing the test and moving to the front of the classroom. Dimitri's head is lowered as he works on grading what appears to be a paper.

I wait at the edge of his desk, but he doesn't bother to acknowledge me. I know he can fucking hear me breathing.

Clearing my throat once, I wait for his eyes to flicker up. When they don't, I release a heavy breath and drop the exam onto his desk. His hand pauses in its scribbling, but his eyes still do not raise.

"I can't take this, Dim—Mr. Gray," I correct.

His hand tightens over the pen.

"I haven't learned the material yet," I explain. "I'm new here, you see, and—"

Without a word, he takes the test, rips it into shreds, and throws them into the garbage can beside him.

I blink at him wordlessly.

"Oh, um...thanks. I was thinking I could—"

"Headmaster's office," Dimitri says in a cold voice. "Now."

I'm probably catching flies with how far my mouth is opened.

"Huh?"

"The consequence of failing one of my exams is a trip to

the headmaster's office," he continues. "You just failed. Head-master's office. Go."

He looks back down at the paper, clearly dismissing me.

All I can do is stand there and gape at him like an imbecile.

Is he for fucking real?

"Sir," Frankie interjects, standing from his seat as well. It's apparent he's been eavesdropping on our conversation instead of focusing on his own exam. "I'm afraid there's a misunderstanding. Violet, here, has—"

"Hand me your test." Dimitri extends his hand, palm up, while one hand writes with red ink on the paper he has resumed grading. His eyes never raise.

"But sir—"

"Test. Then the headmaster's office. Now."

Frankie, visibly bristling, stalks forward with his own test. He hands it to Dimitri who wastes no time ripping it up and tossing it in the trash can.

When we both remain standing there, at a loss for words, Dimitri raises his head once more.

And pierces me with ice blue eyes.

"Go. Now." With a grunt, he forces his gaze off of me and back on the paper he's grading. It almost appears as if his hand is physically shaking.

"Fine, whatever," I huff, gripping Frankie's arm and drag-ging him along behind me. Frankie still seems shocked, eyes glazed over, but he allows me to pull him out of the classroom.

Away from Dimitri's penetrating stare.

What a prick.

CHAPTER 19

VIOLET

I'm *fuming* by the time I get to the headmaster's office, in the lower basement of the academic building.

I probably planned Dimitri's murder five hundred times in a million different ways. My favorite? It involves monkeys, yellow paint, and a dick.

The receptionist greets us with a stern-faced scowl and a nod of her head.

"He'll see you in a second," she says, no doubt having been told why we're here.

One glance at her confirms she's some sort of...other monster. Webbed fingers that must make typing a *pain*. Feathers on her neck and cheeks. Fangs poking her bottom lip.

Maybe some sort of bird lady?

Frankie and I sit side by side in the sparsely furnished lobby. It consists of a dozen or so chairs arranged in a semi-circle against the wall, annoyingly red carpeting, and a single receptionist desk.

After a moment, the door behind the desk opens, and a tall, domineering man emerges.

The headmaster.

He regards Frankie and me with disdain before making a come-hither gesture. Both of us immediately rise, but the crooked finger turns into a palm.

"The girl only," he says ominously, and Frankie gives me an anxious glance. I nod my head once, trying to convey with my eyes that it'll be okay. He doesn't look convinced but reluctantly sits back down.

Grabbing my backpack, I follow the headmaster into his office.

It's a combination of reds and golds, just like the lobby, with accents in golden tones. There's a bookshelf against the far wall, the books devoid of dust and obviously well-loved, and a suit of armor in the corner. The man himself sits behind the table in a high-back leather chair. He steeples his hands together and levels me with a serious look.

"Do you know why you're here?" he asks—and since I forgot his name, I'm just going to refer to him as Headmaster. A very hairy headmaster. Didn't Dad say he was a descendent of the Wolfman?

"Not really, no," I answer honestly.

He nods his head once, picking up a statue and turning it over in his hands. It appears to be a cow with ruby red eyes and a silver, nondescript body.

"I got a strange message from Mr. Gray that you were disrupting class. Care to explain?"

Yup. I hate that guy. Death to professors is my new life motto. Except for maybe Ms. Stevens. She seems kind of cool. Maybe Dimitri needs to fuck her and get some of her happy juice inside of him.

Wait...

No.

"I wasn't being disruptive," I try placatingly. "I was just questioning the logistics of taking a test on my first day of school. I didn't know the material, and I thought it was unfair."

There. Straight to the point. I should consider a career as a lawyer if the whole monster gig doesn't work out.

"That may be, but here at Prodigium, we follow a strict regimen. If you're not up for the task..." He trails off, ripping his eyes from me to stare down at his cow thingy.

"I'm up for the task," I assure him. "I'm super duper up for it."

He pauses once more.

"It's a shame Mr. Gray decided to have his exam today. And it's even more a shame that you were removed from his class. We planned on sending recruiters from the Roaring, and I think you would make a fine athlete."

I barely, just barely, keep from snorting. Me? An athlete? Hilarious.

I run for food and sex, that's it.

Do you know what it's like to run with big boobs? They fucking jiggle. You can be wearing the best damn sports bra in the world, and they'll still billow in the breeze. And don't even get me started on chub rub.

Frankly, my body is *not* meant for activity. At least not the physical kind.

Okay, at least not the physical kind that doesn't involve at least one orgasm.

"Am I in trouble, sir?" I ask, bracing myself. Dad is going to be *pissed* when I tell him.

"Should you be?" he counters with a severe frown.

Trap. This is a trap.

"No?" My statement turns into a question, and I inwardly wince.

But Headmaster seems to take my words at face value and nods his head. I almost sag against the chair in relief.

"Fortunately, Mr. Gray demanded that I not expel you. But do not, I repeat, do not disrupt class again. Next time, fail the exam the old fashioned way. Understand?"

"Understood, sir." I'm eager to escape the stuffy office. I have one more class scheduled for the day, and then it's sleep, sleep, sleep.

Mama likes her sleep.

And…

I should stop referring to myself as Mama. People might get the wrong idea.

"You're excused." I all but scramble out of the chair, stubbing my toe in the process. "Don't bother sending Mr. Frankenstein back here. You are both excused until your next class. I recommend you two make the most of your free hour. Maybe talk to the Roaring recruiters?" He sounds so hopeful, so optimistic, that I shrug my shoulders. Why not? I have nothing better to do.

"Thank you, sir," I say, running out of the room. He grunts in reply.

Frankie is sitting anxiously in the uncomfortable chair, fingers twitching. When I exit, he jumps to his feet to meet me.

"Are you okay?" he asks, eyes roaming over me. I capture his hands with mine, holding them between us.

"I'm fine," I assure him. "And we're free to go."

"Both of us?" He glances hesitantly over my shoulder, towards the closed door, but when Headmaster doesn't come charging out, he relaxes.

"Both of us." I send him a relieved smile, and we both head back into the empty hall. "Maybe you can show me your lab now?" I ask, kicking my leg out nervously.

He pauses, and a slow smile begins to form on his handsome face.

"Or maybe…" He takes a step closer, the toes of his shoes touching mine.

"Or maybe?" I breathe.

"We can do something else instead."

My stomach flutters like thousands of butterflies have been set free. I really, really like the way this sounds.

"YOU'RE SUCH AN ASSHOLE," I GROAN.

"You need to catch up," is Frankie's unperturbed response.

We sit in the moderately empty library, a stack of books piled on the table before me. The library is exactly how I'd picture one to look in a gothic castle—maybe even the Beast's library in *Beauty and the Beast*.

It has ornately carved wooden shelves, stacks upon stacks of books, and a few tables scattered throughout.

"This sucks," I groan, burying my face in a text that dictates life as a monster in the early eighteenth century. Riveting stuff, I'll tell ya.

"And you're behind," he says reasonably.

Before I can protest, a pretty redhead steps up to our table.

"Frankie, can I talk to you for a second?" she questions, and something about her—whether it's her behavior, or her perky breasts practically spilling out of her shirt, or the fact that she's talking to Frankie in the first place—puts me on edge.

Frankie doesn't glance up from the book he's looking at with me.

"I'm not working right now. Please come back during my office hours," he replies dismissively.

Her lips purse into a thin line.

With a sly glance at me, she turns once more towards Frankie.

"I need to talk to you. I want you to take a look at the breasts you gave me. Make sure they're still up to your standards." She's practically purring at the end of it.

When Frankie remains silent, still staring intently at my textbook as he struggles through a passage, the redhead whips off her shirt.

Yup.

That happens.

I'm suddenly face to face with two perky breasts. Two *perfect* breasts. Very symmetrical and round.

Frankie did a damn good job.

"I'm sure they're fine," Frankie says in a bored voice. Turning towards me, he asks, "Did you read the history of Dracula? Absolutely fascinating. I think we should start there. It'll help you with your origins."

Little Miss Perky Breasts *still* can't get the memo. She's fondling them, pinching her perfect nipples, winking seductively at an oblivious Frankie.

I kind of want to kill her.

Like, girl, stay in your lane. He's obviously here with another girl and isn't interested in you.

But when she touches him, leaning forward so her bare fucking breasts brush his arm, I see red. Something inside of me just...snaps.

So yeah.

That is how I got detention my very first day at Monster Academy.

CHAPTER 20

MASON

I'm in an unnaturally good mood.

Granted, that could be the drugs coursing through my system, but I think it's something else. Or, more accurately, *someone* else.

Violet.

Pinkie.

I have a swarm of gnats in my stomach, and just the thought of her causes them to buzz with a vengeance.

It's been a day, and I'm already pussy-whipped. Proudly so.

I couldn't even concentrate in a class I once adored. Okay, so maybe I fucked the teacher, but I'm a changed man now. A one-woman type of man. When the slimy professor attempts to keep me after class for a quickie, I smile coldly and offer her my middle finger. She can do with it what she wants, even shove it up her ass.

Vin and Jack fall into step with me as we hurry down the

hallway. We're an odd pair, the three of us. Errr...odd triplets, the three of us.

"Pinkie, Pinkie, I'm coming for Pinkie," I sing, dancing on the tips of my toes.

"Can you shut the fuck up?" Vin snaps.

I simply wrap an arm around his neck and sing at the top of my lungs, "Pinkie! I need my Pinkie!" Lowering my voice to a whisper, I breathe, "Pinkie. I want my Pinkie," before quickly snaking my tongue out to lick his ear.

He shoves me away in disgust, flashing me a frosty glare. I roar with laughter, and even Jack flashes a small, albeit hesitant, smile.

"You're an asshole, you know that?" Vin sneers, wiping the saliva from his ear. He grabs the hem of my untucked flannel and cleans his fingers on there. "Save your saliva for Vi."

"Vi. Vin. Pretty similar sounding names," I muse, my mind stuck on the thought of using my saliva on my mate. Fuck yes. My cock twitches in my pants, and I know it will only be pacified by the sweet, sweet mouth of my sweet, sweet mate. Or her sopping wet pussy. "Maybe you are related," I finish distractedly.

Vin flashes me a fucking horrified look, and I can't stop myself from breaking into laughter once more. I slap my knees, bending over, and Vin whacks me on the back of my head.

"Don't be an asshole," he mutters, still sounding slightly sick to his stomach at the prospect of being related to Violet.

I'm not stupid, despite contrary belief. I see the way he looks at her even when he pretends not to. Vin, in all the years since I have befriended him, has never once apologized. Not once. Not even when he fell asleep on a girl in the middle of sex because she was taking too long to orgasm. Not when he accidentally stabbed the wrong guy in the back on a hunt. Not when he punched me in the face after that bitch, Cheryl, seduced me.

But Violet? He was practically groveling at her feet, begging for forgiveness. She has his balls wrapped inside her dainty hands, and she doesn't even realize it yet.

I also know he was only trying to protect her in the cafeteria this morning (was it really only this morning?), and that he had obviously changed his mind about keeping his distance. What changed?

I know it's impossible for them to be mates—Van Helsings don't have fated mates, for one—so I can't discern what his fascination is with her. It should bother me, this obvious lust and infatuation, but it doesn't.

I mean, sure, I'd like Violet all to myself, but I know she'll never be truly happy with just me. She needs Jack's kindness to balance her out. Vin's steadfast protection. Hux's devotion. Even Frankie's unemotional worldview. I understand that, and I accept it.

There's no pain at the thought of the other men with Violet, no jealousy. Hell, I wouldn't even mind joining in when—or if—one of them takes her.

The thought of my Pinkie has me hurrying the last few steps down the hall, stopping in front of Dimitri's door. Their class still appears to be in session, so I lean against the wall and cross my arms over my chest. Vin moves to mimic my position, and Jack shoves his hands into his pockets, looking unexplainably pensive.

Before I can question his strange behavior, the door to the class opens, and students begin to filter out. I'm practically bouncing, craning my neck to and fro to catch a glimpse of her golden hair.

"Pinkie, Pinkie, Pinkie," I sing beneath my breath, and Vin flashes me a disgruntled look.

"You're such a child," he hisses.

"Takes one to know one," I retort—probably proving that I am, in fact, a child.

When the last of the students leave the classroom, and Violet still hasn't revealed herself, my excitement turns into panic. Could something have happened to her during the short time we were away?

Vin strides forward, unsheathing his fucking sword like a badass motherfucker. Seriously, where did he keep that thing? I've definitely not noticed anything on his person the last couple of hours.

"Where is my precious treasure?" Hux's dark voice hisses. He has discarded his glasses and pushed his hair behind his ears. Like Vin, he takes an intimidating step forward. I try to trail along behind looking similarly badass. But to be frank? A guy in a beanie with a glazed look in his eyes can't be badass. It's literally impossible.

Dimitri Gray stands in the doorway and leans against the frame. The man...

He's a scary motherfucker. Rumor has it that, before he became a teacher, he was an assassin for the monster government. He looks as sophisticated and elegant as always, the epitome of calm. I imagine nothing can ruffle this man.

"Where is Violet?" Vin asks through gritted teeth, brandishing his sword. His jaw is clenched so tightly I'm afraid it'll break.

I stand behind Hux and Vin, debating the pros and cons of removing my beanie. On one hand, that's a sure way to get Dimitri's attention and compliance. On the other, the hallway is teeming with students, the majority of which are already staring at our ragtag group in rapt fascination.

I don't know if they're staring because Vin Van Helsing is threatening a teacher, the dreaded Dimitri Gray, or if it's because Hux has come out to play.

Either way, my snakes will just make another spectacle we don't need.

"I'm afraid I had to send her to the headmaster's office," he replies coldly, and I bristle at his tone. "Now, have you guys met my friends? They're recruiters and judges for the Roaring...which I'm sure you guys are participating in." He steps back marginally to reveal the two men behind him. One is tall and willowy, bedecked in a gray business suit, while the other is a mountain of muscle. One glance confirms they're brothers of some sort...perhaps a descendant of the Yeti if their white hair, scarves, and thick winter coats are any indication. Maybe even Jack Frost.

"What does this have to do with my precious treasure?" Hux snaps, appearing as disgruntled as I feel.

"We're interested in recruiting Ms. Violet Dracula as an athlete," the muscular man responds easily.

I stiffen.

I trust my girl to take care of herself, I do, but the games are extremely dangerous. Only the best of the best athletes are permitted to compete. The consequences of losing isn't just hurt pride...it can potentially be death.

Call me a hypocrite, but I don't want my mate anywhere near that shit.

Dimitri gives us a look I can't quite decipher before turning back to the two men.

"I'll have her contact you," he assures them, and the taller one nods seriously.

As one, the two Yeti men step into the hall. Their shoulders brush Vin's and Hux's, both of who are glaring daggers into their backs.

"What's this about, Dimitri?" Vin hisses. "Why did you send Violet to the headmaster? And why the fuck are you recruiting her for the Roaring?"

Hux looks as if he wants to punch something or someone

but can't decide who. I subtly move out of his immediate arm range.

My face is too pretty to be damaged.

"I'm not recruiting her for anything," Dimitri snaps, pinching the bridge of his nose with two fingers. "But the administrators for the Roaring are quite adamant that she competes."

"Why?" I ask.

He levels me with a glare I can't quite read.

"Does it look like I know?" he barks. "All I know is that Violet *can't* compete in the Roaring."

His ominous words cause goosebumps to skate up my spine and arms. I scrub at the skin absently.

"Is that a threat, Gray?" Vin asks, venturing a step closer and still holding that fucking sword like he's preparing to cut up some meat. His muscles are flexed, and his face is contorted into what I'm beginning to think is his "I'm going to fuck you up" expression.

"No," Dimitri says briskly. "It's a warning. Now, if you Neanderthals don't mind, I have papers I need to grade." Without another word, he slams the door in our stunned faces, and I'm left reeling from the exchange. What the hell just happened?

"What the heck?" Hux whispers, and I spin towards him. His glasses are back in place, and his stringy hair once more obscures his features from view. Not Hux, then. Jack.

He blanches, pushing himself against the wall, as a group of students hurry in our direction, talking about some hot girl-on-girl fight. Normally, I would be heading that direction as well to reward the victor and console the loser. But again, a changed man over here. My cock and heart only function for one female—see? I can totally be romantic.

"Do you think Dimitri knows something we don't?" I ask,

reaching into my backpack pocket and grabbing out a joint. I made a promise to myself not to smoke in front of Violet.

If she really wants me to stop, I will without question. But for now, I allow the sensual high to liquify my veins. I exhale, watching a cloud of smoke materialize around my head. I work on contorting the shape in the air, changing it into a heart, and smile blissfully.

Stoned off my ass.

"If he does, I'll cut off his dick and feed it to him like a dog. Make him get on his hands and knees and bark for his dog food," Vin replies darkly, and both Jack and I blink at him.

What the everloving fuck? I always suspected Vin was in to some kinky shit, but this is next level.

"That's adorable," I settle on at last, sidestepping another group of men heading in the direction of the library. I distantly hear raucous laughter and chants of, "Slap that tit."

That is *some* girl fight.

The farther we get from the fight, the quieter it becomes. We find ourselves standing in the headmaster's office, staring pointedly at the feathered receptionist.

A receptionist I may or may not have banged at one point.

Don't judge me. I was high as a kite and had also consumed about...oh...five gallons of fairy alcohol? Give or take? And it isn't like I'm the only guilty party. Vin tag-teamed that one with me, and I'm pretty sure he *was* sober.

The receptionist smiles and flutters her lashes, no doubt remembering my poor, unfortunate mistake.

Hell, I didn't even remember it until a week later when I found a feather up my...um...

We'll just pretend that never happened.

"Where's Violet?" Vin demands, cutting right to the chase.

Birdy's—yes, that's her actual name—lips turn down, and her eyes harden.

"Who?" she asks snidely.

When Vin looks ready to strangle her, the muscles in his neck twitching, Jack steps forward to alleviate the tension thickening the air. His attempt to pacify Vin's rage is admirable, I'll admit that.

He shuffles towards her desk, head lowered, and politely states, "Excuse me, ma'am, but I'm looking for my friend, Violet Dracula. She was supposed to be here according to Mr. Gray. Do you know if she's still here?"

I can see Birdy's resolve weakening, her maternal instincts coming out to play when faced with this timid boy. She sighs heavily, refusing to make eye contact with me or Vin.

"She left a little bit ago with Frankenstein's son," she admits, and I feel marginally better at the knowledge Frankie's with her and keeping her safe.

Keeping her out of trouble.

"Do you know where—?" Vin begins, but he is cut off when the glass door is pushed open and a red-faced library worker pants, "There are two naked girls fighting in the library. One of them is Dracula's daughter."

Jack and I exchange a look before racing after the librarian.

What. The. Fuck?

CHAPTER 21

VIOLET

She dies choking on a cock.

Okay, so I might need to backtrack a little bit. I can't just jump right to the good stuff, now can I?

After the admittedly pathetic fist fight—one that involved a lot of titty twisters and boob punches—I'm dragged to a small classroom where I'm told to sit and behave.

I'm the only occupant of said classroom, and I pace anxiously for a solid minute.

Longest minute of my fucking life, let me tell you.

After the allotted sixty seconds are over, I try the door handle, unsurprised to find it locked.

"Hello?" I call, peering through the rectangular glass window on the door. "Is this detention?"

When no one immediately replies, I sigh heavily and move back to one of the desks.

The classroom, as previously stated, is tiny. Only nine desks are organized in rows of three. There's a larger desk at the front for the teacher and a chalkboard.

I vaguely remember being pulled in one direction while Titty McFlapperson is pulled in another. Frankie had hurried after me, mouth set in a determined line, only to be blocked off by a professor I still had yet to meet.

Alas, I am here.

Alone.

In some random classroom on some random floor. I think it's the top?

Either way, the silence causes my skin to break out into goosebumps like it would with hives. If I'm going to be punished, I just want to get it over with.

"Headmaster?" I call. "Anyone?"

Silence.

I perch myself on the edge of the teacher's desk and kick my legs. I sing a song I used to listen to a lot. Something about hitting a baby. Or maybe it's the baby hitting me? One more time.

I've just gotten to the bridge of the song—somehow, my one-woman concert has involved me getting on my hands and knees and singing seductively to the desk chair—when the door of the classroom is pushed open.

I scramble to my feet, dropping the chalkboard eraser I've been using for my makeshift microphone, and turn towards the now opened door.

Only to find it empty, the hallway plunged in darkness.

Now, I don't know about you, but me? I see a dark, abandoned hallway, and you bet your ass I'm not going out there. I've watched horror movies—and though I'm lovable and cute, I consider myself more the comedic relief character instead of final girl material.

"Not today, Satan," I whisper into the classroom. "Not today."

I half want to close the door once more, but again, I'm not

stupid. The second I go over there, something will grab me and pull me into the darkness.

Yeah, fuck that.

I settle for huddling behind the desk, clutching a stapler to my chest. It'll be hard enough if I need to whack someone over the head. *And* I'm a badass vampire with super speed and strength.

Huh. Maybe I am final girl material.

I debate whether it'll be beneficial to use my speed and race to the exit. Maybe find a teacher and figure out what kind of hellish detention this is. But then again, I'll also be liable to run into a wall and knock myself unconscious.

Dark halls? Unfamiliar landscape? My clumsy ass?

Not a good combination. On a scale of one-to-live, I'll be a negative twenty. I'll probably kill someone else with me.

It feels like hours later when the hallway light flickers once before turning on completely. I stare at the white hanging bulb distrustfully.

Horror movie one-oh-one. That light? Yeah, it's a ploy. A way to lure you into a false sense of security before ripping it away from you. Don't ever trust the light.

I'm still in my huddled position when I hear a strangled sob and the sound of footsteps pounding against the linoleum tiles. I freeze, pushing myself further against the desk until I'm practically an extension of it. My breathing saws in and out, and my heart pounds in tandem to the racing footsteps.

From the hallway, a malevolent voice whispers, *"Run, run. I'll always find you."*

My "fuck this" mentality just escalated to "fuck everything."

Nope. Nope. Nope. Nope.

The footsteps slow down suddenly, and a breathy moan escapes someone who is obviously female.

Okay, so a creepy-ass man and a female. Noted.

Now, what the fuck is going on?

I'm frozen. My entire body is hewn from ice. Hell, I'm pretty sure even my heart has glazed over at this point. I'm *terrified*.

Moans begin to escape the female followed by a third voice, "Fuck me. Oh yes. Yes."

I'm not going to lie. A lot of things confuse me. Walking, for one. Basic conversation. How some people can eat like a pig and not gain weight.

But this?

I don't even *want* to know what the fuck is going on. At the same time, I really, really do.

Remember how I said I'm not final girl material? Well, my curiosity gets the best of me, and I find myself ambling to my feet.

Each move is cautious, tentative, and I clutch the stapler like a lifeline. When I get to the door, I hesitate very briefly. I know this is probably a terrible idea. Hell, I've already mentally written my eulogy...which, come to think of, is actually pretty stupid because I'll be dead and no one will get to hear it anyway.

With bated breath, I peek out the door.

The hallway is still illuminated by half a dozen hanging bulbs.

At the very end, three figures are silhouetted.

I strain to make out any individual faces or features, and my breath leaves me in a swooping exhale.

There's a girl on the floor alright, sucking the cock of an unknown male. I recognize the girl as Titty from the library —still wearing the nasty shiner my smug ass gave her. A second male leans against the wall, cloaked entirely in shadows tinged with green.

Only one monster looks like that.

I've heard stories from my dad. Even *he* was scared of him.

The fucking Boogyman.

From this angle, I can't see the first guy's face, but from the pink waves emanating from him, I figure he must be an incubus or a siren eating Titty's life force.

Wait…are those wings?

What I thought was just an abnormally large back is actually red, feathered wings.

Realization slams into me like a bag of falling bricks, and horror swamps me.

It's Cupid.

Yup.

For detention, the assholes put me in a hallway with the fucking Boogyman and Cupid himself.

As Cupid tilts his head, cock still inside the mouth of the now dead girl, I stealthily walk backwards into the classroom.

Please don't find me. Please don't find me. Better yet, please don't know of my existence.

"*Little vampire,*" a voice purrs, and this time, I'm positive it's the Boogeyman. Only one creature is capable of having a voice like that. It grates on my nerves and instills uncontrollable fear within me. "*Come out, come out wherever you are. Come play with us.*"

Yeah, no. I'll stay right here, thank you very much.

"Do you have to be such a cliché?" Cupid asks the Boogeyman snidely.

"Did you have to kill the girl?" he counters.

"I didn't mean to take so much," Cupid responds, and he sounds forlorn, almost. Despondent.

There's silence—briefly—before I hear what sounds like…moaning? Lips crashing together. The ruffle of fabric hitting the tiles.

What the fuck?

"Do you like my big cock in your asshole?" Cupid pants, and a manly whimper echoes down the hallway. "Do you like that? Take all of me. Take it all."

Oh my God. I'm witnessing monster audio porn.

I hear flesh hitting flesh, and then the inevitable roar of completion by both of them. During that time, I have meandered back towards my little happy desk and have posted myself underneath it.

I was once told that if I believed something hard enough, it'll become true.

I'm a plant. Just a plant. Nothing to see here, folks. Nothing to see.

"Let's go find the little vampire, shall we?" Cupid asks, and I hear what sounds like a belt buckle clicking. The Boogeyman chuckles darkly.

Footsteps echo just outside the classroom. My entire body is frigid, but my heart is—contrary—beating erratically, shooting fire down my spine. It's the only working organ in my body.

I use my hand to stifle my gasp, and then I squeeze my eyelids shut.

I'm a plant. Just a plant. I'm a plant.

The footsteps abruptly stop, and I hear someone inhale sharply.

"*She's in here,*" the Boogeyman purrs, the sound causing full body tremors to cascade down my back.

You don't see me. Nope. Not me. Because I'm a motherfucking plant.

"She's under the desk," Cupid adds in a singsong voice.

"No, I'm not!" I call, and both men freeze in their pursuit.

"Did she just...?"

Debating my very few options, I scramble to my feet to face my tormentors. The murderers. On closer inspection, I see that Cupid has light red hair that matches his mammoth red wings. The Boogeyman has dark skin and vibrant green hair.

"Don't kill me. Or put your cock in my mouth. Or whatever it is you're going to do," I plead, raising my hands to fend them off. I turn towards Boogeyman pointedly. "And please, for the love of all that's holy, stop with the creepy, echoing voice. It's weird." Two identically devilish smiles grace their handsome faces. "I have a much better idea that I feel will benefit all of us."

CHAPTER 22

VIN

I'm running from the library, my sword already drawn.
Mason keeps pace with me as we take the stairs two
at a time, our breathing even despite our haste.

"Top floor?" Mason questions, and I nod in response.

All I can think about, all I can focus on, is Violet. My
damn, suicidal mate. Doesn't she realize how deadly detention is?

I have only gotten it once my first year at the Academy,
and it still haunts me to this day.

As we run, I periodically check my phone, waiting for the
confirmation from Jack that he has disabled the cameras and
the alarm on the door.

Perfectly timed, his text comes through just as we
stumble to a stop in front of a thick metal door on the top
floor. An impenetrable door, locked by a keypad.

Jack: You have fifteen minutes.

Fifteen minutes to grab my mate from whatever hell they

had planned for her. And then spank her perfect ass for giving me gray hair before I'm thirty.

You see, students don't just sit in a classroom during Prodigium's detention, nor do they write line after line on the board under the watchful eye of the professor.

Instead, they're fed to the monsters.

We're all monsters, admittedly, but there are some who are so bad, so deadly, that they're secluded in an upper level of the Academy. Their meals are the troubled students.

Which monsters did they send after Violet?

I can still feel her presence in my chest—flickering embers. Once we cement our mating bond, it will roar like a bonfire, according to my research.

For now, I know she's alive. That's all that matters.

And if something happens to her…

I will burn down this entire fucking school.

I silently hand Mason my extra dagger as he wrenches open the door.

The hallway is dark and silent, the monotony of darkness broken apart by the intermittent flash of a hanging bulb. Cobwebs adorn each corner of the hall.

There's a chill in the air—a chill that shouldn't be present in a hallway devoid of any windows or doors leading to the outside. I'm suddenly grateful I'm wearing a long-sleeved jacket.

"Violet?" Mason calls, charging forward. I grab his arm to pull him back behind me.

Whose great idea was it to bring along the guy high off his ass? Certainly not mine. If Jack wasn't needed to turn off the cameras and unlock the door from his computer, then I would've brought him along instead. Or Hux. Either would suffice.

Even Frankie would've been a better choice, but he was

stuck answering questions from the headmaster. I can tell he wasn't pleased by that decision—the aloof Frankie wanted to run into battle.

If I hadn't seen it with my own eyes, I wouldn't have believed it either.

"Vi?" Mason's voice is softer now, cautious. His eyes scan each opened classroom door. "VIOLET!"

Before I can stop him, he's racing towards a fallen body.

A dead body.

My heart is hammering in my chest as fear consumes me. I'm drowning in it, tumbling through a never-ending whirlpool.

It can't be her.

It just can't be.

I don't know how she expects me to live if she's no longer alive. She's my mate—I may have only just found her, I may not have been expecting her, but she has dominated my life in the short span I've known her.

I can't exist without her.

That may seem like morbid thinking, especially since I barely know her, but it's the monster way. When we find our mates, it's only ever them. It can *only* be them. Losing your mate is losing your heart and soul.

My steps are more hesitant, more tentative, as I step up to Mason and the small body. Every muscle within me relaxes when I realize it's not my Violet, but some other girl.

"Is it fucked up that I'm relieved it's not Violet?" Mason whispers, still staring down at the dead body with an unreadable expression.

"I feel the same way, brother," I reply, gripping the sword in an iron vise.

"She didn't get stabbed or eaten or anything like that," Mason says, stepping back towards me. His hand is clutching the dagger so tightly his knuckles are white, blue veins protruding. "She looks drained. A succubus, perhaps? Incubus?"

Only one incubus is deadly enough to warrant such treatment from the staff.

Cupid.

If he's here…

If he's roaming these halls, hungry...

Fear thrums through my veins as I throw out my own cautionary warnings. I need to find her...and fast.

"Violet!" I scream, cupping my mouth to amplify my voice. "Violet!"

"Vin?" a sweet, beautiful voice calls. The world around me stills, suspended in time, as I gravitate towards my heaven.

Mason's hand on my shoulder is the only thing that stops me.

"What if it's a trap?" he whispers. He looks pained, and the hand holding the dagger shakes. I can tell he wants nothing more than to run to her, but for once, he's being the cautious one instead of the reckless idiot. "What if it's a mimicry or a shapeshifter?"

I know he's right. Mimicries and shapeshifters are both common monsters, having the capacity to steal characteristics of their prey, such as their voice, or shapeshift into them entirely.

But the voice sounds exactly like my mate's…

I nod to show him I understand and cautiously inch forward. The sword is raised above my head, seconds from striking.

You better be okay, babygirl, or else this whole school will pay.

The voice came from what appears to be an abandoned teacher's lounge—no surprise, the top three floors have been deserted for centuries. Two figures are leaning against the large oak table, while another is swinging her legs on the countertop.

Violet.

The ache in my chest intensifies once before alleviating; the draw to her is undeniable.

My mate.

My Violet.

"Oh, thank Zeus," Mason calls when he catches sight of her. Before I can warn him to stay on guard, to be mindful of the two figures watching us curiously, he runs forward and takes her in his arms. "Pinkie," he moans, burying his face in her hair. He practically lifts her completely off the counter, swaying back and forth with her in his arms.

Only when he puts her down, stepping back, do I venture a step forward and check her for injuries.

Her hair is ruffled, but I imagine that's from Mason more than anything else. Her beautiful, luscious lips are curled into a small smile.

"Hi, Mason. Hi, Vin," she whispers, and my name on her tongue causes my body to tense and my cock to harden. I just barely resist the urge to run to her and hold her as Mason did. Instead, I stay back, watching her warily. I'm not sure if my affection would be appreciated.

"That's the asshole who mocked you in front of the cafeteria?" one of the unfamiliar men asks, giving me an appraising look. He has green hair and dark, onyx skin. "Do you want me to kill him?"

As per my Van Helsing gift, I immediately catalogue what monster he is, and icy horror slithers down my spine like a snake.

The Boogeyman.

"Violet, step away," I warn her, moving to stand in front of her. The Boogeyman rolls his eyes at me as if my antics amuse him.

"Do you want me to pull out my sword and compare which one is bigger?" he asks scathingly. Cupid—red wings and all—elbows his stomach.

"You know it'll be yours," he assures him placatingly.

"Vin, Mason. Meet Barret and Cal." Violet points towards the Boogeyman and Cupid respectively. "We're having ice cream."

She nods towards a half eaten bowl of ice cream sitting discarded on the counter. Mason eyes the chocolate for a long moment before snaking a hand out and dipping his finger in. He sucks on his finger for a long moment, eyes closing in bliss. Violet's throat works as she watches him.

"That's good stuff," he says seriously, noting my incredulous expression.

"Why the hell are you hanging out with Cupid and the Boogeyman?" I ask Violet, still keeping my eyes trained on the monsters in question. They both eat their own ice creams with innocent smiles on their faces. "Do you realize they killed the other girl in detention?"

"It's Cal and Barret. I told you that. They don't like those other names—says it gives them a bad rep. And about the girl...well...we've all killed someone before, haven't we? We're monsters. You can't blame them for lashing out when they're locked in here like prisoners just because they're different. Cal was starving," she defends, and the red-haired Cupid gives my mate a look I really don't like.

"We haven't had a girl in months," he says. "I can't always feed off Barret."

Once more, his eyes fixate on Violet with unnerving intensity.

"My mate goes into detention to be sacrificially slaughtered and leaves as the best friend of the monsters who were supposed to kill her," Mason mutters, too low for anyone but me to hear. "Just fucking great."

Great. That's the beginning to a twisted joke. A vampire, the Boogeyman, and Cupid walk into detention together...

The Breakfast Club: Monster Edition.

CHAPTER 23

VIOLET

The next couple weeks are relatively uneventful.
I'm swamped down with homework and exams, all of my professors adamant that I make up what I missed before I arrived. Who knew there were so many ways to dispose of a body?

And...

Now I'm thinking about Ali's body. Dead. In the woods. With perfectly placed wounds on her neck. Honestly, that's a dead giveaway that she wasn't actually killed by a vampire. No vampire is that clean when we eat. Heaven only knows how many shirts I stained.

Three words: Ripping. Open. An. Artery.

Well...four words, but you get the idea.

It isn't a clean job. Blood goes *everywhere*.

My week consists of lessons, extra tutoring in the library with Frankie and sometimes Jack, training for the Roaring, and a whole shit ton of men. Vin has taken it upon himself to feed me in one of the private rooms.

At first, I had vehemently refused. The last thing I needed was another embarrassing showdown. I know now—or, at least, suspect—that Vin's behavior was some twisted plan to protect me. He groveled, I forgave him, so we should be good. I told him I could easily feed from a donor, but what did the asshole do?

He growled at me. Fucking growled.

I call him my blood bitch now.

I haven't seen Cal or Barret since detention, and I miss the bastards. They're probably getting all murdery without me.

Cue: an exasperated sigh in French.

Why French? No reason. I just think it's a sexy accent, and I love the way it flows from a man's lips.

Currently, I'm sitting on the bed in my dorm attempting to struggle through my practical theory homework in Mr. Pumpkin's advanced theology class.

"Are you almost done?" Cynthia grouses from the bed beside mine. She has already removed her eyes, ears, and limbs for the night, her head buried beneath a mound of blankets.

The window is open, providing a light breeze that ruffles my blonde locks. Moonlight slices through as well, mixing with the artificial glow of my bedside lamp.

"Move your eyes and ears to the closet," I rebuke, flipping a page in my textbook and copying the answers down. "Then you won't hear or see me."

"You're fucking annoying, you know that?" she rumbles, shifting in bed so her back is to me.

"You're the one in bed before nine every night." The chapter I'm currently on depicts the origins of Halloween...otherwise known as Devil's Night. It's the one time of year that all monsters get set loose on the world and make it their playground. *Our* playground.

One month until Devil's Night.

Two months until the Roaring.

And a billion years until graduation—at least, it feels that way.

"Why can't you just move in with your boy toys?" Cynthia continues, interrupting my reading of a riveting passage about a human who claimed to know about the existence of monsters and murdered dozens of people on our behalf. Like, fuck, John, we may be monsters, but we don't just murder random people without just cause. The details are both gruesome and enthralling.

I lift my head from the book and blink at Cynthia.

"Boy toys?"

"They all live in that big fucking house together. I'm sure they won't mind a fifth roommate." She pauses, shifting restlessly on the bed. "Shit, if you don't move in, I will. I will bang all of them with or without my retractable vagina. Except for maybe Frankenstein's son. I don't fuck fat kids. And I especially don't fuck failed science experiments...which is what he is."

I'm out of my bed and on top of her before I even realize I'm doing it. Possessive indignation roars through me, silencing even the rapid beating of my heart. The thought of Cynthia touching any one of those men makes me see red. And to hear her cruel words about Frankie? A beautiful man with a beautiful, albeit scarred, heart?

I want to rip the rest of her hair from her body. Remove her legs and arms. Pull her apart like a fucked up Mr. Potato Head and reassemble her with an ass for a face.

I want to—

A knock on my door interrupts my savage thoughts, and I stare down at Cynthia's blank face. My knees and arms are resting on either side of her, not touching any skin, and her face is once more an empty canvas complete with dark eye-sockets, a gaping hole where her mouth should be, and a missing nose.

Her mouth still talks from where it's seated on the nightstand beside her eyes, nose, hands, and feet, oblivious to my presence over her body.

"Who the fuck is that?" she says about the door.

Slowly, carefully, I remove myself from above her—being extra careful not to unintentionally touch any part of her body.

What the fuck is wrong with me?

I was going to rip her apart...and laugh.

Maybe I'm wrong. Maybe even monsters have no redeemable qualities.

Shaking my head rapidly, I move to the door.

"I'll see who it is."

"Wait!" Cynthia exclaims. "Use my eye."

"Your eye?"

With her stubbed arm, she pretends to go bowling, cheering victoriously when she knocks down invisible bowling pins.

Understanding, I grab her eyeball—the grossest thing I've ever touched in my life (and I accidentally touched a hairy werewolf penis)—and roll it under the door. I swear there's slime remaining on my fingers.

"Make sure it doesn't go too far," she hisses. "I don't want it to get stepped on."

Muttering a curse beneath my breath, I crawl to my hands and knees and hold the eyeball just under the door, facing it upwards.

Cynthia lets out a squeak, and I'm instantly on my feet, alert.

"What?"

"Help me get presentable, dammit!" Cynthia staggers to her feet...before remembering she removed them and falling on her ass. "Where are my boobs? Grab me my fucking boobs!"

If that isn't something I hear everyday.

Ignoring her, I wrench open the door, realizing it must be one of the guys because—like a normal woman with bras—Cynthia only requests her boobs when they're around.

It's a guy alright, but it's not one of mine.

Not mine, I remind myself stoutly, staring into the face of my professor.

Dimitri Gray looks as impeccable as always with his hair slicked into a low ponytail and a suit on. On closer inspection, I see a splotch of blood on his white collar.

The guys' warning about him being an assassin comes back to me. Or maybe I heard it from students gossiping.

"Ms. Dracula." He bobs his head, apparently unconcerned that it's the middle of the fucking night and he arrived at my door with blood on his shirt. One inhale confirms that the blood belongs to a female—but that's all I can gather from the penny-sized drop.

"Mr. Gray." I attempt to mimic his formal tone and nonchalant-head-nod-thingy.

Behind me, I hear Cynthia mutter, "Where the fuck are my E-cups? I swear to Hades that if you used them I'll destroy you."

Yes, Cynthia, because I would really use your boobs for my own enjoyment. I think that's as taboo as sharing underwear—but don't quote me. This is new territory for all of us.

"You left this in my classroom during class today," Dimitri says stiffly, holding out the black, faded textbook. I eye it with bemusement.

"That's not mine," I say shortly. "I have mine in my backpack."

"I would recommend checking, Ms. Dracula, for you have a quiz tomorrow on chapter seventeen."

I frown at this new development, but obediently step back inside my room and to my backpack resting against the wall. Dimitri follows me inside, lips twisting in distaste as he surveys the small, sparsely-furnished—but surprisingly claustrophobic—room.

His eyes stop briefly on Cynthia—currently on her hands (arms?) and knees, rummaging under the bed for her boobs—before turning to me with a disgruntled huff. For a moment, we exchange a look I would almost describe as mutual amusement, the type of look friends would give each other if they found something funny. Just as quickly, his expression smooths over, and he scowls at me.

I remember then that I hate him and want a bunch of bees to sting him and a leprechaun to put his ass at the end of a fucking rainbow. Nasty little critters.

I make a noise of disbelief when my search for my book proves to be futile.

"I could've sworn I put it in here," I murmur.

"Found it!" Cynthia calls gleefully, holding a pair of boobs in her teeth. She spits it out suddenly. "Dammit, that's the b-cup set."

Ignoring her, Dimitri places the book in my hands and levels me with a stern glare. "Take better care of your property, Ms. Dracula. It would be a shame if something happened."

With that ominous...errr...threat? Warning?

With that ominous *statement*, he stalks out of the room. I watch him go with more confusion than I care to admit.

What the hell just happened?

"Next time I'm woken up by a hot assassin in the middle of the fucking night," Cynthia begins, her voice coming from the opposite corner of her body. "You need to be a good friend and help me find my fucking tits."

CHAPTER 24

VIOLET

J ack is waiting for me at the entrance to the dorms, body hunched over the book he's reading. I take an unobstructed moment to appreciate him. Even with his too large glasses and long hair, the man is beautiful. Unlike the others, he doesn't exude an alpha dominance or a cold power that makes my skin bristle.

Some monsters look at kindness—compassion—as a grave sin. A weakness. I see it for what it really is: a chance to save this fucked up world.

Sure, brute strength and a commanding tone is nice and all, but have you ever sat in front of a fire, content in a gentle man's arms? Having him rub your hair and whisper how beautiful you are?

Jack is the type of man I could dominate in bed. Control. Milk his cock for all it's worth—

What the fuck, Vi? I scold myself. *How did you go from thinking about his shy, sweet demeanor to imagining dominating him in the bedroom?*

Maybe it's because of the stereotype. You see someone like Jack, someone sweet, nerdy, and timid, and automatically assume he'll submit to you.

He *could* be the opposite. I've read romance novels before, and the shy ones always end up being freaky in the sheets.

Not that I would mind.

My cheeks flame as I picture Jack controlling me, dominating me, the sculpted planes of his tanned chest on display.

He snaps his book closed suddenly, head lifting to meet my penetrating gaze. I know my cheeks are probably bright red, and my lips are unbearably dry. My tongue snakes out to lick them...before I immediately think about licking *other* things.

"How did you sleep?" Jack asks, stepping towards me. He meets my eyes, blushes, and then looks away. He combs his fingers through his shoulder-length hair, the movement revealing the jagged edge of his scar. When he notices me staring, he darkens further, ducking his head and kicking his feet.

"It was weird," I begin, walking beside him down the curving, wooded path to the cafeteria.

"Weird how?" Before I can respond, he slips my backpack off my shoulder and shrugs it over his own. At my scathing glare—because I'm an independent wannabe badass woman —he smiles sheepishly. "You looked tense. I didn't want you in pain before fighting class today."

He is just too damn adorable at times.

I open my mouth to tell him about Dimitri's impromptu visit before snapping it closed. The last thing I need is for Hux to make an appearance and go all "macho possessive" on me.

Hux doesn't like a lot of people around me, particularly men. Hell, he freaked out the one time I mentioned I've seen Cynthia's boobs and demanded I move in with him.

He is just too damn adorable at times.

Shrugging, I change the subject, hoping that Jack doesn't notice my evasion of his question. "How's Hux doing, by the way?" Then, speaking directly to Hux, I add, "How are you doing, Chocolate Bar."

Yes, I have decided to nickname Hux "Chocolate Bar." No, it hasn't been sticking, if the looks I receive from the other men are any indication.

Jack's brows furrow as he concentrates. After a moment, the skin smooths over, and he flashes me a shy smile.

"He said, and I quote, 'Tell my precious treasure she looks radiant in the fall lighting. A vision of beauty.'"

My heart threatens to burst from my chest, and I lower my head, suddenly shy.

"Tell Hux he's not too shabby himself," I murmur like the dumbass I am. Sometimes I wish I was like Frankie or even Hux: a walking dictionary full of poise and grace.

Instead, I'm a human trainwreck who responded to a beautiful compliment with *that*.

Jack is silent for another long moment, conversing with his other half.

"He says thank you, and that he will strive to never be shabby until the end of time," Jack responds at last, and I can't help the girlish giggle that escapes me.

We arrive at the cafeteria, and I instantly head into the private feeding room. I expect Jack to continue on towards our table, as he usually does, but instead, he follows me inside and locks the door.

"Where's Vin?" I ask, surveying the empty room. It sort of reminds me of an interrogation room from those cop movies. A simple metal table sits in the center with a chair on either side. There are no windows, and the only exit is the door we came through.

Such a fire hazard.

"He has to do something for King Tut's class," Jack says, shuffling from foot to foot. Yeah, apparently our combat instructor, Mummy, is actually King fucking Tut. And boy, does he like to be referred to as such. Even with the wrappings, I can tell he has a big head.

"Oh." I try not to sound disappointed, but I'm *starving*. And, as pathetic as this sounds, I was beginning to think of our feeding time as a bonding experience. It's one of the few times he lets his guard down around me, allows me to see the man underneath.

We've never gone any further than feeding. Even with his raging boner poking me in all the right places, Vin refuses to take that next step. Whenever I ask him about it, he mutters that it's not the right time.

"Don't worry," Jack says quickly. "I can feed you. Despite having Hux inside of me and immortality, I'm still human. At least, my blood is." When I don't immediately respond, his face slackens with horror. "Only if you want to, of course. I don't want to make an assumption. I can go find a donor, if you want." His eyes steel at the offer of me feeding off someone else, jaw clenching, but he doesn't take it back, despite being uncomfortable.

"Jack," I begin, taking a step towards him. He gulps. "Thank you. But do you know what you're offering? Do you know about the...um...?"

"Lust? Endorphins you release? Yes, I am well versed." He nervously pushes up his glasses with his pointer finger. "I can swap with Hux, if that would make you more comfortable."

"No, Jack, you're enough. If you're sure," I whisper, my mouth dry as I stare at his vulnerable neck. At the power flooding through his veins. While his blood may be human, it smells better than any source I have ever drunk from before, rivaled only by Vin's. The smell alone causes my senses to sharpen with a primal need.

"Where do I...?" He looks around before eventually perching on the chair. While it does have a back for him to lean back against, both of the arms are gone. It makes feeding *much* easier.

"There's perfect." I stalk towards him slowly, giving him the chance to change his mind. When he doesn't, I straddle his lap, my legs on either side of his knees.

Caging him in.

His breath picks up speed, and I can see his pulse pounding in his neck. His eyes are slightly glazed as he mechanically tilts his head to the side, offering himself to me.

"Is this okay?" My breath fans against his skin, eliciting goosebumps. I hear him swallow, and his voice is breathless when he finally responds.

"More than okay."

My hunger consumes me as I plunge my now elongated fangs into his neck. His body jerks, convulses under mine, and a groan travels through him and into me.

His hands, lying hesitantly by his sides, become braver, gripping my waist and holding me against his growing erection. The heady scent of his arousal fills the room.

He begins to groan out my name and other compliments and praises, words nearly incoherent. His blood fills me, completes me—his power and life force pulses through my veins.

Like with Vin, the strength of our connection takes me by surprise. I continue to slurp at his neck desperately, hungrily, passionately. My hands tangle in his hair, both playing with the silky strands and holding his head in place.

I nearly jump out of my skin when his own hand moves to my breast, kneading the orb through my shirt and bra. I moan against his neck.

It feels *so* fucking good.

A second hand sneaks underneath my shirt, underneath

my bra, and tweaks my nipple. It's such a contrast to the hesitant squeezes coming from the first that it almost feels like there are two different people playing with my breasts.

Two different hands.

I grind against his hardness as one hand lightly cups my still fully-clothed breast and the other destroys my nipple, pinching, plucking, and twisting it.

I don't know how long we stay like that—locked in an embrace capable of burning the whole building down—before I reluctantly pull my face away from his neck, using my tongue to heal the marks.

Jack's breathing is heavy, sawing in and out. Coming to his senses faster than me, he drops his hands from my tits and jumps to his feet.

The movement pushes me off his lap and onto the floor with an "oomph."

Why do I *always* find myself on the ground after a feeding? And not even on my back with a cock between my legs.

Damn, I get jipped.

"I'm sorry," Jack blurts out looking extremely distressed. "Crap. I'm sorry. That shouldn't have happened." He extends a hand to help me to my feet. Only when I'm steady does he release me as if I'm toxic. I'm not going to lie: that hurts. A lot. More than I thought it could.

"Next time I'll use a donor," I say, voice stiffer than I mean it to be. "I'm sorry for bothering you."

"Crap, no, that's not what I meant. I shouldn't have...I shouldn't have taken advantage of you like that!" His voice is nearly a scream, and I can see the anguish emitting from his eyes.

I gape at him.

"Huh?" I ask smartly.

"You were feeding, and I know that lowers your inhibitions." Jack paces, pulling at his hair and occasionally clutching his head. "Frick, Hux is freaking out." The last statement is muttered under his breath, not necessarily meant for my ears.

"Jack," I begin.

"I shouldn't have touched you like that without your permission. I'm a freaking idiot." There's so much self-loathing in his voice, so much pain, that I can't stop myself from shouting.

"Jack! Hux! Listen to me for a damn minute!" Jack stops pacing and meets my stare worriedly. He braces himself, flinching away when I step closer.

"I was in complete control of my actions, understand? Everything that happened was because I wanted it to. If anything, I should be the one apologizing to *you*."

"Me?" His voice is high with disbelief.

"My bite can make you...well...it's meant to seduce and entice. So I'm sorry—"

In a span of a second, Jack is in front of me, gripping my shoulders.

Hux is in front of me, gripping my shoulders.

His glasses are still on, his hair still hanging in front of his face, but I know it's him without question.

"Are you sure you're okay, my precious treasure?" Hux asks—well, more like demands. His shrewd eyes assess my reaction.

When I nod my head vigorously, assuring him I am more than fine, he exhales in notable relief.

"I never want you to feel uncomfortable. If we go too far, tell us immediately. And if anyone *else* goes too far, tell me, and I'll handle it." His tone darkens on the latter statement causing goosebumps to ripple on my skin.

I'm fucking terrified and aroused by the prospect of Hux handling it.

"Of course, Chocolate Bar," I say with a megawatt smile,

and his answering one is glorious. Hands still on my shoulders, he leans forward and presses a tender kiss to my forehead.

The hands loosen slightly, and Jack peers down at me.

"You okay?" he asks anxiously.

"Better than okay," I echo his words back to him, and he smiles softly.

Our moment is interrupted by a scream from the cafeteria.

Jack pushes me behind him, facing the still locked door of our windowless room. He stands with a stillness that belies the tension I know he's feeling.

After a moment, a familiar voice screeches, "Oh my Hades! She's dead!"

Well, fuck.

CHAPTER 25

VIOLET

I t was Blowy found dead in the cafeteria bathrooms.

Unlike Ali, her throat was ripped out.

I hear the names they're calling her murderer: savage, beast, monster.

Ironic, really, considering this entire school is full of them.

After an hour of trying to convince the headmaster that I had nothing to fucking do with Blowy's death, our meeting is interrupted by Birdy hurrying into the office. After conversing briefly with the secretary, the headmaster releases me, claiming he has found a witness to collaborate my whereabouts the hour of the crime.

Not suspicious at all.

I retell the story to Cal and Barret, kicking my legs against the countertop in the abandoned teacher's lounge on the top floor. Mason sits beside me, eating his ice cream straight from the carton, that heathen. Thanks Jack's retrieval of the door's passcode, we're able to visit them whenever we want. And yes, it's we. The guys dictated that one of them has to be with me at all times for "protection."

Silly, foolish boys. As if I'll listen.

The only reason Mason is with me now is because he caught me sneaking around and offered to come with. He's the chillest out of all of my guy friends—sort of like a river, following the predetermined current.

"And you think they're going to find your venom on her neck?" Barret surmises, attempting to steal a bite of the chocolate ice cream I bought specifically for Cal. Apparently, Cupid has a sweet tooth. Who knew? Cal swats Barret's offending hand away with a possessive growl of "mine." When I stick my own spoon into the chocolatey goodness, Cal moves it even closer so I don't have to reach as far.

I can't help the smug smile I send in Barret's direction. He flips me off in response.

"Someone's framing her," Mason says darkly.

"But the question is who, Pretty Boy," Cal jests, pointing with his spoon. As always, Mason's face darkens with annoyance at the nickname, but he lets it slide. It doesn't make a lot of sense to start something with the two most fearsome monsters in existence.

Not that I think they're that scary. Total marshmallows. All bark and no bite.

Okay, total lie. They *did* kill a girl by cock. I'm pretty sure there was some biting involved with that death, if you know what I mean.

"Let's make a list!" Barret suggests eagerly, reminding me distinctly of a besotted, energetic puppy. He opens one of the drawers and grabs a paper and pen.

"A list?" Mason parrots, voice dry. I lean back so I'm snuggled against his arm. Mason always emanates this heat—a product of his lineage. Combined with his earthy scent, I want to curl up against his body and...well...I didn't think that far ahead.

Cal and Barret focus on the minuscule distance separating our two bodies. Cal almost appears curious, but Barret's face is blank.

"That's a good idea!" I say, and Barret's blank face turns into a triumphant smile at my approval. He practically preens. "Thanks, Boo Bear."

Note to everyone out there: I am the only person in the world allowed to call him that. Don't try to unless you want your insides to fill with bugs, crawling through your intestines and erupting from your mouth and eyes. Seriously. Don't.

"So first, who was the witness that came forward with your alibi?" Cal taps his spoon to his chin, unintentionally getting chocolate all over his face. For a sex demon, the man's a hot mess.

"Your roommate, perhaps? A professor?" Barret lists.

"It could be." Sheepishly, I duck my head. "Dimitri visited my room last night."

Three male voices rise in protest; Mason tightens his arm around my shoulder, pulling me even deeper into his side.

"Did he touch you?" he asks into my hair. Something about my scent seems to calm him. If it was Vin or even Hux, I would say he is attempting to tame and reign in his beast. But, for all I know about Medusa's son, he doesn't have a monster lurking just beneath the surface. And he sure as fuck doesn't have anger issues like Van Helsing. He's the calmest guy I know...except for now, when he's holding me in an iron vise, heart pounding erratically.

There's still a lot I don't know about my friend, apparently.

"No," I say quickly, realizing how my words could be

construed. "He was just delivering my book. But…" I bite my lower lip anxiously.

"But?" Barret hedges, and I risk a peek under Mason's arm to see the Boogeyman flexing his biceps. The man looks lethal. It's times like this I remember there's a reason why he's locked away from the other students.

"But," I relent. "He had blood on his shirt."

The men are silent, processing that declaration.

"So you think he murdered Tiffany, went to your room to return your textbook, and then admitted to the headmaster that he was with you the time of the murder?" Mason says, voice dubious. All I can focus on is the name of the victim. Huh. I'm a horrible person for not asking sooner. "For one, professors are not allowed to engage in romantic relation-ships with their students—" I open my mouth to protest that nothing fucking happened when he continues, "I know nothing happened, Pinkie. But to the headmaster, it would seem weird for him to visit your room in the middle of the night."

"Unless they both know something we don't," points out Cal. He ruffles his red feathered wings, accidentally hitting the back of Barret's head. Barret's swivels around to glare at him, scooping some of his ice cream into his spoon and throwing it at his face. "Or maybe the headmaster lied about receiving confirmation of your whereabouts." Cal, unper-turbed with the ice cream dripping down his face, leans forward to rest his elbows on his knees.

In sloppy scrawl, Barret writes down Dimitri Gray and Headmaster Asshole.

I smirk at the nickname before realizing this is a serious conversation, and as such, I have to remain serious. I'm so fucking serious I should be wearing a pencil skirt and have my hair in a perm.

"What about the Van Helsings?" Cal continues, and I feel

Mason stiffen beside me. I run a soothing hand up and down his thigh.

"Vin wouldn't," Mason says briskly, resolutely. His tone leaves no room for argument.

Barret grunts.

"He wouldn't!" Mason defends. "He's…" Abruptly, he trails off and glances down at his hands. "He just wouldn't."

"He wouldn't," I agree. Cal and Barret exchange another one of those eloquent looks before sighing, turning back towards me.

"His sister? Your designated best friend?" Cal queries.

I purse my lips.

"I don't think—"

"Put her on the list." Mason's voice is quiet but firm, and I whip my head to stare at him in surprise. His hand rubs soothing circles into my shoulder blades, but he doesn't meet my questioning gaze. "Add Cheryl as well."

"Who's Cheryl?" Barret demands, but he writes her name down.

"Gills," I fill in, and both monsters nod in understanding.

During detention, we had a *lot* of time to gossip. I'm pretty sure they're more enamored with my life than I am.

We add a few more names. All of the professors, for one, and all of the vampires. I want to defend my brethren, but I don't bother. I've lost count of how many times I tried to convince everyone that vampires weren't responsible for the bite marks on both girls.

"Don't be mad," Mason tells me sternly before taking the marker from Barret's hand and adding one more name.

When I see it, my vision turns red, and my hands curl into fists.

"What the hell, Mase?" I demand, jumping to my feet. The ice cream bowl residing in my lap clatters on the floor.

"I said don't get mad," he pleads.

Ignoring his shouts—combined with the roars released from Cal and Barret at him for upsetting me—I storm out of the teacher's lounge, down the hall, and back into the stairwell. I'm fuming, my anger almost a physical manifestation of fire in my mind. I want to burn this whole fucking place down.

My father's a lot of things, but he does love me. I know that he does—in the sick, demented way only he can.

Dracula's name does *not* belong on that list.

CHAPTER 26

HUX

I move swiftly, stealthily, through the woods. Critters scuttle through the forest floors, their vexing chatter grating on my nerves. A bird chirps noisily overhead, and I hear what sounds like a grasshopper. While the noises are not aesthetically pleasing to my ears, they help mute the sound of my footsteps as I slink through the forest.

"Up ahead," Jack whispers, and I whip my head up just as my target slips through the door of a small building. *"A shed,"* Jack supplies helpfully.

It's a small, dilapidated thing with loose boards and no windows. According to my calculations, it sits a few miles away from campus, in a stretch of woods devoid of any walking trails.

"What's the plan?" I ask Jack, crouching behind a collection of tree stumps and twigs. I can feel one of my own forming in the recesses of my brain, and a sly grin curls up my lips.

"We're not murdering anyone," Jack declares in clear exas-

peration. When I open my mouth to protest, he adds, *"And no torture either."*

Damn him and his moral conscience.

"Violet will be upset," he adds gently, and those words have the intended effect. The fight drains from me, and my shoulders slump forward.

"Can I at least maim?" I plead.

"Hux..." he warns.

I'll take that as a no, then.

It's still a strange sensation to have Jack's voice in my head. For as long as I can remember, Jack has been nothing more than the other soul inhabiting my vessel. I remember we would leave notes for each other before each switch, a way to solidify our bond as brothers.

Until he trapped me in my cage.

Fury momentarily burns through me, but I smother it like I would an out-of-control fire. We have to work together, at least for now.

For my precious treasure.

My hand tightens in my pocket around the melted chocolate bar she had given me. One of the greatest gifts I've ever been given, falling just behind the gift of her presence.

With her, I don't feel alone. She's the light breaking apart the monotony of darkness I've grown accustomed to.

She had seemed angry in fight class today. Vengeful. She hadn't even looked at Mason who tried desperately—futilely —to garner her attention.

I had asked if she was experiencing the Great Period, but that only caused her to huff away, muttering under her breath about oblivious, stupid males.

I don't like when my precious treasure is angry with me. It causes a gnawing pit of despair to settle in my stomach.

After this mission is over, I will gift her more chocolates

to help combat the Great Period. She will no longer fight it alone.

"We need to get closer," Jack insists.

"But no maiming?" Sometimes I need clarification. Apparently, it's not appropriate behavior to kill *everyone* who wrongs you. Just some.

With a dismayed grunt in my head, Jack urges me to move forward.

I stay low, relying on the minimal shadows of the shed to obscure my location. It's a dance. A game. My feet barely touch the ground as I move towards the broken window with grace and agility.

If my precious treasure could see me now…

I balance on the balls of my feet, straining my ears to hear anything transpiring inside. After a moment of silence, I risk poking my head up and peering into the "shed."

It appears to be a nondescript, one-room house complete with a cot, a white bowl that serves to hold your poop (a toilet, Jack tells me), and a white rectangle (a fridge to keep your food cold).

Our target is nowhere in sight.

My suspicion grows just as I feel something sharp touch my neck. Jack's anxiousness amplifies as he begins running a long, drawn out list of possibilities to escape this situation unscathed.

I'm very, very upset that none of them involve murder.

"This isn't very nice," I say pleasantly to the man holding a knife to my throat. I hear a masculine snort, and the blade presses down harder, cutting skin.

"Why are you following me?" he demands.

He grabs my shoulders and pulls me to my feet, spinning me around. I know he wouldn't have been able to move me without my compliance. He's strong, but he's no match for my monster.

Dimitri Gray stands in the tiny shaft of sunlight piercing through the boughs of trees, eyes glacial. His light hair is pulled back into a low ponytail, and he's bedecked in black pants and a black shirt.

He's every inch the fearsome assassin.

But he doesn't scare me.

Raw fury climbs up my throat at the sight of him.

"What do you want with my precious treasure, Assassin?" I growl, hands balling into fists.

I can hear Jack inside my mind, attempting to placate me. Calm me. But my beast demands release.

Anyone who dares to harm my love will get their heads served to them.

"Your precious treasure," Dimitri repeats dryly, finally dropping the knife, spinning it around his fingers once, before returning it to its sheath. "You mean Violet?"

A low rumble reverberates through my chest.

"I was merely being a good professor and returning her textbook for the quiz today," he says in that same, monotone voice. His expression is just as dispassionate—a blank, impassive mask. "Not that she bothered to show up to my class anyway."

I know that Violet snuck away to visit her friends in detention with Mason. She thinks I don't know, but she's wrong. I know everything about her.

The question is: does Dimitri?

I search his face carefully, but his mask doesn't slip. Not even a twitch.

"If you hurt her, I. Will. Destroy. You." The mere thought of my precious treasure under any duress causes my brain to lose cells. I would tear this damn world apart with my bare hands.

At my dogmatic confession, a tentative smile finally

graces Dimitri's face. The smile is as cold and cruel as the rest of him—thousands of secrets lurk behind it.

"We're a lot alike, Hux," Dimitri says, almost conversationally. He takes a step backwards, eyes fixed on me with that damn sly smirk on his face. "You want to know what's different between us?"

"I want you to stay away from Violet," I growl. "I want you to tell me why you're framing her for murder."

His expression doesn't change at my accusation, much to my displeasure and rapidly growing anger.

"The difference is that you wear your vulnerabilities on your sleeve. You allow the world to see what you care for. *Whom* you care for. That's dangerous in this world. Very, very dangerous."

I don't know if his words are meant as advice or a threat, but either way, I release a guttural roar and lunge for him. Dimitri easily steps out of my way, the dagger once again held casually in his hand.

"You know nothing about me, Hux. Nothing."

"Stay away from Violet," I hiss once more. I hope he can hear the threat in my voice, see the promise of violence in my eyes. The crazy man throws his head back in raucous laughter, the cold noise more unnerving than his silence.

"Kind of hard to do when I'm her professor."

I want to growl at his smartass reply—I want to attack—but Jack's voice once more attempts to calm me. I can sense my brother's unease and suspicion, but he knows fighting Dimitri will be futile. The man's a trained assassin, and though we're skilled, we're nothing compared to him.

But I *will* find a way to kill him if he lays one hand on my precious treasure. I will tear him apart limb from limb until all that's left is his smug smile shoved up his ass.

"Have a safe walk back to campus, Hux. And tell Jack I said hi."

With a cheery wave that doesn't quite match his icy disposition, he saunters away, whistling.

"What do we do now?" Jack questions nervously. I eye the assassin until he disappears from view.

"We watch. And if he steps out of line, we kill."

CHAPTER 27

VIOLET

My days at Monster Academy begin to follow a pattern. Breakfast in the dining hall, where I alternate eating from Vin and Jack. Classes. And then studying in the library with all of the guys. One—or all —of them will always walk me back to my door just as the sun disappears behind the orange and red tapestry of leaves.

There have been no more murders, thank fuck, and conversation around the school quickly steers away from Ali and Blowy to Halloween fast approaching.

Living with Dad, I didn't overly celebrate the holiday. Sometimes, he would drag me to a fancy Devil's Night party. Most times, however, he would stand outside on the front porch scaring the poor kids who tried to trick-or-treat. I remember once he buried himself at the edge of the long driveway. When the children came, bright-faced and eager, he would grab their ankles while cackling malevolently.

My dad is a little...strange.

"Any big plans for Halloween?" I ask as I arrive at our

lunch table. Vin trails behind me looking dazed and disheveled, his shirt untucked and a drop of blood on his shirt collar. I lick my lips at the sight of the blood, yearning for another taste.

Mason's eyes are fixated firmly on my mouth, eyes heated.

After a few days of ignoring him, I'm grateful when he finally caved and apologized. I had missed him—the dopey, perpetual smirk on his face and his beanie.

I watch him through my fluttering lashes, totally notching up the charm. I'm a sex fucking goddess. The epitome of sex. The reason why vaginas exist in the first place.

Mason is staring at me intently, and I continue to flutter my lashes.

Bow down to the sex goddess.

And then…

"You have food on your face," Mason says at last, reverting his attention back to his plate.

"Such a fucking slob," adds Vin good-naturedly.

"Are you okay? You're not having a seizure, are you?" Jack asks worriedly.

I fucking hate all of them.

"So Halloween," I say quickly, changing the subject. "What's the plan?" When no one immediately answers, I sigh heavily. "What do you guys usually do on Halloween?"

At this, the guys exchange uncomfortable glances.

It's Frankie who answers first, clearing his throat. "I usually work in my lab." At my flabbergasted expression, he shrugs sheepishly. "To me, Halloween is just like any other day."

Jack nods his head. "Same. I usually retire early that night."

"Mason? Vin?" I glance at the two men who are both

looking anywhere, everywhere, but at me. "What do you usually do?"

"They usually do *me*," a sly voice says curtly from behind me. I stiffen, the tiny hairs on the back of my neck standing on end. I sort of wish that those hairs were razor blades I could use to stab the bitch.

Cheryl sashays forward with an exaggerated sway to her hips. She looks as annoyingly beautiful as ever. It's *so* not fair.

"Vinny Poo," she purrs in what she probably thinks is a suggestive voice.

It totally is. Even I want to dry-hump her.

"Masey Bear," she adds, dropping a manicured hand onto Mason's shoulder and kneading the flesh there.

Masey Bear?

I know about her and Vin. But her and Mason?

Mason shrugs her hand off him, face unnaturally cold. It's such a contrast to his normally jovial grin and sparkling eyes that I resist the urge to do a comedic double-take.

"I wanted to officially invite you to the Halloween Spectacular," she purrs, undeterred by Mason's obvious dismissal. I have to give the girl credit: she has balls.

Or very strong ovaries.

The Queen of Ovaries.

Her Vaginasty.

This is why I don't have any friends.

"Leave, Viper," Vin hisses darkly, and a petty part of me— a very, very petty part of me—is jealous he gave her a nickname.

Even if that nickname is Viper.

"What's the Halloween Spectacular?" I cut in, and she flashes me a look of pure annoyance. I sort of feel like a child caught putting a severed hand into their dad's shoe...oh wait. That's not a normal part of childhood? Whoops. Anyway, I feel like a child about to be reprimanded by a parent.

Her lips curl back over her teeth, but she answers reluctantly. "It's a Halloween party the student council puts on," she admits.

First: we have a student council?

Second: we have a fucking student council?

"So does that mean it's open to *all* students," I say with a slight smile. "After all, it is a school event."

I bat my eyelashes innocently.

Her face twists, and she opens her mouth to no doubt argue, before snapping it closed. Through gritted teeth, she says, "Yes."

Turning away from her, I smile at the assembled guys. Mason and Vin both look as if they have eaten something sour. Frankie is volleying his gaze between me and Gills with fascination, and Jack is silent as usual. When they spot my smile, wariness flashes across each of their faces.

"We're going to the party," I say resolutely.

"No," they chorus back to me. I pout.

"Please. Pretty please. Pretty please with sparkly dildos and dicks on top?" I beg, pushing out my bottom lip and folding my hands together as if in prayer.

"We'll talk about it later," Vin hisses at last, ripping his gaze away from my puppy-dog eyes to glare at Cheryl. "Now leave."

"But I miss you—"

"Leave, Cheryl. Now." His expression is as unyielding as his voice. Cheryl remains for a moment longer, seeking support from the other guys at the table. When they all continue to glare at her, she huffs, flicks back her orange hair, and stalks away.

"I feel kind of bad for her," I admit when I'm sure she's out of earshot.

Four incredulous gazes swivel my way.

"What?" Vin sputters. "Why?"

"Because she's lonely and bitter." I shrug my shoulders. "She has no one who truly cares about her, and no one who she truly cares for either. Her one friend died. She's surrounded by a lot of people, yet she's never smiling. I don't think she knows how to. Add to that her unreciprocated lust —not love—and she's a walking, life-sized form of loneliness." I shrug once more as the guys gape at me wordlessly. After a moment of silence, I ask, "What?"

It's Jack who looks away first, something akin to respect and awe shining in his eyes. "You're perceptive."

Feeling suddenly self-conscious, I fiddle with the sleeves of my shirt. "I just know what it's like, that's all."

The silence this time is more pronounced, the tension following my confession thrumming between us like a live wire.

"Well, you don't have to worry about loneliness ever again," Vin says gruffly, and my heart elevates, gaining little tiny wings and fluttering against my rib cage.

Frankie shoves the remainder of his food into his mouth, scrambling to his feet.

"Where are you going?" I ask. We still have a little more than an hour until our first class begins. Usually, we chat amongst ourselves or play a stupid game Mason comes up with.

A full piece of toast held between his teeth, he mumbles, "Lab."

"Oh!" I jump out of my seat as well, clapping my hands together eagerly. "Can I come? Please? Please? Please? I'll be good! Promise! I'll sit and listen and won't touch anything!"

I expect a quick, harsh no. Frankie isn't cruel by any means, but he's the iciest of my new friends. He has these impenetrable walls erected around him, walls that I'm incapable of breaching. His lab is his sanctuary. Even his clients are only allowed in one small portion, from what I hear.

So you can imagine my surprise when Frankie nods without hesitation, quickly swallowing the rest of the toast.

Surprised—but not willing to look a gift horse in the anus, or however that saying goes—I grab my backpack and hurry after him, waving goodbye to the others who are watching me with soft smiles on their faces.

I'm practically skipping as we wander down the wooded trail and into the main academic building. Frankie leads me to the *Employee's Only* door he had pointed out before and then down a long, steep staircase.

"Lights on," he demands, and one by one, bright white lights spring to life overhead, illuminating the spacious lab.

Lab seems too tame a term for the room I'm in. It's *glorious*. If I was into science—and knew more than just "inertia is a property of matter"—I would orgasm everywhere. Make the white tiled floors a slip-and-slide.

Counters are lined around the perimeter of the room, each holding an assortment of machinery and equipment. A glass cabinet over one of the shelves shows a bunch of vials, each holding a strange, undefinable liquid. There's a section closed off with dividers, but through a crack, I can see an operating table and a tray of tools.

"You work here?" I ask in awe, spinning around in a circle. Frankie shrugs nonchalantly, but I can see heat rising to his face. He's *embarrassed.* It's a strange thing to see on the serious man.

"I either make potions for my clients, or they come to me." He shrugs his shoulders, one hand snaking up to ruffle his hair. "Being a scientist is in my blood, I suppose."

His blood?

From what I heard, Frankie is a product of one of Frankenstein's experiments, not a blood relative. I don't dare ask him, though, as he pulls out a stool and gestures for me to sit down.

Once I'm settled, he leans against the counter next to me, eyes intent as they trace my face.

"What?" I ask, bringing a hand up to rub at my mouth. "I still have something on my mouth, don't I?"

Fucking hell. I talked to Cheryl like this.

Frankie's lips twitch, and he nods. "Just a little." Eyes hesitant—cautious—he reaches for me. When I don't shy away, he uses the pad of his thumb to wipe away the remainder of my breakfast. My heart flutters in my chest at the contact.

Clearing my throat, I ask against his thumb, "What's on the agenda today? Fairy drugs? Happy gas? Boob transplants?" My voice turns bitter at the last suggestion. For a reason I don't want to look into, I hate the prospect of Frankie touching another girl's boobs.

At the same time, I know how important Frankie's work is. Sure, a lot of the students use his services to get bigger breasts or a thicker penis, but what about the people trapped in their own bodies? Frankie's providing them with an opportunity to be themselves. For the person who identifies as a man to have a working penis. I'll be damned if I allow my jealousy to get in the way of the good he can be doing.

Frankie smiles softly, as if he understands the reasoning for my suddenly sharp tone.

"Hair removal," he says, removing his thumb from my lips and turning back towards the counter. He scribbles something on the pad of paper before grabbing a bottle of some strange, yellow liquid.

It sort of looks like pee.

"I'm very selective about my clients," he says conversationally. "I haven't taken on any body part transplants or enhancements in a month, and I don't plan to without talking to you first."

In a month.

Since I arrived.

My heart flutters even as my confusion grows. It almost feels as if he wants my permission. I can't deny that makes the green monster inside of me feel better, but I don't understand why he feels the need to ask me first. Is it because I'm his first true friend, or is it for another reason?

He isn't blushing at his statement. He speaks as if it's a known fact, as if it's common sense.

Knowing that awkwardly laughing isn't appropriate in this situation, I swivel back and forth on the twisting stool.

"So, did you want to be a scientist just because of your dad? Or is it something you wanted as well?"

He freezes, pen hovering over the paper, and his back stiffens. I immediately wish I could take back my question. Obviously, it's a touchy subject.

Way to go, Violet.

After a moment, Frankie relaxes, but his head doesn't lift from where it's tilted over his pad of paper.

"Nobody ever asked me that before," he says softly.

"Well, I suppose I'll be your first." My cheeks instantly flame when I realize how my words can be construed.

I could totally be his first.

Oblivious to my slip, Frankie shrugs before his face turns thoughtful. "I guess I don't really know. Ever since I was younger, it was drilled into my brain that I would be a scientist. A doctor. It's all I've ever known." His shoulders hunch. "But I like it. I like...creating things. Fixing them. It's the one thing I'm good at."

"I'm sure you're good at a lot of things," I protest quickly. Once more, I'm gifted with that rare twitch of his lips I'm beginning to crave.

"Do you want to help me make the potion while we wait for my client?" he asks, nodding towards the vials and beakers. I nod my head eagerly, jumping to my feet.

The next fifty minutes consists of Frankie teaching me

what each jar is and how to properly measure the ingredients. He explains which ones to mix and which ones should never touch. He even allows me to create my own potion designed to enhance eyesight.

He's a surprisingly patient teacher. He painstakingly walks me through each step, hand guiding my own.

Remember those obnoxious butterflies? They're back with a vengeance. I need to start taking bug spray to them if they keep this up.

It's only when the fifty minutes are up—and we have to get to class—do I notice the furrowing of his brows.

"Everything okay?" I ask gently as I remove the gloves he made me wear. He smiles softly, reassuringly.

"Yeah, fine. I'm just surprised my client never arrived. She hasn't missed an appointment yet, and we have one every week."

Unease clenches my stomach. Another student disappearing?

"What's her name?" I ask, nibbling my lower lip. Are we going to find another body? Another female drained of blood?

When Frankie frowns, hesitating, I raise an eyebrow at him. "Really? You meet with her every week, and you never bothered to learn her name?"

His cheeks turn red, and he ducks his head, flipping to one of the pages in his notebook.

"It didn't seem relevant," he admits, scrubbing at the back of his neck. "But her name is Marie." He points triumphantly to the name scribbled in unintelligible scrawl. I roll my eyes.

"You're lucky you're cute," I mutter, and his cheeks burn even *brighter*.

"You think I'm cute?" he asks as we climb the stairs and exit back into the hall teeming with students. He freezes suddenly, eyes narrowing on a petite female leaning indolently against the wall texting on her phone. I hurry to keep up as he stalks forward. "Maria," he addresses curtly, and her head snaps up.

"Marie," I correct around a fake cough.

"You're looking rather hairless this morning," he says suspiciously, and I resist the urge to cough again and warn him that's *not* the way to talk to females. "I missed you at our appointment today."

Marie shrugs one shoulder, eyes lowering back to her phone.

"Found a new supplier," she says dismissively.

Frankie's left eye twitches. Literally twitches.

"Who is this supplier?" he asks through gritted teeth. Something in his tone causes her head to snap back up and her face to drain of color.

"Um...Mikey," she admits sheepishly. I don't know who this "Mikey" is, but Frankie's face goes even darker, hands curling into fists.

"Mikey," he repeats in a cold voice. Marie nods.

"He set up a shop in the basement of the cafeteria. Cheap products." The bell rings, indicating the beginning of the first class. Marie stares at Frankie for a moment longer before hurrying down the hall, periodically looking over her shoulder as if she expects him to follow her.

Without a word, Frankie storms out of the academic building and towards the path that leads to the cafeteria. I hesitate only a moment before following behind. Hopefully, Ms. Stevens won't be too upset if I skip her class.

Shit is going down, and I'll be damned if I miss it.

CHAPTER 28

FRANKIE

I f I was a dragon, I would be spouting out fire from my nostrils and mouth.

There's a certain calmness to my anger, something that lurks just beneath the surface. On the outside, I'm calm, if a bit impassive. On the inside, I want to set the world on fire. Watch it fucking burn.

Mikey is stealing *my* clients.

Mine.

The deep-rooted betrayal grows in my stomach, climbing up my throat until all I want to do is scream. Instead, I keep my face perfectly blank.

He'll pay for what he's done.

"Frankie! Wait!" a familiar, angelic voice calls from behind me. That voice is accompanied by the soft thumping of footsteps followed immediately by a muffled curse. I turn just as Violet scrambles off the ground—where she had no doubt face-planted. The movement pulls up the tantalizingly short skirt she loves to wear, revealing a flash of creamy white thighs.

My cock hardens, and my anger towards Mikey momentarily dissipates.

She's so beautiful that it's a physical pain. With her golden hair haloing around her face and dirt smearing her cheeks, I'm utterly smitten. My tongue feels like cotton in my mouth; thousands of words come to mind, but I can't find the will to speak any of them. All I can do is stare, enraptured. Captivated.

"So what's the plan?" Violet asks, scampering up to stand beside me and linking her arm with my own. "Do I need a tarp?"

I blink at her wordlessly, wondering what the hell goes through that pretty little head of hers.

"A tarp?" I repeat blankly.

She nods seriously. "To catch the blood."

My heart warms exponentially. Before I can stop myself, I press my lips to her head.

Both of us freeze. My breathing is labored, and I don't dare look at her.

Why the hell did I do that?

Heart racing, I detangle my arm from hers and take a step away. Distance. I need distance. She's as addictive as the drugs I love to sample. If I don't stop soon, I'll never be able to. Her intoxicating scent. Her luscious curves. Her sparkling eyes.

Everything about her calls to me. If I wasn't certain she was a vampire, I would believe her to be a siren or succubus.

I think I see a flicker of disappointment in her eyes, but it's soon replaced by her normal, jovial spark.

"So, what's the plan?" she repeats.

We reach the now empty cafeteria, and I open the door

for her to enter. A delicate blush stains her cheeks as she slips through.

"I'll handle it," I assure her, my anger manifesting once more. I feel...betrayed. I'm not used to the onslaught of emotions assaulting me. "Are you sure you want to be here with me?"

She gives me a look that makes me feel instantly chastised.

It doesn't take long to find the door leading to the basement. I step in front of Violet instinctively as we descend the long staircase, automatic lights flickering on overhead with each step.

When we reach the bottom, all I can do is stare in horror. Violet releases a startled yelp.

It's not a sterile lab in the normal sense. Sure, I spot an operating table, a collection of beakers, and a few expensive pieces of machinery, but that's where the similarities to my lab end.

This?

This is a fucking sex club.

The low, hypnotic music combined with the flashing colored lights heighten the sexual environment. Bodies are everywhere—fucking, sucking, and...peeing.

I have the sudden urge to cover Violet's eyes against the penis assault.

Mikey sits on a chair near the back of the room, dark skin flickering in the artificial lighting. In front of him, two girls are kissing passionately, kneading each other's bare breasts and tweaking their nipples. At his feet, a male sucks his cock.

"What the fuck?" Violet exclaims, echoing my own thoughts. The familiar scent of unicorn magic—otherwise known as lust magic—permeates the air.

Grabbing Violet's hand to keep her with me, I stalk past the twitching bodies and straight up to Mikey.

"What the hell?" I ask Merlin's son with barely veiled contempt.

The man currently sucking his cock pulls his head up, licking the...errr...cum from his lips. For a moment, I don't recognize the eyes glaring daggers at me from where he's perched at Mikey's feet.

Until I see his dick.

It curves around his hip in a move that shouldn't be possible, saluting me.

No, saluting *Violet*. My Violet.

A low growl starts low in my chest, but I pull my gaze away from the cock *I* created and face Mikey's smug, triumphant grin.

"Frankie! Here to join in the festivities! I'm surprised, honestly. I didn't think you were into this kind of thing."

"What the hell is this, Mikey?" I ask, risking a step closer. The girls—perhaps sensing the tension thrumming in the air —scurry away. Mikey watches them leave in disappointment before turning to me with a quirked brow.

"Whatever do you mean?" he asks.

"Frankie," Violet whispers. "It's *twitching.*"

Her eyes aren't on me, but on the forked cock that is, in fact, twitching like a snake tongue.

"Stop looking at it," I hiss, possessiveness and jealousy rearing their ugly heads. I don't understand why, and I don't dare look too closely at it.

"I want to say thank you," Snake Cock says snidely, moving to sit back on his heels to face us. His cock unwinds from around his waist, once more pointing up at Violet. The two halves of it begin to slither and twist like coiling snakes. "I thought you fucked up my life with your failed experiment. But the girls actually really, *really* like it in their cunts." He punctuates this statement with a wink at Violet.

I glare, moving to step in front of the shell-shocked female.

Whose gaze is still fixed firmly on the cock with a mixture of horror and wonder.

"It's like two mini cocks," she whispers.

"Why are you stealing my clients?" I address Mikey. "We were friends. I gave you a cut."

Mikey is a skilled and powerful mage—no surprise given his lineage. For as long as I can remember, he has been a part of my business, providing supplies and magic for my experiments.

"You gave me twenty fucking percent," Mikey hisses. "Your experiments would be *nothing* without my magic. I deserved more than what you offered me." He leans back and nods towards his dick. Snake Cock immediately leans forward once more to suck it.

I really, really don't want Violet looking.

Mikey groans in satisfaction, clasping his hands behind his head, elbows bent.

"It's...it's wrapping around Mikey's dick," Violet whispers in horror. One of the halves of Snake Cock's dick is curling around Mikey's, tugging.

It's the strangest fucking thing I've ever seen, and I *made* that cock.

Ripping my gaze from the demented sight, I glare at Mikey.

"So you decided to take one hundred percent," I deduce.

"I decided to take your measly business and create an empire." He spreads his arms out to encompass said empire— the thrashing bodies, flickering strobe lights, and thumping music.

My anger strengthens at his words. He turned my business, my hard work, into a fucking joke. I pride myself on being level-headed and calm, on controlling my emotions.

But I've never wanted to punch someone as badly as I do him.

I won't, of course. It's just not in my genetics to engage in physical combat. I wouldn't call myself a pacifist, per se, but I've been programmed to resist the allure of violence.

Violet lets out a strangled gasp, and I immediately drop my gaze to the forked cock, wondering what captured her attention this time. When I see nothing out of the ordinary— the cock still wrapped around Mikey's like a snake choking its prey—I turn towards Violet.

Her gaze is drawn to the corner of the room, mouth parted in shock. Mikey makes a strange noise in the back of his throat as he follows her gaze. His face pales dramatically.

A rage I have never felt before trails an icy finger down the nape of my neck to the middle of my spine. While my previous burst of anger had been white hot, fiery, this one is icy. A coldness seeps into my very bones as my vision funnels.

Standing against the wall, dressed in a bikini top and thong, is Violet.

Or, a version of Violet.

Mikey had fucking *cloned* her.

Before I can say anything, Violet storms towards the vacant eyed creature. Her face is turning purple the closer she gets, and her tiny hands are in fists.

"What the *hell* is this?" she demands, spinning on her heel to face a still naked Mikey who'd followed us. Forked Cock, thankfully, has remained behind, eyes fixed firmly on Violet's ass. I'll deal with him later.

Mikey rubs at the back of his neck awkwardly, almost as if her discovering his fucked up clone is a mild inconvenience.

"I can explain," he begins in a hurry.

"Is that a leash?" Violet continues, aghast. "Is she some sort of dog?"

"Don't!" Mikey warns, but it's too late.

Dog, apparently, is a programmed word in the Violet Clone's vocabulary. To my horror, the creatures drops to her hands and knees and begins to pant, sniffing around our feet.

"What. The. Fuck?" Violet asks slowly, carefully, and Mikey blanches as yet *another* command is unintentionally issued.

At the word fuck, the Violet Clone drops to her back, hands and legs in the air.

"You made me a sex toy?" Vi asks dangerously.

Mikey holds up his hands pleadingly. "Let me explain."

"What is there to explain?" she demands. "You made me into your fucking bitch!" The dog version of Violet Clone appears once more as she sniffs the ground and barks happily. "I feel violated and disgusted!" Violet Clone lifts up her leg to pee on Mikey's leg—a fact that fills me with great satisfaction. "Stop!"

The Violent Clone immediately stops.

"What other words did you program me...her...it with?" Turning towards the sex toy, Violet says, "Simon says put your hand on your head."

The toy places her hand on her head.

"Simon says Jump."

The doll jumps.

"Master."

At this, a long whip materializes from the clone's robotic hand, and she cracks it against the ground. Violet glares at the creature, more annoyed than angry.

"Simon didn't say." She pauses, tapping her finger against her chin. "Simon says blowjob."

At that, Violet Clone scrambles to her knees, and her jaw

drops to just above her chest, the movement so unnatural and grotesque I have to look away.

Violet's eyes are wide with terror.

"What type of cock are you *putting* in me?" she asks in horror, gaping at the big fucking hole.

"There's a market for these toys," Mikey says in a rush. "Dracula's daughter. The sexy blonde vampire. It's nothing personal. Just business."

My anger burns through me. Chills me. The contradictory feelings make me nauseous. Before I can rethink my actions, I slam Mikey against the wall. His head bounces, eyes tightening in pain.

"How many of them did you sell?" I rumble. When he doesn't answer, I slam his head against the wall once more. "How many?"

"None!" he gasps at last. "Dude, I swear it. I only made the one."

"And that's the only one you'll *ever* make." My anger propelling my actions, I throw my arm back and punch Mikey square in the nose. How dare he?

How fucking dare he?

Shaking out my sore fingers, I turn towards Violet who is petting the clone's head softly. The clone's blank eyes stare absently at a spot on the wall, the lights reflecting off her pale, nearly translucent, skin.

"She is *sooo* cute," Violet sings. "Can we keep her?"

CHAPTER 29

VIOLET

And *that* is how I find myself shoving my sex clone into the back of my wardrobe. It took an admittedly long time to find her off switch (the back of her neck), but I was thankful when her body hunched over, hands brushing against the floor and hair hanging.

I'd made the mistake of saying "shit" before I turned her off.

I'll have nightmares for years.

Shoving a body in such a small space is *not* as easy as it looks. There's a lot of twisting and maneuvering you're forced to do. Her poor head ends up between both her legs, and her arms are haphazardly tossed above her head.

I am just about to shut the wardrobe door when Cynthia enters the room. She takes one look at me then one look at my clone before asking, "You have one too?"

I do *not* want to know.

Panting, I shove the door closed and rest my back against it.

"I'm fucking heavy," I pant, attempting to get my ragged breathing under control.

"Do I even want to know why you have your dead body in the closet?" Cynthia asks with a quirk to her brow. I'm shaking my head vehemently before she even finishes.

"Nope. No you don't. And I'll appreciate it if you'll keep this between us?" My demand turns into a question, my voice quivering. Cynthia blinks her abnormally large eyes at me.

"Noted."

Without another word, she grabs a textbook from her desk, shoves it into her backpack, and backs slowly out of the room. She keeps her eyes trained on me the entire time.

As she opens the door to leave, Frankie is coming in, his hand raised as if to knock.

Cynthia flickers her eyes once more between me, Frankie, and the scantily-dressed doll in the closet.

"You do you," she tells me seriously—taking those words to a *whole* new level—before practically racing down the hall. Frankie watches her go with a perplexed look.

"What was that all about?" he asks, moving into my room with a bag of my favorite candy. After the whole Mikey-and-clone incident, Frankie has been in a mood. It's strange to see the normally calm and collected man past the breaking point. I sent him to grab me chocolates in order to calm him down. Frankie, I realize, needs a purpose. Needs a job. He's not the type to sit idly by twiddling his thumbs.

"Cynthia saw my clone," I say with a nonchalant shrug. Frankie's face darkens significantly at my words, and I hurry towards him. "This is a good thing," I insist.

"Cynthia seeing your sex clone?"

"No." I shake my head. "I think it might be connected." When he simply raises his eyebrow, waiting for me to elaborate, I add, "The murders. The sex doll. I think they're connected."

"How the fuck is it connected?" He scrubs a hand through his hair, making the normally immaculate strands stand on end.

"You heard Mikey. People have been *paying* to use that doll." His face grows redder, a vein in his neck bulging. I scramble to finish before he blows a gasket. "What if one of those people paying for the doll is the same one framing me for murder? It would make sense."

"I think you're grasping at straws, Violet," Frankie says, voice surprisingly gentle.

"Or it's a lead," I point out. "If we can figure out who has been buying my—errr—*her* services, we can have a solid understanding of everyone in the school who is obsessed with me."

"But there is a difference between lust and hate," Frankie points out. "And the murders are definitely acts of hate."

"Yes, but how big of a difference?" When he remains silent, I take another step closer, curling my hand around the wrist holding the candy bag. "Whoever is murdering those people is angry...whether it's anger towards me or Dracula, I can't tell. But it's anger. What better way to take out their anger than on a life-size version of me? Who says that the doll was only used for sexual favors? Though that still fucking disgusts me to even think about. Frankie, it's the only viable lead we have."

Before Frankie can answer, there's a knock on the door followed by Mason's voice.

"Pinkie, open up!"

I whip my head towards the door and then back to Frankie, not above pleading with the stoic son of Frankenstein. "Please don't tell them about what happened. They'll freak and *murder* Mikey. I don't like the asshole, but we need him. At least for now."

I can see hesitation clearly on Frankie's face. His thick

lips purse, and his dark brows furrow. After a moment, he nods reluctantly.

"Fine. For now. But after we talk to Mikey, we're going to tell them everything, okay? We don't know how dangerous these clients are. We don't know if they'll escalate from a doll to the real thing."

I haven't thought about that, and the pain in my stomach intensifies. I nod solemnly.

There's a lot of sick fucks in the world. Both monster and human. It makes me nauseous to know some of them are after me. The doll is just further proof of how far some people can go. Who used it? What did they do to it?

I don't know if I can stomach the answers to those questions.

Bracing myself—like I would against a hurricane—I open my dorm room door and allow the men inside.

Mason immediately goes to sprawl out on my bed, and Vin cautiously perches himself on my desk chair. Hux strolls in the room with his hands in his pockets and hair pushed back, the epitome of strength and confidence. A cocky smirk pushes up the corner of his lips.

"And what is my precious treasure up to?" he asks in that mouth-watering accent I want to make babies with.

"Shoving a sex doll clone of me into my wardrobe," I blurt out.

Smooth, Violet. Real smooth.

Frankie facepalms himself.

Silence.

And then all of the men break into raucous laughter. Mason stares at me fondly, eyes twinkling.

"You're a strange one, Pinkie. Very strange."

I attempt to laugh as well before realizing I sound like a dying hyena and toning it down a notch.

"Yup. Because I was *totally* joking," I say. "I'm just a regular, old jokester. Just call me the queen of jokes. Queen Joker. Joker Queen. Joker—"

"Too much," Frankie mutters under his breath to me.

I immediately stop talking.

The rest of the conversation flows easily—the guys talking about the upcoming Halloween party I'm forcing them to attend and the Roaring. Soon, I find myself cracking up as Mason shares a story about his mother and Zeus and a pickle dipped in poison. Thoughts of sex dolls, obsession, and murder disappear from my mind completely until I feel like a normal monster enjoying the company of her friends.

But I know that nothing can stay perfect forever. The monster world is full of darkness. It's inevitable that it'll find me.

This is why monsters are never seen in the light: because the darkness continuously tries to claim them.

I'M EARLY TO MS. STEVENS' CLASS THE NEXT MORNING HOPING to apologize for my absence the day before.

She's sitting at her desk, hair braided away from her face and a red pen in her hand. She glances up when I enter.

"Violet." She sounds almost relieved. "How are you?"

I move to sit on the top of the nearest student desk, dropping my backpack onto the ground.

"Super sorry," I answer. Her lips lower into a frown. Before she can comment, I hurry to explain. "For missing class. I'm sorry. I plan to copy the notes from Jack."

"Violet, it's fine. You guys have lives." She offers me a wry smirk. "I was a student not that long ago too, you know. I was more worried than anything. With all the murders…" Her face twists with disgust. "And now with the new student council decree."

"New student council decree?" I ask, mind flashing to Cheryl and her snakelike smile. No, *shark*like smile. She belongs in the fucking ocean, thousands of miles away from me.

Ms. Stevens' expression turns sympathetic. "Last night, they ruled that *all* vampires have to send a sample of their venom to the school for testing."

That revelation causes me to jump to my feet, anger swamping me. Devouring me. *Consuming* me. I see nothing but red, as if someone had drawn the curtains of a stage closed.

"What? They can't do that!"

"They can, and they will." Ms. Stevens' expression shows me *exactly* how she feels about that. I imagine it's a mirror of my own.

"They're bigots!" I hiss. "They're not asking Mason to send over his snake venom. Their not asking for the cum from the incubi!"

"Violet, I know." She stands as well, graceful and elegant in her pantsuit. "It's not fair. I know that, and you know that. The murders..." She sighs, forking her fingers through her orange hair. "They're scared. Anyone with eyes can see that the bites didn't come from vampires, but unfortunately, we have a lot of anxious students. They see dead bodies and Dracula's infamous daughter, and they jump to conclusions."

I'm livid. Positively livid. This is just like the witch hunts in the sixteen hundreds. They see us as predators, as beasts. They're willing to hunt us down under this deluded mentality they need to protect themselves.

The problem is, we're *all* monsters.

A gnawing sensation pulls at my stomach.

When will this end? When will this hunt stop? How many rules will they implement before we're not allowed to even step outside?

People fear things they don't understand, and we're the epitome of unpredictable.

Soon, the vampires are going to be locked in the top floors of the academy with the other dangerous monsters.

"It's—"

"Violet Dracula," a cold, familiar voice says from the classroom doorway. "Deidre Stevens."

We both turn, Ms. Stevens' lips pursing into a warped scowl.

Dimitri Gray stands in the threshold, God-like in his perfection. His almost white hair is brushed into a low ponytail, and he wears a form-fitting button up and black pants. I hate that I find the man so attractive. He moves with a predatory grace and stillness fitting of his position as an assassin.

"What do you want?" Ms. Stevens—Deidre, apparently—hisses, the sound causing goosebumps to ripple up my arms. Dimitri's smile turns almost taunting.

"I require Violet before class begins," he says.

"But—"

"And permission from the headmaster," he adds with a delightful grin, relishing in her annoyance. At the mention of the headmaster, my vampire teacher physical deflates, crossing her arms over her chest and fixing him with a stony expression.

"What if I don't want to go?" I ask harshly, cocking my hip out to the side. Dimitri stares at me with an unreadable expression, but I could've sworn I saw laughter dancing in his golden-flecked eyes.

"I'm afraid you don't have a choice," he boasts after a moment. Sighing—and realizing that arguing would be futile —I grab my backpack off the ground and take reluctant steps towards the deadly, attractive professor. "Have a good day, Ms. Stevens. I'll see you in a few minutes."

She supplies a noncommittal grunt in reply.

Finally in the hallway, I allow my feet to drag. The last thing I want to be is stuck in a room with Dimitri Gray. The man's dangerous; even his pinkie exudes more power than my entire body. I imagine he'll be capable of killing me with the textbook in my backpack and make it look like an accident.

"I'm afraid you'll be skipping Ms. Stevens' class today," Dimitri says conversationally. I don't bother humoring him with a response.

I'll see what he needs...then get the fuck out of there.

We arrive at his empty classroom, and he opens the door for me. If I didn't know he was a scary motherfucker who visited girls' rooms at one in the morning, I'd think he was a gentleman.

On the desk in front of his, a simple packet sits with a sharpened number two pencil and eraser.

"The quiz you missed." His husky voice sounds in my ear, and I can't stop the goosebumps erupting all over me. And they're not from fear.

"Now? Seriously?" I drag myself into the indicated seat and glare down at the offending paper.

"You missed the last quiz. And as I told you before, naughty students get punished." His voice takes on an almost raspy quality on that last word, and I whip my head up to stare at him. He's sitting in his usual seat behind his desk, but his eyes can almost be described as heated. The intensity of his gaze unnerves me while at the same time evokes a primal need I never knew existed.

"Do you do this with all your students, sir?" I whisper, and I might've been mistaken, but I could've sworn his eyes flared brighter at the addressment.

A slow, sultry smirk pulls up his lips. "No," he answers simply.

Electricity shoots through my nerves, lighting me up.

There's an insatiable need within me, one only he can feed. I don't know if it's because of the power he emits in palpable waves or if it's because he's just so damn beautiful that I'm helpless to look away. Either way, my heart somersaults in his intoxicating presence—in both fear and desire.

We're playing a dangerous game, but I can't seem to stop myself.

"How would you punish me, sir?" I ask, barely recognizing my own voice.

With my enhanced hearing, I hear his sharp intake of breath. His expression, however, remains blank.

"There's a lot of ways to punish a misbehaving student, Ms. Dracula, but I can assure you, the message will be received."

"And what about you?" I dare question, peeking up at him through my fringe of lashes. He stills at my question, back going ramrod straight.

"What about me?"

"How can I punish you if you misbehave?"

He's not breathing, but, then again, neither am I. His eyes capture mine, holding me in their relentless snare. I'm once again struck by the beauty that is Dimitri Gray. The harsh, sharp planes of his face are juxtaposed by the surprisingly soft lips, plush and entirely kissable. His hair looks like silk, and I imagine it'll feel like it as well.

It's him who looks away first with a heavy sigh, and I'm grateful for the reprieve.

"The lust you're feeling now is not real," he admits on a breath. "It's part of my allure as an incubi." His unreadable eyes flash to mine. "I have a darkness in me. A darkness you've probably seen before. I'm not good. I'll never be the good guy, the hero. But you have my vow, Violet, that I'll protect you with all the darkness within me."

I hold his gaze, speechless. I have the distinct feeling that something monumental has just transpired. Something I can't quite put my finger on. The air around us crackles with electricity. His words enter me, consume me, empower me.

What did he mean?

Why did he say that?

Before I can respond, there's a scream from just outside the window. Without a second thought, I race towards it, Dimitri on my heels.

My breath leaves me, and my lungs struggle to refill.

On the steps of the academy, a floor just below us, is a dead body, an unfamiliar girl standing over it in horror.

His dark face is ashen, bloody incisors in his neck.

Mikey.

I turn, horrified, towards Dimitri who has moved back to his desk, leaning against it with a somewhat bored expression. When he notices me looking, he nods towards my unstarted quiz.

"He's dead," I whisper in horror and disbelief. How can he expect me to take a quiz at a time like this?

Dimitri flashes me a crooked grin. "At least you have an alibi." His smile abruptly fades. "Now get to work. I don't want to have to punish you."

CHAPTER 30

VIOLET

Anti-vampire rhetoric gets worse after Mikey's death.

We are regarded with barely veiled contempt and disgust. Some people, like Cheryl and her bitchy friends, are not afraid to say it to our faces. I've been spit on, laughed at, and ridiculed all in the ensuing days.

Ms. Stevens' is the only teacher willing to send students to detention—though even that is a futile attempt.

Students don't want to listen to "Fangs," as they dubbed us.

Dimitri will only get students in trouble if they're seen bullying *me.* I lost track of how many classmates he sent to detention or the headmaster's office, that frosty glare firmly in place.

It took a really, really long time for me to convince Barret and Cal *not* to murder anyone. But a good scare? I can get behind that. Nearly three dozen students left detention with shit in their pants or urine cascading down their legs.

I feel so proud.

It's been a week since the murders—a week since the violence and bullying against vampires has escalated— when I find myself back inside Mikey' lab/sex shop/cloning location.

"Why the fuck are we here?" Vin asks icily as he stares around the now empty room with distaste. This time around, there's no blaring music. No flashing lights. Instead, the lab appears almost ominous, as if the shadows carry more secrets than ever before. I wonder if Vin can smell the pungent stench of cum and lust the way I can. Though there are no writhing bodies, the large room reeks of sex. Discarded clothes cover the cold cement floor, and I spot more than one used condom.

"We need to figure out why Mikey was targeted," I say— though it's only a half truth. I don't add that I need to find the list of names who rented out my clone.

Frankie gives me a pointed look as he rifles through papers adorning one of the counters.

"I *love* the smell of freshly brewed sex on this fine morning," Mason purrs, and I honestly can't tell if he's joking or not.

"Nothing beats that enticing aroma. Sure to start any day off with a bang," I add with a wicked grin.

"Why are you so cute?" Mason asks, dancing towards me and pulling me into his arms. He spins me around, my feet hovering above the disgusting, sex-slicked/sweat-slicked floor.

"Less spinning. More looking." Vin, of course. He's holding a piece of fabric between his thumb and pointer finger with a horrified look.

Smirking, I tap Mason's shoulder until he obediently puts me down, and I skip to Vin.

"That's a bra," I say slowly, as if he'll have trouble understanding such a concept. He stares at the abnormally large red lace with horror before turning towards me. One thing is certain: that bra did *not* go on Clone Me. My boobs are big, but that bra must belong to a giant.

"I know what a bra is," he stutters, throwing the offending fabric down. I screech, covering my face with my hands and curling away.

"Be careful!" I hiss, peeking through one eyelash at the bra.

"What? What? Why?" Vin swivels his head in both directions, searching for what has startled me. I point a trembling finger at the bra.

"Don't you know that we usually keep bombs in there?" I ask. He stares at me. "Our bras are our weapons. I know my cups can serve as Bazookas as well."

Silence. He blinks at me wordlessly.

"Don't you wonder why we always take our bras off when we go to sleep? Or when we're in the safety of our own home?" No answer. "It's because we no longer need the protection. And the last thing we want is to accidentally explode ourselves when we go to sleep."

Completely silent, Vin turns on his heel and walks away.

"Don't try to do that joke with Hux," Jack says from behind me with a timid smile. He wears a pair of spandex gloves as he sifts through a pile of garbage. "He'll demand we make all your clothes into an arsenal."

"Who said I was joking?" I reply seriously.

Now, it's *Jack* staring at me with an unreadable expression.

Changing the subject, I tentatively ask, "Is he here? Hux?"

Jack sighs, returning to his task once more. "He's around. I mean, I can feel him in my head. But sometimes, he...goes away."

A metaphorical bucket of ice water is thrown onto my

head. And I do mean the bucket, not just the water. It hits my head, rendering me momentarily speechless with horror. I work to regain the ability to speak, to function, to do anything other than stare at Jack like an imbecile.

"It's nothing to worry about…"

"Nothing to worry about!" I screech, garnering the attention of Mason who is closest. He flashes me a worried look, but I nod to reassure him that I'm okay.

But I'm not. Okay, that is. The prospect of Hux going away completely…it terrifies me. Numbs me. It leaves me unsteady and disoriented, as if the lightest brush of wind could blow me away completely.

I *care* about Hux. A lot.

"He probably does it on purpose," Jack reassures me quietly. "He sometimes likes his space. Silence."

Jack removes the spandex gloves one at a time, shoving them into his pocket. Venturing a step closer, he pauses when he's an inch away from me. Quickly—so quickly that if I were to have blinked, I would've missed it—Hux's trademark smirk pulls up his lips.

"What did my damn brother do to make my precious treasure so upset?" The ire in Hux's voice makes his accent more pronounced, but the anger is clear enough.

I'm so fucking relieved that I sag against him, briefly resting my head against his muscular chest. I feel him stiffen beneath me before he releases what sounds like a contented purr.

"Shit! Sorry!" I say, coming to my senses. I push off of him and take a step backwards, my knees hitting a low table. Hux has a dopey, blissful smile on his face.

"My precious treasure is allowed to hug me whenever she so desires."

"Awww! I knew you loved me!" Mason sings, eating up the distance between us and throwing his arms around

Hux. Hux lifts his eyes to the ceiling as if asking for patience.

"You have five seconds before I remove your dick, feed it to you until you're performing oral on yourself, and then roast your balls over an open fire. One. Two. Five."

Mason pulls away with a rather girly squeal.

"What happened to three and four?" he demands.

Hux flashes a malevolent grin, teeth shining in the dim lights.

"I really wanted to cut off your dick."

As Mason runs away from a pursuing Hux, hiding behind an annoyed Vin, I turn towards Frankie who is bent over a sheet of paper resting beside a now opened vault.

Nodding towards the vault, he explains, "The bastard had the passcode as one, two, three, four." Frankie slides his hands into his pockets, carefully avoiding my gaze.

"What is it?"

He blows out a breath.

"I found the list." When I quirk a brow, he continues in a hurried whisper. "The list of people who paid for…"

"A ride in my choo-choo train," I supply. When he remains silent, head still bent over the slip of paper, I extend my hand. "Can I see it?"

Silence.

I'm not even sure he's breathing.

Finally, he releases another long breath and holds the paper out to me. Most of the names I don't recognize—at least for now. You can bet your ass I'll hunt down each and every one of them and serve them their-own-cock-sundae.

But there is one person who signed me out more than the others. Almost every single day.

"What the fuck?" I whisper, glaring at the name. "Is this correct?"

"I don't see why it wouldn't be." Frankie still won't meet

my eyes. His hands are gripping the table so tightly I can see his veins. "I'm not a violent person, Violet. But seeing all those names...Violet, I *know* some of those people. I've talked to them. And to know that they..." His lips press together in a thin line as he attempts to regain his control. "I'm going to kill them."

"After I question them," I say, my eyes fixed on the one familiar name written in elegant scrawl. "Then, we can tag-team murder them, okay? Talk about a bonding exercise."

But first, I need answers.

CHAPTER 31

VIOLET

The men on the list are *not* murderers.

Just sick fucking perverts.

I make my way down the list with Frankie, my teeth gritting together the longer I'm forced to endure the jabs said by bigoted pieces of shits.

The current guy we're talking to has slimy brown hair, chocolate eyes, and large bat-like wings protruding from his back. Some type of demon, I presume, though the man—Teegan—insists he's *bat* man. Two words. Not capitalized. No relation to the other, more famous Batman.

His eyes flicker from my breasts to my face and then back to my breasts. I'm beginning to think that my boobs have some type of magnet in them. This is the sixth guy who hasn't been able to look away.

Don't murder him, Violet. Don't murder him.

After that helpful mental pep talk, I smooth my features and level him with an indolent stare.

"So you admit that you, um, partook in activities with my

sex clone?" I ask, and I notice Frankie's grip tighten on the armrests.

"If you meant did I bang her? Yes. Yes, I did. I've always wanted a piece of vampire bitch ass."

Before Frankie can stop me, I'm out of my seat and pounding my fist into his smug face. He releases a guttural roar, hands raising to fend me off.

"You." Punch. "Fucking." Punch. "Asshole."

His face is a canvas of bruises and blood. Livid eyes peer back at me through the mess that is his face. I *may* have gone a little overboard. Again.

I'm a solid six-for-six.

"I did it fucking once!" Teegan hisses. "Just to see what it was like. It's like fucking a celebrity." His dark gaze slides to Frankie. "And it was fucking amazing."

Frankie's face remains blank, eyes bored behind his thick framed glasses. Only someone who knows him well enough can see the banked fire just beneath the surface, the inferno seconds from exploding.

I tug on Teegan's head until his eyes are locked with mine. He struggles, releasing a string of curses, but I stop him with a blast of my power.

Persuasion usually only works after I've just fed. As such, I've been carrying around a bag of disgusting human blood. It's not nearly as potent as Jack's blood or Vin's, but it will have to do. It's not like I can ask them. What could I say?

"I'm going around questioning the men who used my body as a sex doll. Can I use your blood to enhance my persuasion power?"

Yeah, because *that* would go over well.

"*Stop fighting*," I whisper, pushing my allure into each succulent word. Teegan instantly stops fighting, body slackening underneath mine. Sort of like a flaccid dick.

Huh. Maybe that's what Teegan actually is. Maybe he's a penis monster.

"Did you kill all those students?" I ask, pushing the command into his mind. I conjure up images of Ali, Blowy, and Mikey so he knows exactly who I'm talking about.

"No," he answers softly. Dreamily. His eyes have taken on a glazed quality.

"Do you know who did?"

"No."

My fingernails dig into his arms until blood is drawn.

"Why did you pay for that doll of me?" My words are an unintelligible growl, all of my anger and hurt flowing through those words. Teegan swallows harshly. He knows something is wrong, knows that he's the prey in this situation, and yet he's helpless to stop it.

"Because everyone hates you. Dracula's fucking daughter. Can you blame me for wanting a taste of the bitch's cunt?"

Overcome with anger, I punch him in the face once more. Hard. He falls over unconscious.

"They're all useless." I stalk towards Frankie, rubbing Teegan's blood on my skirt. "They're all just fucking perverts, not psychopathic murderers."

"But we did learn something," Frankie points out, his analytical mind turning the information over and over again in his head.

I laugh humorlessly. "That the entire fucking school wants to see me dead? That everyone hates me?"

His eyes shine with soft understanding, and I realize that he understands better than anyone what I mean. While Vin and Mason are both popular, Frankie is more reserved. Before me, he didn't have a lot of interaction outside of his clients. Even with those men and women, he looked at them like science experiments instead of human beings.

We're both lonely and secluded. Hated. At least now we have each other.

"We still need to interview the last name," he says slowly, carefully. His eyes gauge my reaction.

I freeze, turning away from him to stare at Teegan's fallen body. Mechanically, I bend down and toss him over my shoulder. We're lucky we asked him to meet us in an empty classroom after classes have been let out for the day. I couldn't imagine carrying his heavy ass across campus—and definitely couldn't imagine the gossip that would transpire if the students saw me carrying what looked like a dead body.

"I'll handle it," I say, waiting for Frankie to open the door for me. The halls of the school are quiet. I'm not used to it.

"You should stay with us at the house," Frankie persists, moving to stand beside me and keeping one eye on the body slung over my shoulder. "It's not safe."

"I'll handle it."

"But—"

I spin to face him fully, hoping he can see the sincerity in my eyes. Hear it in my dogmatic words. "Frankie, please. I'll handle it."

His face is conflicted, but after a moment, he nods with a defeated sigh. If it was Vin, Hux, or even Mason, they would demand that I submit to their every whim.

But not Frankie.

He trusts me. Trusts my judgement. I need to take poison to the sudden surge of butterflies fluttering about in my stomach.

We move silently up the staircase and to the upper floor. Frankie plugs in the combination on the keypad, and the heavy metal door swings open.

A voice whispers from the shadows, *"Come out, come out, wherever you are."*

"Barret," I call with an eye roll. There's a pause, and a

moment later, Barret appears in front of me, green hair slick with blood.

"Another present?" Barret says, eyeing the body over my shoulder with an excited gleam in his eyes. Cal appears a second later, angrily scrubbing at his sleeve.

"I got *blood* on my sleeve. Blood. Do you know how hard blood is to get out of clothes?" he complains.

"You're still perfect, Cal," I say with an eye roll. I learned early on that I needed to constantly appease his inflated ego.

Cal beams.

"You're perfect as well. Ohhh! What's this? Another one? That's the sixth one in an hour." His expression darkens suddenly, and his eyes narrow into slits. "Are these men that you keep bringing here hurting you?"

I shrug. "Something like that."

I may or may not—depending on how you look at it—have been bringing the men on the list to Cal and Barret for...um...reformation. Therapy. Whatever you want to hear.

Frankie snorts at my understatement, and Cal's eyes widen in understanding.

"Okay, give him here." Cal takes Teegan's body from me. "Can we kill him?"

"We talked about this," I say slowly. "No murder. No lasting scars. No maiming. Just scaring."

Cal's eyes flare brightly. "But if he's hurting you..."

"Hurting? What? Who?" Barret demands, refocusing on the conversation. I love Barret, I do. He's the sweetest man in the world...but he's not the sharpest tool in the shed, if you know what I mean. Half the time, I'm not even sure he's paying attention.

But when he flexes his biceps intimidatingly, I know he would make a dangerous foe. Fortunately, he's firmly in the "friend" category.

I don't want the Boogeyman as an enemy.

"No murder," I state one last time before turning on my heel and retreating the way I came from.

I hear Frankie whisper something that sounds like, "Make them all eat their own shit," before he joins me.

And then the Boogeyman's low, chill-inducing voice, *"I'm coming for you, little boy. You can't hide from me."*

Five masculine screams follow. Soon, they'll be six.

What can I say? Karma's a bitch.

CHAPTER 32

VIOLET

By the time I'm back in my room, I'm exhausted. My body is leaden and tired, and all I want to do is curl beneath the covers and sleep for eternity.

It takes convincing, but Frankie reluctantly separates from me at my dorm room. I can tell he isn't happy about it —lips pressed into a straight line and eyes narrowed—but he doesn't fight me. Instead, he reminds me that their house is a short walk away and that I'm welcome anytime.

That declaration gives me the warm fuzzies, and I can't stop the stupid grin from lighting up my face.

My smile instantly fades.

Cynthia sits at her desk, mechanically removing both her eyes and nose. She's still dressed in her trademark flowing white gown, a combination of a night dress and a wedding dress.

"I still can't decide what I'm going to be for Halloween," she says conversationally as I move to sit on my bed. I eye her cautiously as I kick off my shoes and curl my legs up underneath me. "I'm debating between a sexy bunny and a sexy leprechaun. I know, I know. There's not much of a difference. But I'm trying to decide how good I'll look in green. Would it dry out my skin? Make my hair pop?" When I remain silent, she lifts an eyeball up to stare at me. It's unnerving, to say the least, to stare at a face with only lips and sockets while she holds a wet eyeball in her hand. "Vi! Answer me!"

"Why'd you do it?" I ask softly, ripping my gaze away from my roommate and friend.

"What do you mean?" She places first one eye and then the other into her drawer. "Take out my eyes? Because I hate looking at your ugly ass face."

"I saw Mikey's records," I begin, voice still a whisper. What is this feeling blooming from my chest like a spider-web? Is it...is it pain? Heartbreak? I don't like it.

She lifts her head up. "The warlock who died?"

I nod, despite the fact I know she can't see me. "That doll in the wardrobe..." My shoulders hunch up to my ears. "The records said you checked her—me—it—out numerous times. Why?"

I wish she had her facial features in. She takes the definition of blank face to a whole new level. The only indication she even heard me and hasn't removed her ears yet is the slightest twitch of her lips.

"I see."

Without another word, she moves to her feet and grabs her eyes and nose from the drawer.

"That's all you're going to say?" I demand, jumping to my feet as well. "I just discovered you bought my sex clone more times than any other student, and you say 'I see?'" I attempt to imitate her voice, but I'll be the first to admit I took some creative liberties. When she doesn't answer, methodically grabbing more of her belongings and shoving them into her backpack, I move to block the door. "Well? Do you have, like, a crush on me or something? Is that it? Was it revenge?"

My mind is scrambling to come up with a plausible explanation. I thought...well...it seems naïve now, but I thought we were friends. Has it all been a lie?

Her sightless face stares at me. "I've been the *only* one to defend you," she says in a hushed murmur. "They call you a murderer, a monster, and I defend you. I always defended you, even at the expense of my own standing in this school. But this?" She laughs humorlessly. "What exactly are you accusing me of, Violet? Because I have a feeling this is about more than just a night spent with a shitty sex doll."

I open my mouth but immediately snap it closed. I don't have any idea what to say, how to fix this. I don't even know what's broken.

"I didn't buy your fucking doll. I don't know what made you think I did, but I never touched it. I didn't even know it existed until you showed up at our room and shoved it into the wardrobe. And you know what? Never once did I think you were up to something notorious. I trusted you. Even when you were hiding your own body." She takes a step closer until her slipper-clad feet touch my own. "If the situations were reversed, I would've known immediately that someone was framing you. Attempting to confuse me. Instead, you think I'm the bad guy." Her voice holds a hint of her banshee scream when she speaks next. "I don't like being accused of murder, Violet, even if it's in a roundabout way."

"Cynthia—"

"Don't." She holds up a gnarled, gray hand. "Just don't. You have just made an enemy out of the Woman in White, Violet. I hope you realize what your accusation has cost you."

"I didn't—"

I'm beginning to think I fucked up. Royally.

What just happened?

"I didn't buy your sex doll," she repeats sternly. "And I didn't murder anyone. I've been your friend. I defended you! And look what that cost me. Now…get out of my way before I make you." My mind still racing, scrambling to catch up, I move to the side. Cynthia purposefully rams her shoulder into mine as she passes. "Whoops."

As she storms down the hall, her backpack slung over one shoulder, I watch her with more confusion than anger or fear.

Again, what the everloving fuck just happened?

"I see that you got into a little altercation with your roommate," a sly voice says as a familiar figure enters from around the bend in the hall.

"Go away, Dimitri." I'm tired. Exhausted, really. Torturing people really takes a lot out of a girl.

"It's Mr. Gray to you," he reminds me, stopping in front of my door. He holds up what appears to be a…pen? "You left this in my classroom."

"Huh?"

Eyes intent on my face, he grabs my hand, opens it, and wraps my fingers around the pen.

"You left this in my classroom," he repeats.

"And you came all the way to my room to return it to me?" I ask incredulously, surveying the red inked pen. I *do* recognize it as being mine, but I don't recall ever taking it out of my backpack. "In the middle of the night? A pen? Really?"

I eye the man warily.

"I was being helpful," he states in that stoic way he says everything. It almost makes me feel like an idiot, like I should be grateful he returned my random ass pen that he probably stole from my backpack in the first place.

"You know what? Fuck you, Dimitri."

"Mr. Gray," he corrects with a wry grin on his handsome

face. An unmerciful, savage kind of beauty I've only ever seen reserved in predators, in monsters. But beauty is beauty, and his ensnares me as artfully as a net laid out to capture unsuspecting prey.

"Fuck. You. Do you think I'm stupid? Every time you're around they find a body. Why is that, Mr. Gray?" I say his name like a curse word.

That damn smile doesn't leave his lips.

"You've just seen what accusations cost you, Violet. You made an enemy out of the Woman in White."

"And am I going to make an enemy out of you too?" I ask, taking a step closer. His words from class before echo in my brain. His promise to protect me with all of his darkness. Is that what this is? Him protecting me? Or was that another lie caught in this fucked up web?

"Would you scream if I said yes?" he asks teasingly, and I cross my arms beneath my chest. That gesture pushes up my breasts, and Dimitri's eyes drop to them instinctively.

"I think, Dimitri Gray, that you'll be the one screaming." His eyes whip up to my face in shock. "Now get the fuck out of my room."

"I'm not in your room," he points out like the smartass he is. He points to himself, standing near the threshold, and then to my room. "And if it makes you feel better, I totally thought Cynthia was behind the murders too."

His words chill me—his intended reaction, if the sly smile is any indication.

"What makes you think that?"

He shrugs a shoulder, nonplussed. "She has been in love with Mason for years now. She may claim to be your friend, but that girl is secretly vengeful. Jealous. Plenty of motive to murder her fellow students and then blame you."

First: Cynthia's in love with Mason? My stomach sinks with dread and jealousy at the prospect of the two of them together. I never would've suspected. Mason barely acknowledges her when we're all together, and I'm pretty sure she hasn't talked to him.

Second: How does Dimitri know all this?

My thoughts must've been clear on my face, for he shrugs once more. "I read her diary."

He read...?

He may not be the murderer, but he's a monster.

"Dimitri," I begin in exasperation. "You don't just read a girl's diary, even if you do think she's a psycho murderer. A girl's diary is...well, it's sacred."

He smiles, unrepentant.

So if Cynthia was telling the truth—and she truly didn't use my doll—someone else did and framed her. Is it related to the murders? And what role does Dimitri play in all of this?

Before I can question him, a scream resonates from down the hall. The assassin's eyes twinkle in the dim hallway lighting.

"Let me guess," I say tiredly. So. Freaking. Tired. "They found another body?"

"A girl named Marie," he answers with an affirmative nod. "An old client of Frankie's."

"And did you have anything to do with the murder?" I ask, giving the professor a critical once-over. There's no doubt in my mind that he knows more than what he's telling me. A lot more. Trying to get answers out of him would be like trying to stop the waves from cresting the shoreline with my bare hands: impossible.

"I can assure you, I did not murder those students," he replies sincerely.

Maybe he's telling the truth. Maybe he's not. The fact of the matter remains that he *is* hiding something. It's no coincidence that he shows up just before a new body is found, providing me with a useful alibi.

Or maybe providing himself with one.

"Don't keep leaving behind items in my class," he warns sternly as another scream joins the first. Doors open and close; the hallway fills with curious students.

"I won't," I whisper.

"Have a good night, Violet." He nods his head once before shoving his hands into his pockets and sauntering down the hallway. I watch him maneuver the throng of crying, terrified students. My heart seems to be growing in a rapidly shrinking vise. Insidious fear slithers through my mind and grasps my heart.

Another murder.

More fuel for the crazy vampire witch hunt.

Can't a girl just go to school in peace?

CHAPTER 33

MASON

Halloween has always been my favorite holiday. The orange and black decorations. The pumpkins adorning each walkway. The skeletons and scarecrows.

Humans have romanticized it with time. It's no longer a representation of the monsters haunting this world. To them, it's some silly holiday where you can dress up and pretend to be Santa.

For us, it's our most sacred day.

Monsters no longer have to hide in the shadows; instead, we're worshiped in the light.

I take another long inhale of fairy weed, staring off into the distance. The sunset has painted the town in soft yellows and oranges. The colors are calming—and a direct contradiction to my tumultuous thoughts.

She's late.

Again.

I don't know why I'm always so surprised. Maybe it's because we never believe the person we love will hurt us until they do. And even then, we still seek out the best in them.

In our deluded minds, the people we love are incapable of actually harming us.

I've been making excuses for her for years.

I drop the cigarette, crushing it beneath my foot, and head back towards the school.

"Not even going to say hi?" There's the click of heels and then a tall figure moves in front of me.

Graceful and elegant, Medusa is every inch the goddess and monster legends portray her as. Her silver gown clings to her front modestly but leaves her back bare. She's taller than most women, even without the heels, coming to about six feet.

And erupting from her head, slithering and hissing, are dozens of snakes. Some are large while others are small. The width and color of each one varies as well.

Mother eyes my own beanie with distaste. She doesn't understand why I hide my snakes, my heritage. I'm not under the impression that the school doesn't know who I am, though.

But I don't want them to constantly fear for their lives either.

The legends are wrong; the snakes don't just turn men to stone. It can turn *anyone* who harms us into a block of cement. Male, female. Young, old. One look into the snakes' slitted black eyes, and you're a goner. I'm terrified I'm going to accidentally get angry and turn some poor soul into a living statue.

Fucking terrified.

"Mom," I say, breaching the distance and kissing both her

cheeks. One of her snakes hisses near my ear while another bites my cheek.

Not pleasant creatures.

To all the people who have pet snakes: fuck you. Those things are menacing. I should know. I have a very, very long one.

That's a dick joke, by the way.

"Sit," Mom demands, strolling gracefully towards the cement bench. Her dress cascades around her like starlit silk.

With great reluctance, I sit on the bench beside her, the school appearing small in the distance.

"I've missed these chats," my mother begins softly. "I've missed you."

I barely, just barely, stop myself from snorting. Mother misses only one thing. Well, two things. Her beauty and Zeus's cock.

Both of which Zeus's jealous wife stole from her.

"I missed you too, Mom," I lie, staring down at my feet. Her gaze pierces me like a knife, but I refuse to lift my head.

"Halloween's tomorrow."

Okay, what the fuck is this? Mom doesn't care enough about me to make idle chit chat.

A part of me wants to demand she cuts to the chase, but I know that would be futile. Her snakes aren't the only ones with venom.

"Yup," I say nonchalantly. "Going to the school's Halloween party."

I go every year, but this is the first time I can honestly say I'm excited. I can still picture Violet's face when she arrived at the house and demanded we help her pick out a costume. I'm still pissed that lingerie model was immediately discarded, but Vin had a good point: would we want others to see her like that? Fuck no.

She'd been bouncing with childlike enthusiasm, her voice wistful as she discussed all she wanted to do and see.

For her, I'll do it all.

"A little birdy told me you've been befriending Dracula's daughter," Mother bites out at last, and I turn to her, startled by the raw anger in her voice. Her eyes are as slitted as her snakes'.

Gauging her reaction, I don't immediately speak.

What's the proper answer? If I say yes, will she go on a rampage about how vampires are the lesser species? If I say no, will that be a betrayal to Violet?

Mother makes the decision for me.

"Don't bother lying to me. I can see it on your face." She huffs, turning her nose up as if Violet's scent still clings to me.

"Mom," I begin slowly. Cautiously. Tentatively. "She's my mate."

The silence this time around could be cut with a knife. It's thick, settling between us like molasses. Only her eyes move to stare down her nose at me. They're dark—not physically dark, but emotionally. I've never seen such an expression on my mother's face before, and she's never been an overly warm woman.

"That...makes a lot of sense," she says at last.

"You know you can't control the mate bond," I continue. I don't know why I'm constantly trying to defend myself to her, defend my actions. I sure as hell don't want to defend my blossoming relationship with Violet.

"I went to the oracle the other day," Mother says after another long moment of silence passes. Her face is tight—a change from her usual apathetic expression.

Mother goes to the oracle like some girls go to the spa. She calls it her "girl's day"—pimps herself out, visits the oracle of the gods, and then bathes in the blood of her enemies. I think her and Violet will get along great if they ever got to know each other. Maybe once Mother gets over her prejudices, she can invite Violet to her girl's day.

The thought makes me smile. My two women.

It's every man's dream for his mom and sort-of-girlfriend to go on a murder spree together.

"The oracle…" Mom begins, seemingly far away. Her eyes are slightly dazed.

"The oracle what?" I ask, irritated.

"She saw *you.*"

I freeze—because what else can you do when your mom says that a seer saw your future? I'm both terrified and curious about what she'll say next.

"And?"

Mom's hands fiddle with the hem of her long skirts. I wonder if they're a gift from Zeus or one of her other lovers. The gods only know how much my mother *hates* shopping for herself.

Don't get me wrong: she loves the act of shopping itself. But she thinks it's beneath her to spend Olympus Silver on clothing or jewelry when a lover can buy it for her.

"And…" Her body heaves with her deep breath.

Why do I have the distinct feeling she's being overly dramatic on purpose?

"And that girl, that *Violet,*" she twists her name into something hideous, something worse than a bug beneath her sharp heel. I don't like it one bit. It feels like thousands of snakes are slithering up my spine, cutting off my circulation —snake pun intended.

"What about her?" I grit out.

I wish I had something to take the edge off. Something to make this conversation somewhat bearable. However, I've been trying to cut down on fairy drugs for Violet's sake. I've regulated myself to only one a day.

"Mason, sweetie…" She places a hand on my shoulder, but it feels more like a fifty pound iron weight than the comforting touch of a parental figure.

"Spit it out," I say through clenched teeth.

"The oracle saw your future. Dracula's daughter is going to be the one to kill you."

CHAPTER 34

VIN

I feel fucking stupid.

Staring at my reflection in the full-length mirror, I wonder if Cupid's "you're now a dumbfuck" arrow hit me in the ass when I slept last night.

There's no *fucking* way I'm wearing this in public. And yet...

I'm totally fucking wearing this in public because Violet insisted and batted those big, beautiful eyelashes of hers at me.

Mason steps into my room, takes one look at me, and then crawls onto his hands and knees to search under the bed.

"What the fuck are you doing?" I growl, crossing my arms over my chest. The costume severely restricts the movement, so I end up awkwardly placing them by my sides.

Mason pokes his head out from underneath the bed, eyes alive with mirth. "Looking for your balls."

Motherfucker.

"What costume did she pick out for you?" I snap, facing the mirror once more. My lips are pulled into a tight scowl, and my eyes are narrowed into slits. Frankly, I look murderous.

"Not that one," Mason says. In the next second, the laughter he was trying to keep inside of him bursts out like a dam exploding. He clutches his stomach, tears in his eyes.

I hope he fucking chokes.

When Violet had told us she wanted us to wear matching costumes, I had argued profusely. The last thing I wanted to be was one of those couples who wore boyfriend/girlfriend cutesy clothes.

Not that we are a couple.

Or cute.

Or boyfriend and girlfriend.

And then she smiled—that gorgeous smile that caused butterflies to flutter in my stomach—and I had conceded somewhat graciously.

I hadn't seen the costume she had delivered...until now.

You see, my girl wanted something ironic. And what is more ironic than monster hunters? When she suggested we dress up as the Scooby Doo Gang, I'd agreed, completely forgetting that there were only two males.

One dog.

And two females.

Oh yeah, you're resident monster hunter isn't even Scooby himself. Instead, my whipped ass finds itself in a pleated red skirt, an orange sweater pulled tight over my chest, and a pair of thick glasses sliding down my nose. To add insult to injury, the crazy girl put a wig in the box for me to wear. A fucking bowlcut, dark brown wig.

Velma.

Fucking Velma.

Mason wipes tears from his eyes with the back of his hand.

"I need to go get dressed," he says, gaining control of himself. "But you...you look fucking fabulous."

"Go eat ass," I grumble. Still laughing, he clasps my shoulder in a show of manly solidarity before exiting the room.

Fucking hell. The things I'll do for my woman.

With one last glance in the mirror—affirming that my ass does look good in the skirt—I stalk downstairs. Frankie and Jack are already seated on the couch when I arrive, Frankie mixing together a strange concoction and Jack's head buried in a book. They both glance up when I enter.

Frankie is dressed as Fred, complete with the white shirt and abnormally tight pants. Jack is our resident Scooby with magically created dog ears and black spots on his brown sweater.

Both men roar with laughter when they see me.

"Laugh it up, assholes. I doubt you'll be laughing as much when Violet's head is under my skirt." With a huff, I throw myself onto the couch between them. They both glance at each other over my head, turn towards me, and break into raucous laughter once more.

On the bright side, I'll get to see Violet as Daphne. My girl can pull almost anything off. But a skin tight purple dress? Fuck yes.

Mason swaggers downstairs, his hands shoved in his pockets and a confident sway to his hips. He still wears his customary beanie, but his flannel has been replaced by a long green shirt.

"Isn't Shaggy supposed to have...like...shaggy hair?" I ask, still irritated with Violet. And myself, if I am being completely honest. I haven't even officially mated with her yet—and we're sure as fuck not in a relationship—but she already has me wrapped around her little fingers.

Hopefully, my dick will be one of those things.

Wrapped, I mean. Around her fingers.

Well...it's not as if my dick can wrap around her fingers, so I suppose, technically, it'll be her fingers wrapped around my cock instead of the other way around.

Or her entire hand.

Or her mouth.

Or her sweet cunt...

"What the hell?" Mason exclaims, eyes flying towards the door. My mouth drops open as Violet enters, Cal and Barret trailing behind her with wide eyes. I've heard that the school releases all of the monsters during this sacreligious holiday, but to see it in person is an entirely different thing. The monster hunter in me perceives them as a threat and wants to stab a sword through each of their bodies. The man in me knows they mean us no harm.

Well, they mean Violet no harm.

"You ready for the party?" Violet asks excitedly, bouncing on the balls of her feet.

All I can do is stare at the little temptress in horror. She's *not* dressed as Daphne. There's actually not a lick of purple on her person.

Instead, her blonde hair is brushed back into a low pony-tail. She wears a long brown trench coat with a black suit beneath it. Cal, the leaner of the two, is wearing a dark green jacket, and Barret is wearing a loose flannel shirt.

"What the *fuck* are you?" Mason continues.

"Monster hunters. Duh. I'm Castiel. And they're Sam and Dean." She indicates Barret and Cal respectively.

I stand up slowly, crossing my arms over my chest.

She takes one look at me...and breaks into laughter.

"What the hell are you wearing?" she asks between giggles.

"Your damn costume," I mutter. I don't necessarily feel self-conscious, but it's not like I want the girl I'm falling in love with to see me this way. Ducking my head, I stare at my currently bare feet…

Until my glasses slide off my nose.

That makes Violet laugh even louder, clutching her stomach and falling into Cal who screams, "Don't mess up the hair!"

I dare a glance up when she says my name.

"Vin, sweetie," she repeats, wiping tears from her eyes. "I don't know what you've been told, but I *didn't* send you that costume."

"I thought you wanted to be the Scooby Gang?" I ask, confused. "You sent me this."

She giggles. "I texted Mason yesterday telling him that we were all going to be different monster hunters, from different movies and television shows. You're supposed to be one of the Men in Black. I sent the costume yesterday as well."

Barret's eyes lower, resting on my bare—hairy—thighs not concealed by the knee high socks.

"He looks good," he says with an unashamed wink. Cal straightens to his full, impressive height, red wings fluttering behind him. I wonder if there are cuts in his jacket for them.

"Not as good as I look," he argues with a huff. Both Barret and Violet simultaneously roll their eyes.

"Get changed." Violet claps her hands together. "We have a party to get to!" She punctuates this statement with a fist to the air and a butt wiggle. Barret immediately copies her until I have Dracula's daughter and the Boogeyman twerking in my living room. While I'm dressed as Velma.

What a fucking day.

"I'm going to murder you," I whisper to Mason as I pass.

"In my closet to the right," he replies—the location of my missing costume. Grumbling, I take the stairs two at a time, easily slipping into Mason's trashed room.

There's a few empty containers of fairy dust on the dresser and more on the bed.

I know Mason wants to quit for Violet, but if he tries to do it cold turkey, I fear what the consequences will be. There's a reason fairy dust is one of the most addictive ingredients in the monster world.

Sidestepping a mountain of clothes on the ground, I head to his closet and grab a black suit and sunglasses. *This* costume I can get behind. Hopefully, Violet is one of those women who can appreciate a man in a suit.

Instead of going to my room, I opt to change in Mason's. Maybe I'll fuck with him and get rid of all his clothes, so all that's left is the Velma outfit.

I'm just slipping the jacket on when a book on his nightstand captures my attention. I honestly can't tell you why. Maybe because it's old, with fading yellow pages and indecipherable words. Maybe it's because I'm a nosey bastard.

Either way, I step over to the nightstand and glance at the page he was currently reading. Most of the words are faded, but there's one section that stands out. My body grows cold; my lungs struggle to replenish the rapidly leaving air.

It's a book about mates and mate bonds.

More importantly, it's a book about how to sever a mate bond.

And kill the recipient of the bond in the process.

CHAPTER 35

VIOLET

The last party I went to involved fancy dresses, bottles of wine mixed with blood, and a wall of chained humans.

As I step through the door, I brace myself for the pungent, familiar scent of blood and sweat to assault my senses. I *do* smell sweat, but thankfully, there are no chained humans.

The party takes place in a house next door to the guys'. Cheryl's and her friends', if the pictures adorning the walls are any indication. My stomach twists painfully when one picture on the wall captures my attention.

It's Cheryl and Vin, the hunter's arm wrapped around her waist. Cheryl is glancing up at him like he holds the moon, but Vin's expression is closed off. Blank.

"I hate parties," Vin murmurs, oblivious to the direction of my gaze. I have to admit he looks handsome, sexy even, in his form-fitting black suit, cufflinks, and dark tie. He looks positively dashing.

Though I do prefer the Velma outfit. Something about seeing his muscular legs…

"Ohhh! Violet! Look!" Cal says, bouncing up and down like an excited little boy. He wraps one of his arms around my shoulders and points with the other. I try to see what he's seeing, but all I spot is a crowded room with blaring music and dim lights. "They're *dancing*. I miss dancing. I don't get to dance often in my prison. Dance with me!"

"Last time I danced I broke my neck," I reply dryly. When Cal pushes out his lower lip, pouting—honest to God pouting—I groan. "Don't make that face at me. You're a grownass monster. You shouldn't *pout*."

"But I want to dance," he whines, attempting to sway my body side to side. I laugh despite myself at his antics. Honesty, Cal reminds me of a large man-baby. His childlike energy is infectious, but I can't blame him. He has spent years hidden in the top floors of the academy with the other dangerous monsters. The only time he is allowed a reprieve is during important holidays, such as Halloween. The magic embedded in his skin forces him back to the academy at midnight.

A real life, monstrous, Cinderella story.

But he's one of my best friends, and if he wants to dance during his night free, then we'll fucking dance.

"Save me one, Pinkie!" Mason calls as I allow Cal to pull me onto the dance floor. Out of the corner of my eye, I spot Barret moving to a game of beer pong, body vibrating with excitement. Vin leans against the far wall, away from the dancing bodies and drunk monsters. Frankie and Jack stand a little bit away from him, deep in conversation. As I watch, transfixed, an unfamiliar female steps up and says something to the two males. An uncontrollable bout of jealousy spears my chest. I can't hear what is said, but the girl walks away appearing dejected.

"Trouble in paradise?" Cal whispers in my ear, body twitching with the music. Literally twitching. For a powerful Incubus demon and the world-renowned Cupid, he has horrible rhythm. His large red wings ram into anyone and everyone that gets too close. When a handsome man, who has danced up behind me, gets knocked on his ass, I have to wonder if he's doing it on purpose.

"No trouble," I say, pretending to push a shopping cart and pulling invisible items down from the shelf. "No paradise."

"Oh please," Cal snorts. He does what appears to be an offbeat version of the sprinkler. "I'm all about love. Literally. I see love and feel love and create love." The last statement is said with a flutter of his wings for emphasis. "And those guys?" He nods first to Vin, Frankie, and Jack, still hiding against the wall, and then to Mason who has partnered up with Barret for beer pong. "They're halfway there already."

Halfway there.

Halfway in love.

My stomach tightens, churns, flutters like a thousand butterflies taking flight.

"Halfway isn't all the way there," I point out breathlessly, unsure if I can believe his dogmatic words. "If we're running a race, halfway isn't the finish line. It means you lose."

I'm babbling, I know it. Sue me.

Cal smiles knowingly. "Believe me, sweetheart. I have had over a thousand women and men in love with me. I know what it is."

"Have you?" I ask, peering up at his handsome face.

"Have I what?" I wonder if he's purposefully being dense. His long lashes flutter as he twists and turns to the music.

"Been in love."

He stops dancing abruptly, and I realize my question hasn't been as obvious as I thought. Warm, golden eyes peer down at me. I suppose I haven't ever paid attention to his eye color before, but they're beautiful. Glistening orbs of molten gold.

After a moment, he wrenches his head up to look at a spot over my shoulder.

"No," he says at last. "I thought I was. Once. Maybe twice. But it's hard to tell what's love and what's simply lust." He shrugs his shoulders, but there's no hiding the brief stab of pain that flashes across his face. Those memories haunt him, torment him. They create the shadows in his eyes—the ghosts only he can see. "But never true love. At least, not yet." His tone turns wistful, heavy with pain, regret, and longing.

"What about Barret?" I ask, remembering the compromising position I found them in. Well, heard them in. Heat floods my cheeks at the memory.

"No, not love. He's my best friend, sure, but I need sex to survive. Sometimes, he's the only person available." He pauses, releasing a heavy sigh. There's such longing in his gaze, such longing dripping from every word, that my stomach tightens. What must it be like to be locked away? To be hidden from the world? What makes him so bad and scary in a world full of darkness that he is imprisoned? His mouth sets into a grim, unforgiving line. "Maybe I'll find love."

I offer him a soft smile. "I'll help." And I will. Whatever he needs. Whenever.

After a moment, he gifts me a tremulous smile.

"We should get you back to the others. I can't hog you... even though I'm prettier than all of them." He pauses, staring down at me with earnest eyes. They burrow themselves in my very soul, chipping a piece of my heart. "Thank you for being my friend."

"Thank you for not killing me and making me choke on your cock," I deadpan.

The expression on his face? Priceless.

As we move through the throng of students, my eyes are drawn to a familiar figure leaning against the wall with a severe expression. Headmaster. When we make eye contact —you all know the type, awkward as fuck—he nods in greeting. I awkwardly wave, spotting Ms. Stevens beside him and another of my professors beside her.

No Dimitri.

"Why are the teachers here?" I query as we move to the edge of the dance floor.

"Chaperones," Cal answers, lips curling in distaste. It's hard for me to remember that these teachers, the same teachers who have been nothing but kind to me (minus Dimitri), have locked him away. "It is a school event after all."

He grabs my hand and drags me towards where Barret and Mason are demolishing the opposite team at beer pong.

"How many of you are up there?" I ask, motioning vaguely towards the ceiling, even though we're not even in the academic building at the moment.

"About a dozen. There's three floors of us."

"And it's only you and Barret on your floor?" I ask, and he goes silent. Pensive. I give his hand a reassuring squeeze, trying to offer him comfort through touch alone. I can't say I understand what he's going through, but I imagine he's lonely. Despite that, there's tenebrous determination hiding behind his soft smile.

"Pinkie!" Mason cheers before Cal can answer, running towards me and spinning me around. The opponents of the beer pong game grumble, but indulge Mason.

"Pinkie!" Barret echoes, taking me from Mason.

Mason's eyes *flare* at his use of my nickname. I half expect him to start growling, lifting his leg to urinate on my leg and claim me as his.

Goodness gracious. Where had that thought come from?

Normal people should *not* pee. Well, they should pee, but

just not on people. Unless that person has wronged you, then you have permission to pee away. Preferably in the mouth.

"My nickname," Mason hisses, and Barret blinks his eyes innocently.

"Fine," Barret concedes at last. "Then I want my own nickname. Hmmm."

"Nothing stupid," I warn. "Or cheesy. Or girly."

"Oh! How about Cheese Curd?" He flashes me a bright grin, showcasing two rows of perfectly white teeth. For a man who eats humans, he has very good hygiene.

"Cheese Curd?" I parrot, but fuck, how can I resist that smile?

Don't give in, Violet. Don't give in.

"It's perfect," I finish, flashing him a smile of my own.

Dammit. No strength.

Mason smothers his laughter with his hand.

"Really, really good," I continue, pleased when my voice isn't belligerent. Barret positively *beams* looking so damn adorable with his green hair and dark skin and flashing white teeth. It's impossible to be impervious to his beguiling brown eyes. The last thing I want to do is take candy from a baby.

Or a cheese curd from the Boogeyman.

"Now," I say, turning back towards the carefully arranged plastic cups. "Who wants to have their ass not beaten in beer pong?"

Unsurprisingly, no asses are beaten but mine. Badly. Honestly, at this point, I would expect one of the guys to show me some mercy.

Instead, they remain relentless, combative predators.

Competitive assholes.

When I lose—again—and Mason whoops like he won the lottery—again—I storm away from the boys and into the kitchen.

Not that I'm a poor loser or anything.

During the hour we've been playing, the party had come to life. More than one monster has a glazed, indifferent look to their eyes. I don't know what the teachers are chaperoning, but it sure as hell isn't the alcohol and fairy drug consumption.

The headmaster is standing at the drink table, eyes intense as he surveys the students. When he sees me, he nods his head once more in a barely decipherable greeting. Wordlessly, he hands me a drink spiked with blood and something stronger. Something pungent. Alcohol, more than likely, mixed with fairy piss. I almost consider declining based on that alone before decide why the hell not? It's a party.

Taking a sip, I wrinkle my nose at the disgusting taste of stale blood. Bagged blood. Nothing like the enticing taste of Vin's or Jack's.

"Your father called me today." Headmaster's slashing eyebrows pull low over glowering eyes.

"What did he want?" I take another small sip.

"He's worried about you." He sounds...aghast by the prospect. Shocked, almost, as if it's difficult to believe that Dracula could care about anyone but himself.

"What did you tell him?"

Headmaster's eyes remain fixed on the writhing bodies on the dance floor. Behind his tangled beard, I can't even be sure his lips are moving.

"I told him that you're safe and well. And that is not a lie, is it?" He finally pierces me with a penetrating glare, one brow raised. I can understand his unease. Dad is extremely powerful in the monster world. If he felt the need, my dad could destroy Headmaster and this school. Wolf Man or not, he has nothing on Dracula.

"It is not a lie." We exchange a glance of solidarity, a silent agreement to keep the horrors plaguing this campus far from my father. Who the hell knows how he'll react?

I move away from Headmaster when I spot a familiar shock of dark hair and a scar marring a scowling face. Hux.

"I always forget how horrid I find these parties," he murmurs when I arrive. I have to admit my monster looks cute as fuck with his puppy dog ears and nose.

"You don't have to stay that much longer," I say.

"For you, my precious treasure, I'll stay for eternity." He grabs my wrist, and I swear warmth migrates from where our bare skin touches, settling in my chest. Heat radiates throughout my body accompanied by a kaleidoscope of emotions.

He can whisper "my precious treasure" all night long. In twenty different languages. Or he can just bark it like a dog. Either way, I'll be one very happy—very thirsty—monster.

"Hux?" I ask as a sudden thought occurs to me. I peer up at his face. It's not traditionally handsome, but then again, nothing about Hux is. There's a feral beauty, a masculine elegance, to his swooping cheekbones and the sardonic twist to his lips. His beauty is raw and untamed, a direct contrast to someone like Vin who wields his good looks as a weapon.

"Yes, my precious treasure?"

I really, really need to stop swooning whenever he says those three words. Soon, my face will be permanently morphed into a wistful-smile-and-glazed-eyes combination.

The question I want to ask him gets stuck on my tongue, my courage waning. I want to know about him: his scar, his history with Jack, the discourse I can sense between the brothers. Instead of asking any of that, I whisper, "I'm glad you're here."

His words submerge me in a warm cocoon. "There's nowhere else I'd rather be."

See? Swoon.

I probably just got pregnant ten times from his words alone.

"Now, I don't know what type of nonsense dancing this is," Hux begins, gesturing towards the bodies thrusting on the dance floor. He pauses suddenly, lips parting with an exhale and eyes widening. "I've just been informed that this is *twerking*. Hmmm. It sounds like something a bird would do." He shakes his head before extending a hand, palm up. "Violet, will you do me the honor of twerking with me."

I place my hand in his much larger one.

"I'd want nothing more."

CHAPTER 36

VIOLET

Note to future self: don't ever, not ever, allow Hux to twerk. Seriously. Don't.

I know what you're thinking: it must be super sexy to see a man as rigid and untamed as Hux letting loose. Maybe in normal circumstances, it would be. Instead, Hux looks like he's trying to take a mean shit while simultaneously singing opera. His brows are lowered in concentration as his ass bends, attempting to replicate the movements of the other dancers. Strange noises emit from his parted lips with each bob of his butt.

There are just some things you can't unsee.

At some point, Hux turns to Jack, and I find myself awkwardly swaying side to side in his arms.

"This party is...a lot," Jack decides at last, eyes timidly roaming over the bodies. I don't have to look over my shoulder to know that a couple is fucking right behind me. Another group is doing body shots, and a third is playing pin-the-nose on the monster. The prominent stench of piss and sweat fills the air, assaulting my senses.

"Not your scene?" I note, my hands clasped together behind his neck. His own rest on my waist, the touch tantalizingly soft through the material of my coat.

Jack snorts in derision. "Not at all."

A sudden burst of heat settles in my core.

And *not* the sexy kind.

"I have to pee," I tell Jack seriously.

His eyebrows raise nearly to his hairline. "Do you need me to come with you?"

"I can go to the bathroom by myself, Jack," I say, a wry grin playing on my lips. He's so damn adorable when he stutters and blushes.

"It doesn't matter to me." He shrugs his shoulders sheepishly. "I just like being with you."

Warmth travels from where his hands sit over my clothes, settling in my chest. I can't stop the large smile from blossoming on my face. Jack, Hux, it doesn't matter. Both men make me feel cared for and protected. Beautiful. A seed of happiness takes root in my heart while my more logical brain warns me I'm encroaching on dangerous territory. Now that this seed has found soil, water, and sunlight, it's growing, growing, growing—growing impossibly large until I fear it will sprout noticeable branches.

These feelings are new to me. Foreign. They infest my body, my heart, my mind, my very soul. I don't know how to react. Words fail me.

Instead, I stare at him like an imbecile.

Stammering out some random shit fact about animal mating habits, I excuse myself to use the bathroom upstairs.

The hallways here are quieter—most of the party has been left behind in the lower level of the house. I pause when I hear familiar, raised voices from one of the bedrooms. The door is open, allowing me to see into a surprisingly sparse room. The black dresser is a startling contrast to the otherwise bright arrangement: a white bedspread, white throw pillows, and a white floor and ceiling. The splash of pink lining the bed somehow demotes the room from masculine to feminine and soft. The stark white and almost inky black otherwise would've made the room seem harshly masculine.

Cheryl sits on the bed, eyes red-rimmed and lower lip trembling. Standing across from her, his back to me, is Vin.

The piercing jealousy momentarily shrivels my lungs until what little air they have been able to hold dies. I instantly stomp on the jealousy like it's nothing more than a pesky, albeit disgusting, bug.

I...I *trust* Vin. And even if I didn't, I don't have any hold over the dangerously sexy hunter. He's my friend and ally, but we've never talked about a relationship.

I know immediately I'm intruding. I can feel the tension vibrating in the air between them like a live wire.

"Vin, please," Cheryl sobs. "I love you."

And that's my cue.

I slowly, stealthily, begin to back down the hall, my eyes trained on Vin's broad, hunched back.

"You don't love anyone but yourself," Vin deadpans.

"But Vin—"

"You cheated on me with Mason." Vin's voice is quiet, but it has the effect of lightning striking. Is that what happened between them? Is that why Vin hates her? But why doesn't he hate Mason?

Cheryl's face twists and contorts at his words. Straightening her thin shoulders, she levels him with a glare capable of cutting skin.

"And you don't think your little vampire slut hasn't been banging him behind your back?" she seethes, and I bristle, momentarily pausing in the hallway.

I haven't banged any of them, thank you very much. No fields have been plowed on this farm. Poor Old McDonald will be rolling over in his grave.

"It's different," Vin snaps. From this angle, I can only see a quarter of his profile, but I know his jaw is clenched tightly and his hands are fisted. I recognize his tone of voice; once upon a time, it used to scare the shit out of me. I call it the voice of death.

"How? Because she's a slut? Because she spreads her legs for anyone with a cock?"

"Nah. Not everyone," I say before I can stop myself. "Just the really big cocks. I'm a little bit of a cock snob." Both Vin and Cheryl swivel their heads in my direction. Vin's expression is blank, but Cheryl's is livid. Disdain drips from her eyes like acid corroding rock.

"How long have you been lurking there?" Cheryl snaps, piercing me with a look that resembles a frosted-over sword. Her mouth is set in a grim, straight line that tightens the longer she stares at me.

"Just arrived." I glance from Cheryl to Vin and then back to Cheryl. "And now, I'm just going to...um...leave."

Violet out.

Keeping my eyes trained on the two unpredictable monsters, I back down the hallway until my back is pressed against the wall. A part of me—a shriveling ball of weeds and decaying flowers—wants Vin to follow me out. To choose me over her.

But he remains in the room with the viper.

He doesn't close the door, and he doesn't take a step closer to her, but it feels as if he did. Pain takes root in my chest and grows until I can feel it in my lungs, my stomach, the soles of my feet. Trying to ignore the sting of his—rejection?—annoyance?—I walk all the way down the hallway, only relaxing when I'm safely locked in the bathroom.

What the hell was that?

It's not as if I walked in on Vin and Cheryl in a compromising position. So why does it feel as if my heart is breaking? Why does it hurt so damn much, like a sword that hasn't quite broken skin?

Ignoring my feelings—something I'm quite good at—I place all of my hurt and pain and anger in a steel box. It doesn't quite alleviate the ache in my chest, but it helps.

Quickly, I pee and wash my hands before leaving the bathroom. A glance down the hall confirms that Cheryl's bedroom door is now shut.

I don't...

I don't understand what that means.

I ignore the voice urging me to break inside and see if Vin is still with her, instead hurrying down the steep staircase and into the throng of partygoers.

I don't see Barret or Mason. No Cal. No Frankie or Jack. No Cheryl. Hell, I don't even see Vanessa. For the first time in as long as I can remember, I feel lonely. It shoots up my spine until I'm practically choking on it. My lungs rapidly try to refill on air. No matter how hard I try, I can't seem to inhale quick enough.

Loud, boisterous laughter echoes from the center of the dance floor, and my eyes are automatically drawn there. At first, all I see is a group of guys. One I recognize to be Ali's boyfriend, but the rest I can't place.

With a whooping battle cry, they begin to pull a string connected to a dummy. The rope around the dummy's neck tightens as her feet lift up from the ground.

I recognize the shirt and skirt ensemble. Pink bats are sewed into the black fabric, and the shirt itself has a heart neckline. The dummy they used has blonde, flowing hair and a petite, elfin face.

It's me.

My sex doll.

Tears burn my eyes as I watch my body hang from a makeshift noose. Her sightless eyes stare down at the bodies around her, utterly expressionless.

Where are the guys?

Why haven't they put a stop to this?

And how did they even find the doll?

One glance at my old roommate's laughing face is the only answer I need.

"Piñata time!" someone screams, and the answering roar causes goosebumps to stand at attention like an army of marching soldiers.

I can't watch this.

I know the body isn't actually mine, that the robot has no emotions, but soul crushing fear wreaks havoc on my insides as they begin to hand out bats and crowbars.

Tears burning my retinas, I brush past the assembled students, ignoring their taunts. Their laughs.

I'm Dracula's daughter, for fuck's sake. I'm a monster that you'll read about in stories. Why am I allowing some senseless bullying to bother me?

I race outside, the moonlight illuminating the single flagpole and two unconscious students, alcohol and what appears to be shimmering fairy drugs surrounding their bodies. My breathing is embarrassingly uneven, and my heart races in tandem.

And fuck, I have to pee again.

I stand in the driveway, debating whether or not I dare step back inside. On one hand, the guys will worry if they search for me and can't find me. And I have to piss like it's nobody's business. On the other, *where the hell were they?*

Anger cresting, sweeping over my vision like a red cloud, I storm in the direction of my dorm. I need to sleep—forget any of this ever happened.

But my monster? She wants to enact vengeance. Murder. Maim. Cut off cocks and give these men anal. Shove the severed dicks so far into their assholes that they're vomiting them out.

I haven't had fun like that in *ages*.

Ignoring my monster, I walk farther and farther away from the party. From the students who hate me. From the sex doll hanging from the ceiling as students beat her with a bat. From the men who left me, abandoned me.

I'm going to piss, then sleep, then—

Something hard hits the back of my head, and tiny white orbs dance in my vision. I stagger, reaching a hand up to rub at my mane of curls. My fingers come away sticky with blood.

"What?" I murmur.

I better not fall unconscious. No fucking way. Nope. Not today, Satan. Not. To—

Darkness cloaks my vision like the bitch I know it to be.

CHAPTER 37

JACK

I've always hated parties. The irritating, incessant chatter, the boisterous laughter, and the sacrificial rituals.

Having a psychopath in my head doesn't help matters either.

"I'll make it painless," Hux assures me, staring through my eyes at the soon-to-be-dead werewolf whose gaze is fixed on Violet's butt. The werewolf indolently lifts his eyes, whispers something to the idiot beside him, before pantomiming slapping her ass. *"On second thought, I'll cut his still beating heart straight from his chest with a pair of rusty scissors before slipping it up his anus until he see stars. And then, I'll take his eyeballs and shove them in both his ears. And his cock? Don't even get me started. I'll eat that fucker for dinner, so help me."*

At least with Hux I never get bored.

"No killing," I tell my alter ego firmly. He huffs, muttering something inarticulate about me being a killjoy. Literally.

I'm not going to lie; the prospect of killing this wicked-eyed werewolf appeals to me more than I care to admit. I too fantasize about beheading him and severing his cock, but alas, Violet would be upset.

I cross my arms over my chest and stare out at the party-goers. There's an infectious joy radiating in the air combining itself with the prominent scent of lust. More than one couple has found themselves tangled together in the middle of the dance floor, uncaring that numerous eyes are on them.

Memories of my feeding time with Violet bombard me. Her breathy moans. Her heaving chest. The feel of her gyrating her hips against my cock.

For the first time in centuries, I had lost control. My *monster* had lost control. I couldn't differentiate where I ended and Hux began. We were one in that moment, each seeking to pleasure our mate. Hux's hand on her breast had been tentative, unsure, his fear of scaring her outweighing his need of her. Mine, on the other hand, had been harsh, tugging and twisting. The feel of her peaked nipple beneath my fingers...

Hux moans in my head.

"She's ours," he says firmly, possessively. I can't help but agree with him.

"Yes."

My cock strains against my pants. I'm overcome by the irresistible urge to bury myself in her sweet cunt. Pound into her until she's screaming my name.

"Like what you see, handsome?" a woman purrs, and I pull myself out of the memory, out of my own head, to take stock of the scene before.

Two naked women sit directly in front of me, breasts bouncing as they rub their pussies together. Quickly, I avert my eyes, heat rising to my cheeks. Not lust, but embarrass-ment. Did they think my boner was from them? *For* them?

"Tell them they're nothing compared to my precious treasure," Hux instructs, scoffing at the notion we would find them more attractive than Violet. *"Tell them they're hags."*

"Yeah, I'm not telling them that," I reply back, hurrying away from the moaning women.

"Tell them they're nothing compared to my Violet, and they should just kill themselves now to save me the trouble of doing it later," Hux continues.

See? Psychopath?

I push up my glasses, annoyed.

"We're not murdering anyone."

Hux literally groans in my head like a petulant child. If he had control of my feet, I imagine he would be stomping them right about now.

"Pinkie! Have you seen Pinkie?" Mason calls, neatly side-stepping a couple lying down in the middle of the floor. His eyes are glazed, mouth opened in wonderment. As I watch, he reaches a hand out to catch the...light? After three ineffectual attempts, Mason shoves his hands in his pockets with a pout.

"Are you high?" I ask, not unkindly. Mason blinks rapidly, as if attempting to orient himself to his surroundings.

"When did you and Hux develop two bodies?" he slurs, stumbling over his own two feet. "Wait. Make that three. I didn't know there was a third one in you."

"He's speaking nonsense. I fear he has no more use for my precious treasure," Hux exclaims in my head. *"Should I kill him?"*

For frick's sake...

"He's broken," Hux continues adamantly. Meanwhile, as if to prove my darker half's point, Mason gets on his knees to serenade Violet who isn't even present. I'm pretty sure he compares her butt to the "fleshiest moon that ever had babies."

His words, not mine.

"I kill," Hux declares resolutely.

"No! Mason is my friend and Violet's. She'll hate you."

That finally gets through that big head of his—errr—that big head of ours.

Violet is his entire world. If there's even a possibility that she'll despise him or be angry with him, he'll work endlessly to rectify it. Thank goodness. The last thing we need is Hux murdering all of Violet's male friends because they are of no use to her.

Movement in my peripheral captures my attention, and I turn just as Violet descends the staircase. Her expression is blank, impassive, as her hand trails over the bannister. She almost appears to be lost in thought, the sullen straightening of her lips a direct contrast to the jovial spark present just a few minutes ago.

"Pinkie!" Mason calls, lips stretching into a wide smile. She either doesn't hear him or chooses not to respond, hurrying out the door.

"We must go to my precious treasure," Hux says...well, more like demands. I have a feeling that if I refuse, he'll take over my body by force.

Dragging a dazed Mason behind me, I hurry outside. The still air belies how cold October has become. The temperature has dropped significantly in the last few weeks despite the absence of wind.

There are two students unconscious in the lawn, but I see no sign of Violet.

What happened when she went upstairs? What did she see? What did she hear?

"If someone hurt her..."

"You'll kill them, I know," I finish for Hux drolly. I can't say I'll blame him; I'll probably even help.

Mason cups his mouth with his hands and screams,

"Pinkie! Where o'where is thou Pinkie? My heart beats for thee Pinkie."

"Please let me kill him," Hux deadpans. I shush him.

A flash of golden hair makes my breath catch; it appears to glisten in the darkness. Even pulled back in a low ponytail, I know without a doubt that hair—like sunlight and moonlight woven together—belongs to Violet.

I grab Mason's collar once more and drag him behind me, towards Violet.

"Violet, it's us," I say, ducking beneath a skeletal branch. When she doesn't slow down, worry bleeds through. "Violet?"

"Pinkie! Get your cute ass over here so I can spank it!" Mason slurs.

She moves behind another tree, disappearing from view. Hux's voice encourages me to run even faster, to keep pace with her. He might not be able to kill me, but he'll damn sure try if we lose her.

Finally, we spill out into a clearing. Moonlight illuminates the towering trees circling it and the frozen girl standing directly in the center.

Something's not right.

Mason, oblivious to the unease migrating down my spine, releases an energetic whoop and races towards Violet. The second he's a foot away from her, he's abruptly yanked upwards, a rope tied around his feet. Upside down, he swings like a pendulum—the shock of his capture momentarily breaking him out of the drug-induced haze.

Hux roars in my head just as Violet turns around.

It's Violet...but it's not. She looks exactly like Dracula's daughter, down to the hideous costume and golden hair. But her expression is listless, her eyes blank. The warmth I always feel in my chest in her presence is noticeably absent.

Before I can stop Hux, he grasps my consciousness with

both hands and yanks me out of the driver's seat. I stumble through the dark abyss of my mind, landing on my knees in the passenger side. I can still see through the windshield, still converse with the driver, but it's impossible for me to steer.

Hux, with all the rage and fury the monster possesses, stalks forward. He intends to confront this Violet fraud, demand where his precious treasure is. It doesn't bother him that he'll be potentially torturing a woman who looks exactly like his beloved. He knows innately that it's not his Violet.

Before he can get farther than a step, a rope tightens around his ankle and pulls him—us—up into a tree until we're dangling upside down.

"Fuck!" Hux roars.

And then Mason: "Why is the Violet clone getting on her hands and knees and spreading her legs?"

CHAPTER 38

VIOLET

Something drips on my face, startling me out of my deep slumber. I groan, desperate to wipe the offending liquid away. My hands refuse to budge an inch.

Huh. Did I fall asleep sitting up?

I peel open my crusted eyelids, shocked to see rough, cavern walls hewn from stone. The only light is a flickering candle mounted to the wall.

What.

The.

Hell?

I've fallen asleep in pretty weird places in my years, but this takes the jackpot.

How did I get here?

And, more importantly, where am I?

My head is fuzzy, cloudy, as if it has been dunked in a cauldron of glittering silver. Numerous aches pulsate down my body. I swear my brain is seconds from exploding.

I vaguely recollect images of the party. Vin and Cheryl. My sex clone. And then...

Fuck, I was kidnapped, wasn't I?

I struggle against the ropes digging into my wrists, staring around the barren room. It appears to be a cave of some sort, complete with stone walls, a few unlit torches, and a large torture table in the center.

Now, I've had my fair share of happy dreams concerning a torture table that looked pretty similar to this one. But in said dreams, I was usually with one of the guys and naked, *not* in my trench coat with blood matting my hair to my scalp.

Girls, you'll be lying if you say you never had a torture sex dream. Thirsty bitches, the whole lot of you.

And yes, I'm calling you out soccer mom Shannon.

I futilely attempt to pull at my restraints. They feel to be just rope, so I don't understand why I'm not able to escape. Unless...

Unless it's rope blessed by the gods.

There's very few things that can contain a vampire, especially one as powerful as me. Oak, for one, doused in holy water. And god-blessed objects.

Whoever kidnapped me has connections.

My eyes desperately scan the small room, searching for a way out. I'm really not in the mood to die down here. My gaze catches on a diminutive critter scuttling from one side of the room to the other. Small gray body, thin whiskers, and abnormally long tail. As I watch the mouse scamper away, an idea occurs to me.

My compulsion works by maintaining eye contact and infusing my powers into my words. I can compel both monsters and humans—who says it can't work on animals as well?

Narrowing my eyes at the little creature, I wait until his own beady ones turn in my direction.

I'm not gonna lie. I fully envision a Disney princess moment. The gallant mouse will hurry towards me, tiny teeth gnawing on my rope until I'm able to escape. I'll name him Gus, and he'll be the Prince of Mouseton for the rest of his little life.

I even go as far as to sing, my words dripping with power as I reach a crescendo.

I could totally be Cinderella.

And then…

My mouse explodes.

Motherfucker.

Alone with only my thoughts, I sift through who could be my kidnapper.

All the vampire fanatics, for one. And the murderer. And the people who bought my sex doll. And the people who hate Dracula. And the people obsessed with Dracula.

I'm fucked.

I don't know how long I sit there, metaphorically twiddling my thumbs, when footsteps echo from around the corner. I sit up straighter, fully prepared to use my compulsion on this asshole.

Until I remember that the god-blessed rope hinders my powers.

Huh. So the mouse didn't die because of an onslaught of power assaulting his tiny brain. He died because of my singing.

Overdramatic bitch.

When the person steps around the corner, candlelight highlighting the orange and gold in his mane of hair, I feel my lips curve into a frown.

Headmaster.

It's *always* the fucking headmaster. Seriously, read a book. Do they ever make any of the school officials good?

He is as impeccably dressed as always in his trimmed gray suit and darker cufflinks. His trademark wild beard has been trimmed slightly, showcasing his rosy cheeks and dimples.

Wolfman in the flesh.

"So it was you," I whisper harshly, watching his back flex as he turns to stare down the cave entrance. I don't know what the fuck he's looking at, but whatever it is ensnares his entire attention. With his hands clasped behind his back, I can almost believe he is in the middle of giving a lecture, not seconds from murdering me.

I fully prepare myself for his evil villain monologue. Maybe a malevolent belly laugh that elicits goosebumps up and down my arms.

Instead, he remains silent, seemingly lost in thought.

"So it was you," I try again, hoping he'll get the hint and fucking talk. Reveal all his evil plans.

Silence.

With a shuddering breath, he turns towards me. Since the last time I've seen him, at the party, he has aged years. Centuries. There are heavy lines on his forehead and cheeks, crow's feet wrinkling the skin around each eye.

"There's been another murder," he confesses at last. He looks surprisingly distraught with that proclamation. Tired. "She was found with vampire bites in her neck."

I watch his face carefully, gauging his reaction.

Before I can speak, he continues, "Your venom was tested and found to be on all of the bodies."

Well if that isn't a sledgehammer to my nonexistent ballsack.

It's what I suspected, after all. I knew that whoever was behind these murders, whoever killed those students, had a vendetta against me. It's why we destroyed the body that day in the woods.

I'm being framed.

I stare long and hard at Headmaster's weary face. There's something glinting in his eyes that gives me pause. Something in contrast to the somber curl of his lips.

A new theory takes root in my brain, painstakingly tended to until it grows and grows. It's all I can focus on as I stare at the man in charge of running this school.

I could be mistaken, but he almost looks...excited.

"Students are scared, so that means *parents* are scared. We can't have that, now can we?" he continues, stalking forward. His pressed suit is at odds with the dirty stone floor and walls. "With all the new evidence, everyone is going to think you did it."

"But you *know* I didn't," I insist, struggling feebly against the restraints. The rope digs into my wrists tightly, irritating the skin.

A tentative smile flickers across his face. There and gone in less than a second. I half wonder if I imagined it.

"The parents and students need to know that the murderer is taken care of," he continues, ignoring my outburst. "So I'll give them what they want."

"A scapegoat?"

"Dracula's daughter," he corrects. "They'll feel safer knowing the menace has been dealt with. And it would bring good publicity to the school."

I don't know whether to be offended or not at being referred to as "the menace."

Not. Definitely not.

Because this "menace" is about to be murdered.

It adds fertilizer to the theory growing in my brain. What if *Headmaster* murdered those students as a way to blame me? Blame the vampires? It's no secret that we're considered scum by other monsters in the community. And, by having me framed for the murders, Dracula would not be able to retaliate without severe repercussions. Headmaster could just say he was defending himself, defending his school, and he'll go down a martyr.

And I'll be fucked sideways, frontwards, and everywhere in between. And to add onto that fuck fest? I have to pee again.

"I didn't murder those students," I repeat. "The real murderer is still going to be out there if you kill me. Unless...unless *you* were the one who murdered them?"

At my confrontation, he doesn't even blink. I'm pretty sure he has zoned out, eyes slightly glazed as he stares at the spot of blood from Gus the Mouse.

He's a horrible villain.

"I'm sorry it has to be this way, Violet. I truly am. But this school is my legacy, and I can't have one vampire ruining it." The asshole sounds almost sincere which only infuriates me further. I half expect him to whisper, "You're expelled," while petting my hair and licking the tears from my face.

Alas, he chose not to use that amazing catchphrase. Shame. It's not like he's going to have another opportunity.

"I didn't—"

"Besides, I have proof that you're behind these murders," he continues, ignoring my half-hearted plea. A moment later, he procures numerous pictures from his pocket. My mind stalls as I attempt to take it all in, understand what I'm seeing.

The first picture is grainy, obviously the work of an out-of-use school camera. It shows the interior of the cafeteria, and a long, abandoned hall that leads to the kitchen. A girl I recognize as Blowy lies on the ground, blood flooding the tiles around her. Standing above her, dead eyes and lips set into a grim line, is *me*.

Well, fuck.

The next picture is just as grotesque. The front steps of the school, early morning sunlight highlighting the macabre scene. And there, on the stone steps, is Mikey. And little old moi.

"That's not me!" I insist, quite stupidly, if I'm being honest. The pictures clearly shows that it *is* me.

Or my sex clone.

What the hell has Violet 2.0 been up to?

"I can explain!" I stutter quickly. "This story involves a realistic sex doll and an innocent vampire."

But I know that my words will fall on deaf ears. He'll never believe me—not that I blame him, with all the evidence he had gathered. Not only that, but I have the distinct feeling that he's the one who framed me in the first place. Call it a hunch. Headmaster wants nothing more than to gain publicity for his school. What's a better way than a serial killer who's revealed to be Dracula's daughter? A serial killer that he eliminates, proving he's capable of keeping the school safe?

He turns towards the cave entrance where a shadowed figure stands.

"Come here, boy," Headmaster calls, and the figure emerges like a besotted puppy.

I feel my breath leave me in a swooping exhale. My heart, which has been surprisingly steady throughout all of this, picks up speed until it's thundering in my ears. Everything hurts. I'd rather be tortured than see his face, see his smile, see the dead glint in his eyes as he regards me like yesterday's trash.

"Violet, I believe you know my personal assistant. He's going to be helping me today," Headmaster says, waving dismissively at the man beside him.

Frankie smiles.

CHAPTER 39

VIOLET

He pierces me with a look that reminds me of a sword coated in ice. All of the warmth in my body drains, leaving me shivering. It shrivels my lungs that are already rapidly losing air. His betrayal is like a repeated kick to my gut, a knife to the chest. He's twisting the dagger until my blood flows freely down his stained hands. Fuck, he's killing me. The pain is unbearable, wreaking havoc on my insides.

He's still dressed as Fred from the Halloween party, but this time, there is no smile playing on his sensual lips. They're pressed into a grim line instead.

"My assistant, Frankie, provided the drug we used on you," Headmaster admits conversationally, unaware that he had just ripped my heart straight from my chest. Tears burn my eyes, and I try to make my anguish evident as I turn my gaze onto Frankenstein's stoic son.

There's no warmth in his eyes, now. They're hard chips of stone.

"What drug?" I ask, wrenching my eyes away from him. It takes considerable effort—every molecule in my body is attuned to his.

Headmaster seems tired of my incessant questioning, but he indulges me anyway. "At the party. It was designed to shrink your bladder. Originally, the plan was to kidnap you during one of your many trips to the bathroom, but you made it easy for me, dear, by leaving the party by yourself." His smile is all male smug satisfaction.

I'm *livid*.

"Why the *fuck* would you do that? Out of all the heartless things! Do you know how badly I have to pee, you mother-fucker? Do you? Do you understand the burning in my vagi-na?" I'm babbling, I know it, but my tumultuous emotions are incapable of being turned off.

I remember reading in one of my textbooks that the best way to survive a serial killer is to open yourself to him (and not literally—I'm pretty sure opening up my chest cavity would only excite the sick bastard). Allow them to see you as a human.

Alternating between Frankie and Headmaster, I begin to plead. "Did I ever tell you about my cat?" I babble, watching Frankie's slashing eyebrows lower over his eyes. Headmaster just appears bored. "It's a funny story, truly. So there was this cat I found in my backyard. A sweet, little kitten who had probably been abandoned by her mother. Matted fur. A chunk taken out of her ear. Tiny little paws. I took her in and fed her. Made her my own. Well, this little cat kept trying to escape the house."

"Why the fuck is she still talking?" Headmaster drolls, giving me a bland look.

That only encourages my damn mouth to talk even faster, the words running together until they're practically inarticu-late. "I never had an outdoor cat before, so I was terrified of letting her go. What if she ran away? What if she got hit by a car? Finally, I conceded and allowed Kitten to play outside. That was what I named her, by the way. Anyway, so Kitten would always come back to my house for meals and cuddles, but she would spend the rest of her time outside. Okay, so flashforward a year later."

"Apply the injection," Headmaster instructs Frankie, and I have no doubt the word "lethal" is implied.

I'm spewing nonsense at this point, a verbal freight train seconds from crashing into a brick wall.

"So it's a year later, and Kitten doesn't make it home in time for her nightly meal. I'm freaking out, thinking the worst had happened. Dad is laughing at me for getting so attached to a cat." Frankie advances on me, a dripping needle held reverently in his hand. "I begin going from door to door, searching for my damn cat. Finally, I cross the forest to the house on the other side. I've never been there, mind you, but the door opens and an older gentleman stands in the doorway. Behind him, eating from a food bowl, is my cat. I'm immediately relieved that this man has taken care of my cat, and I tell him so. The man's face scrunches up in confusion as he stares between me and Kitten. My cat, obviously hearing my voice, comes to weave between our legs with a contented purr. I show the man the picture of me and Kitten, explaining I had taken her in a year ago and how she's an outdoor cat through and through. The man then shows me a picture of *him* and the cat, telling me that he found her a year ago as well and had made her his own."

Frankie is now in front of me, the needle glinting in the flickering candlelight.

"And *that*," I finish the story with a ragged breath, "is how I discovered my cat was two-timing me." My eyes desperately search Frankie's face, looking for any sign of the man I care for. When his expression remains impassive, I whisper, "Why?"

That one word, one question, will haunt me.

"Because," Headmaster answers staunchly from behind. "He's an experiment, Violet. A creation. He doesn't even have a heart, let alone a soul."

But I don't believe that. Not my Frankie. Not the man who comforted me, cared for me, laughed with me. Not the man who patiently worked with me in his lab.

The needle lowers until it's centimeters from my skin, and my body begins to shake. What is it going to do to me? Eat away my insides? Make me grow hair that eats away my insides? Create bugs that eat away my insides?

Why do I have a feeling it's going to eat away my insides?

The second it would've broken skin, Frankie turns away from me with a ferocious roar, aiming the needle at *Headmaster's* neck instead. I have the pleasure of seeing the werewolf's eyes widen in shock as Frankie barrels down on him.

Candlelight catches on something in his hand, and I've only just opened my mouth to scream Frankie's name when he falls to the ground, a knife protruding from his chest.

My anguished sob gets caught in my throat as Headmaster advances on me. He doesn't even look ruffled after the fight, as meticulous as ever, not a hair out of place.

With an annoyed grunt, he picks up the needle Frankie discarded and advances on me. I can't even look at him, at the man who will inevitably kill me. My eyes are locked on Frankie still lying on the ground.

He tried to save me. He attacked Headmaster for me.

He didn't betray me.

As if he can read my thoughts, Headmaster crowds my vision. His eyes are pinprick black orbs, startling against his tanned skin. "I knew the monster couldn't be trusted. Started asking too many questions." He clicks his tongue disapprovingly. "This is why you shouldn't have feelings. Look at what they do to you! Look at how they destroy you!" Something dark, harsh, distorts his features. "Did I ever tell you about my late wife?"

Ahhh there it is. The evil monologue.

"Let me guess?" I monotone. "Dracula killed her?"

His eyes widen slightly, almost imperceptibly. "No. Why the fuck would you think that?"

Now, it's my turn to scrunch my brows in confusion. Did I just totally misread this moment?

"Because you have me tied up and want to kill me. I'm pretty sure it's because of some vendetta against my father or vampires in general."

"Not at all," Headmaster assures me. "You're father is actually a pretty good monster, and I have nothing against vampires. I'm killing you to stop the bad press all these murders are giving my school."

I was *way* off the mark.

Shaking his head, he continues with his story. "Anyway..." He pierces me with a look that warns me to keep my mouth shut. "We were in love until she left me for another man."

"Dracula?" I assume, desperately attempting to search over his shoulder for Frankie. Is he okay? Is he...?

I don't even want to think about the dreaded d-word. I know a piece of me will die with him. A piece of me I'll never be able to get back. The strength of my feelings migrates down my body, settling in my core and tightening my chest. Piece by piece, these men have chipped away my defenses I once thought were impenetrable. They have wiggled their way into my twisted, dark heart—I can't lose them. Any of them.

Even if they did betray me.

Headmaster makes a disgruntled noise in the back of his throat, pulling me back to the conversation at hand.

"Why do you think everything has to do with your family? That's pretty vain, if I do say so myself," he reprimands. "Now, if you don't mind…"

For the second time in minutes, a strange substance is inches from my neck.

Motherfucker, this is *not* how I expected my Halloween to go when I woke up in the morning. Go to the party, they said. You'll have fun, they said. Never mind that it was my idea in the first place.

Once more, before the needle can be injected into my neck, Headmaster releases a guttural roar. He throws his head back as red seeps through his suit.

Frankie stands behind him, twisting the dagger he had quite literally used to stab him in the back. My eyes roam over Frankie's body and face, searching for injuries. I gape at his blood-free chest, the only evidence of his wound a cut in his shirt.

"You're okay!" I sob. Frankie's smile is shy, uncertain, as if he doesn't know how it's going to be received.

"As he said," he nods towards the Headmaster on his knees. "I don't have a heart."

There's so much hesitancy on his face. The mask has been broken, ripped to shreds, and in his place is a forlorn little boy. How long has he known about Headmaster? Why didn't he tell me? Those thoughts echo in my head, and I can't stop myself from flashing him an accusing glare. He lowers his gaze demurely.

"I'm sorry," Headmaster rasps.

A second later, he lunges for me, hand outstretched. Not even Frankie can stop him from sticking the needle in my neck and pushing the disgusting liquid into my body.

My wide eyes meet Frankie's terrified ones.

If the apathetic Frankie is scared…

I'm fucked.

CHAPTER 40

VIOLET

I brace myself for the pain—afterall, there's *always* pain. I've learned to compartmentalize it, to group it into tiny boxes before burying each one.

There's the least harmful pain. A tiny sting or ache, barely on your radar. A paper cut, maybe, or your stomach after you eat spoiled meat.

And then there's the medium pain: getting your leg chopped off, having your throat sliced, and even getting your still beating heart removed.

Finally, there's the excruciating pain. The one that makes you curl into a ball as tears drip down your cheeks. The one that makes you beg for death and all it has to offer: period cramps.

When no pain immediately comes, I allow my eyelids to flutter open. Frankie has Headmaster pinned to the ground, an enraged roar flooding the room. It's an odd sight to see— for as long as I've known him, Frankie has been gentle and quiet. The type of man to watch from the shadows instead of stepping into the light. He's a monster, but he's never been like the others. Frankie's gentle. That's not a word I usually use for monsters—and it sure as fuck isn't one they like to hear—but it's the only word capable of encapsulating Frankie's silent strength.

He's not vicious or cruel nor is he cold. There's a warmth that radiates through him, even when he's staring at me with dead, glacial eyes.

As he pounds his fist into Headmaster's face, some of his warmth transfers to me causing my whole body to tingle.

He cares.

Probably not the time to think about that when you're seconds from dying painfully.

And it's *definitely* not the time to get the warm fuzzies over a crush.

"Enough already," a cold, deadly voice snaps, and a second later, Dimitri Gray steps into the dimly lit room. His light hair is pulled back into a low ponytail, and he wears all black making him one with the shadows.

He slinks forward, a stealth to his gait I couldn't even begin to replicate without tripping and dying. The next moment, he has Headmaster on his feet and a knife to his throat.

"What the fuck is going on now?" I exclaim. My mind feels sluggish, as if I'm wading through swampy waters. Seaweed tangles around my ankles, impeding my forward progress. Still, I forge on through waist-deep, disgusting water.

There are answers somewhere in this room, and I'll be damned if I don't get them.

Ms. Stevens hurries into the cave, high heels clanking against the floor. Her wide eyes take in the scene with horror before she rushes to me.

"Diedre, if you would be so kind as to remove Ms.

Dracula from the room," Dimitri instructs, a clinical detachment to his voice that belies the fury radiating throughout his body. Ms. Stevens appears slightly dazed, but she complies, easily slicing through the ropes.

She must have a god-blessed knife. Only those are capable of cutting through this particular type of rope.

Once I'm free, wrists raw and bloody, I hurry to where Frankie still sits on the ground. He blinks rapidly, almost as if he's attempting to focus. There's a nasty bruise already forming around his right eye, and scratches mar his cheeks from Headmaster's wolf claws. I'm grateful there's no lasting injuries—bruises and cuts will heal.

When his eyes feast on me, he glances away quickly, almost as if he can't bear the sight of my face. That hurts. Immensely so.

For reasons I don't want to divulge, I want him to look at me. See me. I want those cold eyes to dethaw the way they normally do.

"How are you feeling?" Frankie asks worriedly, eyes still locked on the ground.

His words remind me of what had transpired only seconds before. Namely, the unknown substance entering my bloodstream. And probably destroying my insides. I sit back and assess my injuries. Aside from my aching wrists and ankles from the ropes, I feel fine.

As if he's privy to my thoughts, Dimitri sneers, "She's fine. I changed out the liquid before you guys came down here."

In some sort of weird synchronization, we blink at him.

The assassin huffs, rolling his eyes to the heavens. He won't find what he needs to deal with me up there. I'm better suited for the warmer place, if you catch my drift.

Cue: a joke about me being too hot.

I'm too tired to think of one.

"I'm not an idiot," Dimitri snaps, turning towards the

Headmaster still held by knifepoint. "I knew about your plans even before the thought entered your mind." His hard gaze flickers towards Frankie, but he addresses me. "I wasn't sure if he could be trusted. I gave him a fifty/fifty chance of either killing you or saving you." Frankie blanches at Dimitri's assessment of him, face paling.

Fifty/fifty chance.

Huh.

Not even a seventy/thirty.

I'm actually kind of pissed that Dimitri has no faith in Frankie. Then again, I immediately thought he betrayed me, so I suppose I can't judge.

"Now," Dimitri continues, eyes glinting like chips of coal as he stares at Headmaster. "I almost didn't accept the job." At Headmaster's questioning gaze, Dimitri rolls his eyes once more. "To kill you, of course. I almost refused the job and let you live. You were a good headmaster, and from what I saw, you cared for the students. I don't just kill every random person." He clicks his tongue disapprovingly. "Unfortunately, you decided to go after a student—"

"A murderous student!" Headmaster interrupts, flashing me a belligerent glare. Dimitri shakes the man's shoulder, knife pressing further into his skin.

"It's rude to interrupt," he says stoically. "Anyway, you only signed your own death warrant when you attempted to kill Ms. Violet Dracula. And now, I even have an excuse for disposing of you. A way for me to remain at the school. I saw you kidnap and attempt to murder a poor, defenseless student. What was I to do? When I tried to stop you, you attacked me. It was only self-defense. Isn't that right, Diedre?"

Ms. Stevens still looks shaken up, but she manages a timid nod. "That's right. I saw the entire thing."

"You lying—"

Before Headmaster can finish his curse, Dimitri stabs the knife in his neck. Blood spurts out, and Headmaster's hands immediately rise to squash the blood flow. His eyes are wide, dazed, helplessly glancing from person to person. They rest on Frankie, an eloquent plea in their murky depths.

Frankie. His assistant.

His partner in crime, apparently.

But Frankie merely turns his head away, expression blank.

Dimitri watches Headmaster fall to the floor in the disinterested way he regards everything. After a moment, he glances towards a pale-faced Ms. Stevens. "If you would be so kind as to escort Ms. Dracula back to the school, please?"

"I...um...yes. Of course. Come on, darling." Ms. Stevens helps me to my feet, wrapping one arm around my waist. The touch isn't necessarily comforting, but I don't want to be that rude bitch who shakes it off after our headmaster was just murdered by an assassin/teacher.

Seriously, why would Headmaster even hire Dimitri in the first place, a known assassin? And who paid for the hit against the Wolfman?

Frankie stands up to follow us out, but Dimitri stops him with a bloody hand.

"Not you," he says curtly. "We need to talk."

"Dimitri—" I say on an exasperated sigh. His eyes don't leave Frankie's face.

"That's Mr. Gray to you. And I want to hear from the man himself how big of a role he had to play in this...adventure." His teeth are bared; his eyes, similarly, shine with an unparalleled fury. It's a look designed to instill fear in his victims.

If Frankie's shaking hands are any indication, it works.

"Go," Frankie murmurs to me. Like Dimitri, he refuses to look at me directly. "I'll be right behind you."

But I can't leave it like that. I *won't*. There's a reason

winter turns to spring. A reason why the snow melts and flowers begin to bloom. A reason why leaves grow on previously skeletal branches.

There's something beautiful about that growth, about the dethawing of ice. Something magical.

I yearn to see the ice diminish from Frankie's eyes completely. Maybe I should be more cautious. Maybe I should be angry at him for not telling me Headmaster's plan sooner. Maybe I should worry about his intentions.

Instead, I whisper, "I forgive you."

Frankie tenses, hands balling into fists, but he doesn't respond. It's okay, I suppose. He doesn't need to. Me forgiving him doesn't mean I'm not pissed as fuck at him.

Dimitri pierces me with an unreadable look, breaking the staring contest he had with Frankie only seconds before.

"You're too kind, Violet. That bleeding heart is going to cost you." All this is said without any inflection, any emotion.

I shrug. It might...and it might not. It doesn't change the fact that I'm a monster. My so called "bleeding heart" only goes so far. I forgive as many people as I murder.

Without humoring Dimitri with a response, I follow Ms. Stevens out of the tunnels.

CHAPTER 41

VIN

I don't know how the fuck I got roped into prison guard duty. Honestly, I blame bad luck. Maybe I'm cursed. You can't have a cock like mine without some repercussions.

Cal and Barret moan and bitch as I lead them to the upper level of the school. When I was asked to escort the two monsters back to their holding cell at midnight, I couldn't refuse. It was in my Van Helsing blood to handle wayward monsters.

And the Boogeyman and Cupid? Definitely wayward.

"Just one more hour," Cal pleads as I type in the now familiar combination on the door. It swings open on silent hinges revealing a pitch black hall of classrooms.

"Unless you want the magic that makes you spontaneously combust to kick in at midnight, I recommend getting your asses inside," I instruct, already tiring of this conversation. I need to find Violet, to explain. I know she saw me and Cheryl together, but I had to make her understand.

When Cheryl cornered me, demanding an explanation for our breakup, I felt it was the least I could do. I never loved Cheryl, but she had been my girlfriend for the better part of five months. She dragged me into her room, tears brimming in her fucking awful eyes, and begged me to take her back. To love her the way I never could.

But it wasn't as if I could tell her I found my fated mate in Violet, now could I? Van Helsings don't have mates, and they sure as fuck don't engage in relationships with vampires. I know my family will not hesitate to kill me and her if they discover I tarnished the Van Helsing's prestigious name by fraternizing with the enemy.

Nothing happened between me and the viper. I told her, in no uncertain terms, to fuck off and leave me alone. Leave Mason alone. I may have threatened to stab her if she refused.

What can I say? I'm a monster through and through.

"I hate it here," Barret says, but he doesn't sound angry, only resigned. "It's dark."

"Is the Boogeyman afraid of the dark?" I ask, lifting a brow.

"I got used to the dark," he admits after a long moment of silence. "I just don't like being alone."

Cal tries for a cheerful smile, but it comes across as forced. More like a grimace. "You have me! And I'm better than anybody. No offense," he adds to me hurriedly.

"None taken." I shrug. "I don't like people. Or monsters. Or anyone, really."

Cal gives me a cryptic look, a look I can't quite read, before saluting me.

"Tell Violet to come visit anytime," he says. Barret's face lightens up at the mention of my golden-haired, vampire mate. He practically bounces on the balls of his feet. "And you don't have to be a stranger either."

As the door closes automatically—right at midnight—I feel the slightest pang in my chest. It almost feels like...pity. I pity the two monsters forced to hide away from the rest of the monster population. Not dangerous enough to warrant a one-way ticket to Revenant, our monster prison, but not sane enough to join society.

What secrets are they hiding? Behind Cal's bright, flirtatious smile and red wings? Behind Barret's empty look and energetic smirk?

They seem relatively normal, so why all the secrets? Why are they kept locked up here, away from us? It can't be just because they're murderers...we all are. I know Cal relies on sex to live, and I know Barret eats human flesh.

But…

Violet drinks blood, werewolves eat humans, and more monsters than not kill humans and monsters alike. Why them? Why Cal and Barret?

Mind wandering, I head back down the steep staircase and through the main academic doors. I know that through the forest, the party will be in full swing. Violet will probably be dancing with Mason right now, giggling at one of his stupid, cheesy jokes. Or maybe she'll be swaying side to side in Jack's arms as he stares at her like she's the only person in the world. Or Hux, with his hard stare that only softens in her presence. Or Frankie, who doesn't quite understand what he's feeling or why.

A couple runs into me as they emerge from the forest. I recognize the man from one of my classes. A wendigo, if I remember correctly. Zade or something. His female companion is not someone I recognize, but the translucent sheen makes me believe she's a ghost.

"You heading to the party?" Zade asks, words slurring.

There's a special type of alcohol that can make a monster drunk. It involves fairies and toilets. But fuck, if I don't drink the piss daily.

"There's a piñata," the girl adds as if I give a fuck.

I scowl at them both, and they giggle, seemingly unperturbed with a face that has once caused every monster to shit themselves in fear.

Am I losing my touch?

At least I'm not still in a skirt. I can't be fucking terrifying dressed as Velma.

Without another word, they run around me—no doubt to find a quiet place to fuck.

And me? I'm going to head back to my room, away from the loud noises, the blaring music, and the girl who hates me.

The girl who I may or may not be falling in love with.

Fuck, what am I going to do?

CHAPTER 42

VIOLET

We emerge inside a familiar, sterile room. White lights flicker on, one after the other, until the room is engulfed in a pale glow.

"How are you feeling, Violet?" Ms. Stevens asks, not unkindly. She sounds almost concerned, a foreign sensation by itself. I'm not used to people caring about me, especially adults.

"Grateful that my insides aren't being devoured by bugs," I answer truthfully.

I allow my gaze to wander around Frankie's lab. Had he sat on one of these stools, creating a formula designed to kill me? What was going through his head?

I don't know if I can classify what Frankie did as a betrayal. Maybe he knew, from the very beginning, that he was going to save me. Maybe.

Or maybe he changed his mind when he entered the cavernous room and saw me tied up. Maybe he had every intention to kill me.

I'm not surprised the cave led to the lab, if I'm being honest. There's a lot I don't know about Frankenstein's son. I didn't even know he was an experiment and not a real person until today.

"I see your mind racing," Ms. Stevens muses.

I shrug. I don't really want to have a heart-to-heart with my professor.

Unbidden, my eyes land on the stool I'd sat on when Frankie was teaching me. His easy-going smile, normally hidden from the world. The patient way he explained each potion, each machine. The laughter in his eyes when I screwed up and caused my pinkie finger to grow hair— fortunately, he had a potion to reverse it.

Fuck, I need to hear his explanation. I need to know what's real and what's fake between us.

We walk out of the lab and into the empty hall. Moon-light splices through the various windows, illuminating the hallway and empty classrooms. The school feels much larger during the night without students wandering the halls.

Ms. Stevens leads me to her classroom, shutting the door behind us and leaning against her desk. She crosses her arms over her chest and levels me with a sympathetic look.

I don't like it. Goosebumps feather across my skin, twisting my stomach and heart. I don't like being seen by her, this stranger. Her eyes seem to stab me. Skin me. It's...unnerving. This feeling of baring my soul and revealing my deepest, darkest secrets to the woman before me.

And suddenly, I know.

I know it as surely as I know the sun rises in the morning and lowers at night. As surely as I know my name is Violet No-Middle-Name Dracula. As surely as I know my name was actually supposed to be Violent, but Dad forgot to add the "n" on the birth certificate.

There's nothing but kindness and warmth exuding from her eyes.

But…

The prickle of unease intensifies.

"I think Headmaster murdered those students," I whisper, watching her reaction. Every twitch of her pretty eyes. Every intake of breath. I have to give her credit: she's a good actress. She inhales sharply, eyes widening in her pale face.

I've always trusted my sixth sense. It guided me, led me.

Behind her compassionate gaze, behind her perfectly curled hair and twitching lips, lies a murderer. A monster.

Dracula always made fun of me when I spoke of my mysterious sense. I never understood it myself—I still don't understand it. But I trust it implicitly.

And this voice, this sixth sense, is screaming that I'm looking at a murderer.

Don't ask me how I know. Again, I wouldn't be able to tell you. At all.

"Or maybe," I begin slowly, cautiously. I barely recognize voice; it's not a growl exactly, but something dark and deadly. It's the voice of my predator approaching her prey. "Someone else killed them. Framed me."

Once more, her pretty eyes widen further.

"What are you thinking?" she asks.

"Why did you do it?" No use beating around the bush. I want answers, answers only she's capable of providing. "Why did you kill those students?"

The mask slips like it never existed. I wouldn't quite compare it Dimitri's expression—not nearly as apathetic or cold—but it still makes me stagger back a step.

Note to future self: don't poke the bear without backup. Seriously. Don't.

"How did you know it was me?" she asks, cocking her head to the side in obvious bemusement. She doesn't bother trying to deny it, which I can appreciate...in a sick, twisted way.

We're monsters, after all. We're immune to the effects of death and murder. If she had framed any other student, any other vampire, I probably wouldn't have cared. Instead, she had blamed *me*. And if there's someone I fucking care about, it's me.

I don't bother telling her about my sixth sense. Instead, I reply with a half-truth.

"You're too fucking nice. No one is that nice in this world."

And that's true. In this world, if you're nice, you secretly have an agenda. You have to learn to look at the world as a murky shade of gray instead of black and white. There are numerous facets of evil. The line between that and good is blurred, unrecognizable.

"You suspected me because I'm too nice?" she asks in obvious disbelief.

Okay, I'll admit. It sounds fucked up even to me.

I don't need logic to be right.

"Just give me your evil villain monologue, and let's get this over with." I wave my hand for her to begin. Already, I'm planning how I'm going to get rid of her.

"Violet, dear, I did it for *you*," she replies earnestly. My eyes bug out of my head as I stare at her. Out of everything she could've said, I hadn't expected that.

What the fuck?

I'm not exactly the most upstanding citizen, but murder in my name? Fuck no. I prefer to do my own murdering, thank you very much.

When I remain silent, gaze blistering, she sighs and crosses to sit in the chair behind her desk. Her entire body seems to deflate like a balloon being popped. Tired eyes stare back at me.

"Even when I was a student, vampires have been considered the lesser species. We're looked down upon. Made fun of. Ridiculed."

"And you think murdering people helps with that?" I ask. Am I the only monster with sense here? When the fuck did that happen?

Ugh. Dad would be so disappointed in me.

"It's funny," Ms. Stevens scoffs, but her voice holds no humor. "We're the inferior race in the eyes of monsters when we're stronger and faster. Why else do you think Van Helsings hunt us? Because the monsters are *scared* of us. Scared of our powers. Scared of what we can do. We combine the strength of a werewolf, the compulsion of an incubus, the immortality of a ghost, and the speed of a wendigo. We're the superior species, and it's about time the others realize it."

I try to process her words, I honestly do. I don't want to say I'm dumb or anything, but...

Yeah, I don't really understand what this speech has to do with the murder of my classmates.

Ms. Stevens—I wonder if I should call her Diedre given that we're murder buddies and all—gives me a dry look.

"I made the murders appear to be from a vampire. Well, technically your...*clone* did. I believe Mikey had three of the Violet sluts," she speaks slowly, as if trying to explain a difficult equation to a child. I would take offense to it, but I'm so damn confused I'm grateful. "But all the vampires *know* that the deaths were faked, designed to frame them. The other monsters? They genuinely believe that the murders had been done by a vampire. They never bothered to think differently."

Okay, that makes sense. She wanted a bridge between the species. The vampires know the deaths were fake—the product of a knife, not fangs.

But the other monsters? They thought we did it because they wanted to *believe* we did it.

Now, the question is why. Why cause discord? Why blame me?

If I was just a tiny bit smarter, I'd probably be able to answer those.

"We need them to fear us, dear. And we need the vampires to unite. What better way than having Dracula's daughter wrongly accused of murder and put to death?" She sounds so fucking sweet, as if she isn't discussing my demise.

"You were going to use me as a martyr," I say evenly. First Headmaster, and now Ms. Stevens. Why can't I catch a break? Why does the entire staff want me dead?

"A necessary sacrifice for the greater good," she replies calmly like the psycho bitch I now know her to be.

"So what now?" I ask, flicking my gaze to the shut door. Can I run? Would I be fast enough? I'm faster than most monsters, most vampires, but am I fast enough to escape her?

Ms. Stevens stands gracefully, smoothing down her skirt. Even on Halloween, she isn't wearing a costume. She looks as impeccable as always in her pencil skirt and blouse.

"I'm sorry, my sweet darling. I'm going to kill you."

CHAPTER 43

VIOLET

I don't consider myself desensitized to death. Not really. Even after all this time, it still affects me. I'm not the type that freaks out when I see blood, obviously. Nor do I freak out coming face to face with a dead body.

But it still chips away a tiny sliver of my soul. Piece by piece, until I'm barely recognizable. Death...it does something to a person, something words fail to articulate.

When Ms. Stevens advances at me, a predatory glint to her eyes and a sympathetic curl to her lips, that same change rushes over me. That feeling you get when you stand face to face with death.

It's not fear coursing through my veins like electricity. It's not even annoyance. It's...a sort of numbness. A cold chill that seeps into my bones and sends ice down my body.

I have no delusion that I'll somehow emerge victorious. Ms. Stevens is older than me, wiser. She probably had years of extensive training. I'm just a vampire who trips over chairs and runs into walls. In a movie, I'm the dumb blonde who dies first—not final girl material.

In her hand, like an extension of her limb, the god-blessed dagger rests. One of the only things capable of killing me.

"I'm truly sorry, Violet," Ms. Stevens says, and there are tears—honest to fuck tears—in her eyes. Why does she have to act nice when she's trying to murder me?

"We can work something out," I begin before lunging for the door. The handle glints in the artificial lights, my reflection visible. The whites of my eyes…

Before I can grasp it, Diedre—I feel as if we've progressed from last names—tackles me from behind. I fall to the ground, my face whacking the floor. Pain explodes behind my eyes and in my nose.

"Stupid fucking bitch," I curse, doing the only logical thing possible in this situation. I toss my head back, my neck flexing unnaturally, and headbutt her.

Pro tip: don't do it. It fucking hurts.

But it has the desired reaction. Diedre releases me with a curse, favoring her now bloody nose. It's only fair, after all, for her to have an injury similar to mine.

For the first time ever, there's a break in her front. A crack in her usual cheery facade. In that brief moment before her mask slips back into place, I see a darkness in her eyes. An abyss. Anger and hatred and jealousy that I can't quite understand.

"Violet," she says in a calm, placating tone. "Don't be difficult."

Don't be difficult, she says.

I'm going to murder you painfully, she says.

Fuck her.

When it becomes apparent I'm not going to comply and

hand myself over for slaughter, her face contorts hideously. Her lips pull over her teeth, and her fangs descend.

"You're being a bitch, Violet," she hisses.

"Heard that one before." I move into a defensive stance, my entire attention fixed on the knife in her hand. The knife capable of killing me. "There is one thing I'm curious about, though. How did you get my venom?"

I understand the rest of it. She sent my sex clone to murder the students. Signed me out using Cynthia's name. But while the doll has numerous similarities to me, she doesn't have my venom. My blood. My DNA.

Deidre's lips curl into a malicious smile. The hairs on the back of my neck prickle.

"Did you know," she begins, almost conversationally, "that you're not really Dracula's daughter?"

Her words momentarily strike me dumb. Freezes me. She could've told me that I had a mouth for a vagina and I'd react the same way.

She's lying, of course. Dracula *is* my father.

"I was with him when he found you," she continues, and this time, there's no hiding the derision in her voice. The disdain.

"Found me?" I parrot stupidly. Why am I even humoring her with a response? She's lying. I know she is. But the tiny, curious voice in my head is screaming at me to shut up and listen.

"You became his world. The golden child." Disgust twists her pretty features. "He forgot about all his other children."

At that, I *did* gasp. I always knew that I wasn't Dracula's only child, but I've never met any of my siblings before. Never even thought about them, if I am being honest.

She must see something on my face, for her smile grows. "Yes. I'm surprised you didn't figure it out earlier, sister."

Sister. I have a sister.

At the same time, I don't know if I can believe her. She's a psycho bitch trying to kill me—I need to take every word she says with a grain of salt.

"He chose you over his own daughter. His sons. His family. You, a monster who wasn't even a vampire." Anger darkens her eyes.

Okay, so she has daddy issues. With my daddy. Wait...that sounds bad.

"We can work something out," I cajole, holding my hands in the air like a prisoner approaching an armed police officer.

"It doesn't matter," she sniffs. "He'll notice me soon enough."

"What do you mean 'a monster who wasn't even a vampire?'" I ask. If I'm going to die, I'll be damned if I don't know everything. Maybe someone will hire a necromancer to resurrect me or some shit.

Diedre rolls her eyes as if my monster status is the least of her worries. "Surely you've noticed that you don't behave like a normal vampire?"

Oh yeah, definitely.

Dumbass.

That is sarcasm, by the way.

"I drink blood," I point out, finally able to turn the tables and make *her* the stupid one. "I'm fast. I'm strong. I'm a vampire."

"You have attributes of a vampire, yes, but you're not one. Maybe you're a hybrid. I don't know. All I know is that Dracula found you abandoned and took you in. Made you his. Even hired a witch to restrain your monster."

She's lying.

She has to be.

I stare at the crazy woman for a prolonged moment. Nothing makes sense. I feel as if I'm on a carousel with no way off. Around and around we turn, but I'm unable to escape. I can never stop turning.

"Enough of this." With a sigh that hints at her incoming strike, she comes for me again. I just barely duck out of the way of her dagger.

"Diedre, please," I begin seconds before her leg connects with my stomach. I stumble, catching my hip on the edge of a desk.

So reasoning won't work...

I allow her to grab at my shoulder, but I use the distraction to punch her face. There's a satisfying sound of bones crunching. Flesh hitting flesh. It shouldn't feel as good as it does.

But hey, can you blame me for being a little vindictive?

She charges me like a bull, the momentum propelling us both to the ground. Her crazed, luminescent eyes zero in on me. Her prey.

Her hand raises with the dagger, and I desperately grab her wrist, holding it in the air. Fuck, I don't want to die today.

"Diedre, stop!" I scream, attempting to infuse my persuasion power into each word. Of course, it doesn't work. Not when she's holding a god-blessed dagger.

Fuck.

She releases a ferocious growl, teeth bared, and a distant part of me knows I'm going to die here today. It's the same way I knew she was the murderer.

But everything within me rebels.

With a roar of my own, I use my strength—a strength that surpasses a normal vampire's—and flip positions. Her frosty eyes spear me sharper than the dagger in her hand could've. There's raw hatred in her gaze. Underneath all that, there's pain. Pain for the family she lost. Pain for Dracula who discarded her. Pain for the love that has been lacking in her life.

I twist her wrist until a sickening crack resonates in the room. She releases a startled scream, dropping the dagger. It clatters against the floor with a thud.

I don't give myself a second to think, a second to reconsider. All I know is that this woman, this teacher, tried to kill me, and she will continue doing so.

I don't like murdering people, honestly. I don't despise it, but it's not like I'm advocating for slaughtering all of your enemies.

Still, I don't hesitate as my dagger cuts through skin and muscle. Her mouth parts in a circle as she exhales—one of her final breaths. There's a glossiness to her eyes, a sheen that I've only ever seen in corpses.

And still, she talks. Her voice is whispered, hoarse. Guttural with blood. I have to lean forward to catch her words. "Don't…" She coughs, blood cascading down her chin. A normal person would've comforted her in her final moments, but I've never been normal. I'm a monster. "Don't trust your men," she rasps at last.

My men?

"What are you talking about?" I demand. "Frankie?"

She shakes her head slowly, more blood forming. "Don't trust them."

Even in death, she's still a cryptic bitch.

"I need more than that." I try to rein in my impatience. It's not her fault she's dying.

"Who do you think I got the venom from?" she croaks. Her breath heaves with a shuddering breath.

And then she dies.

On the floor in front of me, the dagger I shoved in her heart protruding upwards.

I don't feel any guilt as I stare at her fallen body. I don't grieve her. She was a murderer herself, and I know without a shadow of doubt she would've continued killing if she had the chance. I did the world a favor. But it's still a dead body— the body of my teacher, no less—and I'm already the prime suspect of numerous other murders.

How the fuck am I going to explain this?

CHAPTER 44

VIOLET

I don't know if I should be grateful or terrified when Dimitri and Frankie enter the classroom. Dimitri takes one look at the dead body, and a single brow quirks.

"It's not what it looks like," I hurry to defend. Dimitri smirks.

"It looks like there's a knife in your teacher's chest, and you're standing over her with a bruised face and blood on your hands."

"Oh." I feel my insides twist in half a dozen knots. "Then it's exactly what it looks like."

Frankie rushes to my side instantly, eyes wide in his face. I have no idea what transpired between Dimitri and Frankie down in the tunnels, and I don't care.

At least, I don't care *now*. I'll probably pester them tomorrow for details. At the moment, I have a much bigger problem—a problem the size of a body.

"Are you okay?" Frankie asks, hands hovering over me but never touching.

"She's fine." Dimitri waves a hand dismissively. Condescending asshole. He ignores the daggers I hurl his way with my eyes, choosing instead to kneel beside Diedre. "Impressive kill. Straight in the heart."

I release a half-hysterical sob. "Oh yeah. I'm just a regular, old assassin."

Without responding, he grabs a white cloth from his pocket and rubs at the hilt of the dagger. His movements are mechanical, practiced. I'm ninety percent sure he's humming under his breath.

"What are you doing?" I whisper, stunned. He flashes me a brilliant smile, showcasing two rows of perfectly white teeth and noticeable dimples. I hate that my heart stutters to a stop at being on the receiving end of such a smile.

"Why, getting rid of fingerprints, of course." He resumes his task, painstakingly slow.

There's so much I want to ask him, want to demand of him, but I know now isn't the time. Why was he with me during every murder? Who hired him to kill the headmaster? Why is he helping me...if that's what he's doing?

Dimitri is an enigma, and I can't tell what team he's playing on. He's the bishop on the chessboard, the player that can change the game completely.

"I'll take care of her," Dimitri continues, indicating the dead teacher with a bob of his head. When I open my mouth to protest, he clicks his tongue. "You have to learn to trust people, Ms. Dracula."

"I thought you said I was too trusting." I wrap my arms around my stomach, suddenly unbearably cold. It could be shock. Though Diedre Stevens isn't my first victim, her death feels different from the others. Maybe because I knew her, talked to her, somewhat befriended her. She betrayed me, and I...

And I killed her.

"That's because you don't know who to trust," Dimitri says evenly, and Diedre's words come back to me.

Don't trust your men.

She was lying, wasn't she? She had to be. Just like she lied about Dracula not being my father. Just like she lied about me not being a vampire. Desperate women will do anything to escape death. She wanted to confuse me, to drive a wedge between me and my new friends. My men.

Right?

"Take Ms. Dracula to her dorm, please," Dimitri instructs Frankie. When neither of us jump to do his bidding, he repeats, harsher, "I said, take Ms. Dracula to her dorm."

Frankie hesitantly places his hand on my lower back, as if unsure of where to touch me. I want to lean against him, show him with my actions that I forgive him, but I don't. My mind is reeling, spinning, and I can't slow it down long enough for me to focus.

"How...?" I face Dimitri. "How are you going to get rid of her?" There's a disconnection between my mind and body. My words and my brain. I feel disembodied, as if I'm floating high above surveying the scene below. The girl standing with her arms around her and a pale face isn't me. She can't be.

It feels like I'm watching a movie in front of me, that I am an actor and not the director, helpless to change the scenes as they scroll across the screen.

Dimitri's smile is cold—as cold as his eyes. "It's amazing what you can do with a mirror, Ms. Dracula."

And with that cryptic response, he dismisses me.

FRANKIE WALKS INTO MY ROOM WITH ME. HE HASN'T SAID ONE word to me, and I haven't said one to him. The tension between us is almost palpable. Already, I'm as taut as a string on a violin.

Diedre's words echo in my head. A continuous loop. I know I shouldn't trust her, but what reason would she have to lie?

I'll need to talk to my dad. Soon.

I remove my bloody trench coat, not bothering to put it in the laundry basket. Knowing Dimitri, he'll steal it when I'm asleep anyway. I rip off my suit jacket and shorts, crawling under my covers in only a tank top and a pair of panties.

The silence implodes with Frankie's heavy sigh.

"Violet…" he begins. He tentatively perches on the edge of my bed, keeping his body a respectable distance away from mine. A part of me wants to breach that distance, the distance that feels like a canyon between us. Another part of me needs space after everything that happened. Frankie scrubs a hand through his light brown hair, body shaking. There seems to be a thousand thoughts running through his brain. Abruptly, he turns to face me. "Compel me."

"What?" I was not expecting that.

"Compel me. Ask me anything you want to ask me. I can't lie if you compel me, and I want you to hear for yourself the truth." There's no denying the sincerity in his voice. The earnestness. He needs me to do this because he knows, as well as I do, that we'll never be able to regain trust without it.

"I don't know—"

"Please, Violet." He implores me with his eyes to give in, to allow him to prove himself to me. They ensnare me, hold me hostage, and fuck, if I don't give in.

"Fine," I huff, crawling forward. Frankie gulps—no doubt his instinctive reaction when coming face to face with a predator—but he doesn't shrink away. *Tell me the truth, Frankie. Did you plan to kill me?*

His eyes glaze over, a dopey smile crossing his handsome face. This close, I can see a slight scar through his eyebrow. No, not a scar. It almost appears to be stitches, dark against his porcelain skin. From when he was created?

"No, never," he answers immediately. No hesitation.

"Why did you do it? Why did you go along with it? Why didn't you tell anyone?"

His eyes twitch—the only indication he's nervous about this line of questioning.

But he's helpless to resist the allure of my compulsion.

"Because I wanted to be a hero. I wanted to be *your* hero. I only discovered what he had planned yesterday, when Headmaster visited me. But even if Dimitri hadn't swapped the elixirs, you would've been fine. The one I created would've made you laugh for an hour. You would've been fine." His words rush together, as if he's desperate to release them all in one breath.

My heart warms. He wanted to be my hero?

Swoon.

But at the same time, I'm furious with him. He put both our lives at risk to fulfill some dumb hero complex. *He could've died.* I can forgive a lot of things, but I can't forgive that. He put his own life at risk to protect me.

Stupid, stupid boy.

"Why would you do all that for me? What makes me so special?" I ask, heart clenching.

And then he says it. Compelled. In my room.

"I think you're my mate."

It's like I've been zapped with electricity. I'm not sure I'm even capable of speech anymore. I stare at Frankie like he'd just suggested we go moon some nuns.

Mate? Me? Him?

Fuck. Is it too late to pretend I don't speak English?

His eyes widen imperceptibly, breaking free of my compulsion, and horror fills his face. I don't know if it's because of my shocked expression or because he told me in the first place.

Mate.

I've heard of mates before, obviously, but the majority of monsters live their whole lives never meeting theirs. And that's if you have a mate to begin with. I can't deny I'm attracted to Frankie. I *like* him.

But I also like…

I like others. A lot.

"I shouldn't have…I'm sorry." Frankie staggers to his feet, stumbling, before darting to the door.

Fix this, Violet! Compliment his dick!

"I'm…I'm sorry," he repeats before I'm capable of forming words, and then he's gone.

Is he apologizing for telling me the way he did?

For being my mate in the first place?

Does he think I don't like him like that?

With a muffled groan, I twist and belly flop on my bed, burying my face in my pillow.

Fuck. Why do you have to be such a fuck up, Violet?

Because that's what I am. I push people away. I had a man declaring to be my mate, and he ran from me.

Mate.

What am I going to do?

∽

I'M RIGHT.

When I wake up the next morning, my bloody clothes from the night before are gone. I don't know how Dimitri got into my room, and I don't care.

I don't care about anything at the moment.

My mind is sluggish as I dress, taking care not to disturb my injuries. Most have already healed, but the rope burns from the god-blessed restraints remain on my skin. The bruises on my face are already fading to a light yellow color —thank fuck for advanced vampiric healing.

After dressing, I exit the dorm building. The campus is surprisingly quiet, most students attempting to sleep off their hangovers, as I move through the woods and to the cafeteria.

Our usual table in the cafeteria is empty. No Vin. No Frankie. Hell, not even Jack and Mason are present. There's a pain in my chest, a clenching sensation, that quite literally stalls my feet. Loneliness threatens to drown me.

I don't like this feeling. At all.

I try to focus on the positives: Diedre Stevens is dead, and she won't be killing again.

I'll ask my father as soon as possible about her outlandish claims.

Until then, I'll attempt to survive school.

A school that hates vampires, particularly me. And a school that has three sex clones running around, but I don't want to think about that.

And boys? Don't need them. I'm making a vow right now: for the rest of the school year, I won't even think about cock.

You heard me right. My vagina will be cockless, as will my mind. I won't think about mates or feelings or any of that emotional shit.

I sit at my usual table, wondering where the guys are— and then mentally berate myself for breaking the sacred rule.

Thou shall not think of cocks.

More than one student throws me a vicious glare, the anti-vampiric movement growing every day, but I ignore them. Hopefully, with the end of the murders, the hatred will die as well.

But I'm Dracula's daughter, despite what Diedre insisted, and I'll survive whatever's thrown my way.

Bring it on, bitches.

EPILOGUE

MASON

"How long have we been hanging here?" I ask, voice catching in the wind. Hux—and I can tell it's Hux by his trademark scowl—bares his teeth.

"Too long."

We're fucking lucky we're not mere mortals. We'd be dead a long time ago for how long we've been upside down. All that blood rushing to our heads...

Our cocks.

My cock.

What if this fucks up Little Mason?

I picture Violet then. Her pouty mouth and soulful eyes. Those long legs visible in the short skirts she likes to wear. Her heaving chest.

My pride and joy stands at attention, eagerly awaiting sweet pussy like a good little soldier. He's as enamored by her as I am.

Hux's eyes are wide with horror.

"Why the fuck are you hard right now?"

"I needed to make sure the Stabber was working properly," I reply. It's disconcerting to be upside down, to see your feet in the air as your arms sway. I'm grateful my beanie is enchanted; the last thing I need is a bunch of angry ass snakes biting my face.

"Stabber," Hux repeats slowly. "Is that a normal thing? Do men of this time name their penises?"

I blanch. "Dude, don't say penises. It's weird. Say cock or dick or Violet's favorite word, Pickle Thumper."

Yeah, I'm an ass. Sue me.

"Pickle Thumper." His brows scrunch in confusion. "Jack is mentally shaking his head at me."

We swing in silence for a moment, but there's only so much peace and quiet I can take before I go insane.

"I'm going to sing," I warn my companion.

"Don't you fucking dare—"

"Pinkie, oh Pinkie! Love me with that Pinkie!"

So I'm really, really an asshole.

At least I have a cute smile.

We hang for another few hours, the sun now high in the sky, when the snap of twigs alerts me to a new presence.

Dimitri Gray stands at the edge of the clearing, arms crossed over his chest. Amusement dances in his eyes.

"Errr...a little help?" I ask.

"Normally, I'd just leave you for dead," he begins, and my heart sinks. "But I'm afraid we have a mutual interest now." He stalks forward and cuts first my rope and then Hux's. I twist at the last second, landing on my back instead of my neck.

"Mutual interest?" Hux demands, already on his feet. Showoff. I'm much more slow to get up, ignoring the stab of pain from my fall.

Dimitri's smile is honestly quite scary. Why can I picture him standing over my bed with that exact smile?

Oh god. Now I'm picturing him popping out of a drain on the side of the road, a red balloon in his hand.

Without bothering to answer, he turns on his heel and walks back the way he came from.

"Why do I have the distinct feeling our mutual interest is Violet?" I whisper to Hux, and I watch him tense beside me, struggling to control his temper.

"If he harms my precious treasure, he'll pay," he threatens, and I don't doubt him.

No, what I *do* doubt is that Dimitri intends to do Violet harm.

Dimitri has a role to play in Violet's life, of that I'm certain. I just don't know which part he plays, which piece on the puzzle he connects with.

"Come," I say to Hux, ignoring the growing ball of unease in my stomach. Everything about Dimitri evokes that reaction, and it's not just because he's a scary as fuck assassin. "Let's get to our girl."

Our girl.

I kind of like the sound of that.

ACKNOWLEDGMENTS

As always, I have a team of people to thank! Thank you to my amazing alphas and betas! I don't know where this book would be without your help.

My family, of course. Thank you. Your unconditional support and love means the world to me. I don't know where I would be without you.

And finally, my readers. Thank you for reading this book. For joining me on Violet's journey. I feel so incredibly lucky I have you guys in my corner, supporting me.

ABOUT THE AUTHOR

Katie May is a reverse harem author. If she's not writing or reading, you can find her playing games with her family, watching horror movies, or skydiving. Just kidding. Feel free to reach out to her anytime! Or join her reader's group for exclusive content Katie's Gang - Katie May Readers's Group.